ELLERY QUEEN'S
A MULTITUDE OF SINS
edited by Ellery Queen

ELLERY QUEEN'S *A MULTITUDE OF SINS* is a collection of 14 stories selected by Ellery Queen as the best stories published in the *Ellery Queen Mystery Magazine*.

The dictionary defines sin as "any violation, especially a wilful or deliberate one, of religious or moral principles," and for its synonym adds "see crime." Thus both crime and sin mean a breaking of the law—" any serious violation of moral or divine law, or of human law.

This volume simplifies the meaning of the word "sin." Only through detection can one uncover the *MULTITUDE OF SINS* held within this anthology.

Other Large Print
Novels by Ellery Queen

THE FRENCH POWDER MYSTERY

THE DUTCH SHOE MYSTERY

ELLERY QUEEN'S

A Multitude of Sins

Edited by Ellery Queen

130462 ✓

John Curley & Associates, Inc.
South Yarmouth, Ma.

Library of Congress Cataloging in Publication Data

Multitude of sins.
   Ellery Queen's a multitude of sins.

   1. Detective and mystery stories, American.
2. Detective and mystery stories, English.   3. Large type books. I. Title.
[PS648.D4M85   1986]   813'.0872'08   86–16573
ISBN 1–55504–175–2 (lg. print)
ISBN 1–55504–160–4 (pbk.: lg. print)

Copyright © 1975, 1976, 1978 by Davis Publications, Inc.

All rights reserved. No part of this book may be used or reproduced in any manner without written permission except in the case of brief quotations embodied in critical articles and reviews.

Published in Large Print by arrangement with Davis Publications throughout the United States and territories; Canada; the United Kingdom and the Commonwealth; and a non-exclusive basis in the rest of the world market.

Distributed in the U.K. and Commonwealth by Magna Print Books.

Printed in Great Britain

ACKNOWLEDGMENTS

The editor hereby makes grateful acknowledgment to the following authors and authors' representatives for giving permission to reprint the material in this volume.

Isaac Asimov for *A Case of Income Tax Fraud*, © 1976 by Isaac Asimov.
Brandt & Brandt for *One for Virgil Tibbs* by John Ball, © 1975 by John Ball.
Curtis Brown, Ltd. for *Generation Gap* by Stanley Ellin, © 1976 by Stanley Ellin.
Barbara Callahan for *Lavender Lady*, © 1976 by Barbara Callahan.
John Gores for *File # 10: The Maimed and the Halt*, © 1975 by Joe Gores.
Joyce Harrington for *Blue Monday*, © 1976 by Joyce Harrington.
Edward D. Hoch for *Captain Leopold and the Impossible Murder*, © 1976 by Edward D. Hoch.
Harold Q. Masur for *Murder Never Solves*

Anything, © 1976 by Harold Q. Masur.

Harold Matson Co., Inc. for *Like a Terrible Scream* by Etta Revesz, © 1976 by Etta Revesz.

Florence V. Mayberry for *Alone with the Witches,* © 1976 by Florence V. Mayberry.

Scott Meredith Literary Agency, Inc. for *A Most Unusual Murder* by Robert Bloch, © 1976 by Robert Bloch.

S. S. Rafferty for *The Pennsylvania Thimblerig,* © 1976 by S. S. Rafferty.

Larry Sternig Literary Agency for *Nobody Tells Me Anything* by Jack Ritchie, © 1976 by Jack Ritchie.

R. L. Stevens for *Five Rings in Reno,* © 1976 by R. L. Stevens.

CONTENTS

INTRODUCTION
  Ellery Queen   1

FILE # 10: THE MAIMED AND
THE HALT
  Joe Gores   3

ONE FOR VIRGIL TIBBS
  John Ball   30

A MOST UNUSUAL MURDER
  Robert Bloch   61

LAVENDER LADY
  Barbara Callahan   85

BLUE MONDAY
  Joyce Harrington   99

FIVE RINGS IN RENO
  R. L. Stevens   122

LIKE A TERRIBLE SCREAM
  Etta Revesz   153

THE PENNSYLVANIA THIMBLERIG
  S. S. Rafferty   171

MURDER NEVER SOLVES
ANYTHING
  Harold Q. Masur   208

GENERATION GAP
  Stanley Ellin   231

ALONE WITH THE WITCHES
  Florence V. Mayberry   257

NOBODY TELLS ME ANYTHING
  Jack Ritchie   281

A CASE OF INCOME TAX FRAUD
  Isaac Asimov   318

CAPTAIN LEOPOLD AND THE
IMPOSSIBLE MURDER
  Edward D. Hoch   348

A MULTITUDE OF SINS

INTRODUCTION

Dear Reader:

Sin is defined as a "transgression of divine law... or any violation, especially a willful or deliberate one of religious or moral principle." And for its synonym, the dictionary reads: See crime.

Thus, simply, both sin and crime mean a breaking of law – any serious violation of moral or divine law, or of human law.

Fraud, kidnapping, blackmail, arson, counterfeiting, assault and battery, embezzlement, vandalism, robbery, the impeding of justice, adultery, perjury – the whole catalogue of crime, the "compleat calendar" from petty theft to multiple murder – all are sins, and many of them appear in this volume, Number 32 in the series of annual hardcover anthologies deriving from *Ellery Queen's Mystery Magazine.*

Oliver Wendell Holmes has told us, and for that matter Sherlock Holmes could have told us: "Sin has many tools" – everything from gun, knife, poison, rope, and blunt instrument to the mind itself; and you will encounter many of these tools in this collection – and learn that "a lie is the handle which fits them all."

But do not despair.

There is hope.

Mystery covers, and detection uncovers a multitude of sins.

ELLERY QUEEN

Joe Gores

File # 10: The Maimed and the Halt

Daniel Kearny Associates (a skiptracing agency with Head Office in San Francisco and branches throughout California) is back in one of the best of the File series; and Patrick Michael O'Bannon, the red-haired field man (one of the best in the business), is up against his old adversary, Colonel Buford Sanders, as clever and audacious a crook as ever flimflammed an insurance company. No mere repo of a car in this ten-year-old feud; no, O'B is investigating a $275,000 ripoff that has baffled all his private-eye predecessors...

The silver-haired man paused at the head of the wide steps of San Francisco City Hall. He stuck his silver-headed black walking stick under one arm while lighting a thin cheroot. With his ramrod posture and his ascetic face he looked like an oldtime riverboat gambler.

Then he started down the steps.

A grimace of pain contorted his features. Only the cane, thumping heavily on each step, kept him from falling. His crabwise downward progress was agonizingly slow; it was like watching a film depicting torture.

"You say *he* drives his own car?" demanded Dan Kearny unbelievingly. Kearny was pushing 50 but didn't look it, a hard-jawed man with a graying mane of hair and a nose bent and flattened by a lifetime of not backing away from trouble.

"Special controls so he can operate everything with the use of only one leg." Meyer Edmunds was pudgy and perspiring, with thinning sandy hair and an insistent cologne. "That man has just finished ripping off Fiduciary Trust Insurance for two-hundred-and-seventy-five thousand bucks. Don't quote me, of course."

"This special car of his – a Cadillac, I suppose?"

Edmunds nodded glumly. "Colonel Sanders always goes first cabin."

"The Colonel Sanders of chicken fame?"

Patrick Michael O'Bannon had thrust his flame-topped head into the crowded cubby-hole office. He pulled the door shut so that outside lights would not dim the moving images on the tacked-up screen.

"Colonel Buford Sanders, USAF Retired," said Kearny.

"*Buford* Sanders? You mean *my* Colonel Sanders?"

"Now you know why I wanted you in here."

Edmunds rewound the film as O'B sat down. Daniel Kearny Associates (Head Office in San Francisco, Branches Throughout California) seldom drew the VIP of a big insurance company as a possible client; it had to be something unusual if their own investigators couldn't handle it. Meyer Edmunds started the film over again.

"O'B, this is everything our boys have gotten on him over the past two years – since the car accident."

The clips, spliced end to end, showed twenty continuous minutes in the life of Colonel Buford Sanders. Some in black and white, some in color, some of theater excellence, others hand-held from moving cars or through fences, one from over a transom.

In all of them Sanders was doing the same thing. Limping.

"Are you *sure* he's faking it?" asked Kearny dubiously.

"No, I'm not, Dan, and that's the hell of

it. I'm the only one who still thinks it's fraud. We've already paid off."

The lights went up. Willowy blonde Giselle Marc had delivered the ice Kearny had called upstairs to clerical for, had collected O'B's wink, and had departed. Drinks were in hand and cigarettes were alight. It was one of the few times, O'B thought, that Kearny's office in the basement of the old Victorian which housed DKA resembled the fictional private-eye's domain.

"Nine Caddys we've repossessed from that man," O'B mused. His seamed, freckle-spattered face blueprinted a middle-aged drinker's life, but next to Kearny he was the best field investigator DKA had. "Nine. Spread out over almost ten years. And this is the first time I've ever seen a picture of the man."

"We haven't had a new assignment on him in thirty months," said Kearny as he consulted the Colonel's bulging file.

"Since the car accident," Edmunds said.

"We picked up four Caddys in California," said O'Bannon, "two in New York, one in New Orleans, one – no, two – in Florida. He plays games, that man does."

"With all the computerized credit checking there is today, how could he even *buy* nine Cadillacs, one after the other, and –"

"He looks so good on paper that the dealers just never bother to run him through a credit-reporting service," said O'B. "He's retired military, gets a fat government pension, has a hell of an expensive home in Seacliff –"

"Dealers are required by law to get a certain percentage of the sales price," Kearny explained, "but no law says they can't balloon six or seven hundred of that down payment and get it a couple of months after delivery. The Colonel never makes the balloon payment and it usually takes us about six months to drop a rock on the new Caddy. By then the bank's eaten the contract and it's on contingent."

"But you have *always* made recovery," Edmunds persisted.

"What's to recover?" said O'B. "Last one I picked up had tires you could read through, a cracked block, no transmission, and a crankshaft dragging on the ground. The client took a twelve-thousand-dollar bath when we sold it for junk in Tallahassee."

Edmunds sighed and stood up. "Ten days of additional surveillance is all I've been able to gouge out of the head office. After that we close the file – unless you turn up *proof* of fraud."

"Why us?" asked Kearny.

"By now he knows all my people by their first names."

"If he blows his nose, I'll be holding the handkerchief," promised O'Bannon.

DKA seldom got to mount a concentrated surveillance on a single subject, expenses unlimited. O'B brought in two other DKA investigators, Larry Ballard and Bart Heslip. Heslip was a black ex-boxer who found the same excitement in manhunting that the ring had once given him; Ballard was a late-twenties blond man, just under six feet and conditioned like an athlete.

"Remember, gents, even more important than uninterrupted observation is the fact that he *must never know*, must never even *suspect*, that someone's staked out on him. If he's been disciplined enough to never give himself away once during two years –"

"But he's already been paid off," Heslip pointed out.

"That's what we're banking on," O'B said. "But remember, this guy can *smell* a setup. He's gun-shy. I've been after him for ten years."

"Unmarried, I take it?" asked Ballard.

"Widowed seven years ago."

"Why not get a woman next to him and –"

"Four insurance-company baggers tried in the last two years." Baggers are female investigators, who often carry tape-recorders in their handbags. "But part of the basis for the high settlement was his claim that the accident made him impotent. Nothing stirring."

"If we could catch him shacking up –" Heslip shook his head and chuckled. "Man, two *years?* That takes *some* sort of cool."

"He's got it," said O'Bannon.

Ballard was thoughtful. "How about – oh, sports? Catch him in a gymnasium? On a weekend hike? Horseback riding?"

"He does go to a gym five times a week – for whirlpool therapy. They haven't caught him taking a weekend anywhere since the accident. Church every Sunday – stands in back because he claims he can't kneel down. Until the accident he didn't go to church at all."

That briefing was on the first morning of surveillance, which was carried out essentially from the garret room of an elegant three-story red brick whose owner owed Edmunds a favor. It was directly across Scenic Way from the subject's distinctive colonial revival with its hipped roof and second-floor Palladian window.

"With a house like that, servants, a

gardener – what's the cat on the hustle for?" mused Heslip.

"You've answered your own question. He *likes* the hustle."

"There he is," said Ballard from the window.

The sandbagged 600mm lens brought Colonel Buford Sanders up close enough, as he laboriously descended his front steps, to count the hairs in his mustache. Click. Click. Click. But O'B knew, even as he took them, that the stills would only support Sanders' claim. He checked his watch and stood up.

"Time for his hour with the Jacuzzi bath. See you gents later."

The therapist, Wednesday lunch at the Presidio officers' club, back home. O'B had the daily routine down pat. It was on the return trip, with Sanders' special Caddy two blocks ahead, that O'B became aware of a new element in the equation. On Thursday, when he popped into the office after business hours, he told Kearny about it.

"Edmunds must still have one of his people second-guessing us, Dan. There was a second tail on Sanders for five blocks yesterday afternoon, and this morning a TV repair truck from a company that isn't in the phone book was parked down the street for twenty minutes. Ballard thinks someone was tagging him, too."

Kearny was already at the phone, having Edmunds paged out of the steamroom at the Elks Club. In a few minutes he hung up.

"Not Edmunds. But somebody else at Fiduciary must have had a bright idea. Edmunds will check around, make sure the field man gets yanked." He was on his feet. "Let's go get a drink."

"You'll find this hard to believe, but I can't. I'm due to relieve Bart in half an hour."

"His girlfriend's back east visiting her folks – so Bart's got nothing better to do. And this *might* be important. You know how good Larry is with women, well, day before yesterday he spotted that good-looking maid of Sanders drinking at a little bar on Lincoln Way and Twentieth Avenue where Larry hangs around."

They shouldered into their topcoats, then paused at the front of the garage to set the alarms and lock up before going out into the chill September evening.

"Coincidence?"

"Can't see it being anything else," said Kearny. "She just likes to drink – with anybody who isn't her husband."

"That covers a lot of ground," said O'B.

"And her with two kids at home. Tsk, tsk. We'd better go speak to the girl."

Jacques Daniels' was not a fancy way of speaking about a sour-mash bourbon. It was a bar owned by two partners, one a small lively balding Frenchman from Algeria who had given his first name to the place, the other a pert little blonde named Beverly Daniels. She and Larry Ballard were talking across the bar when O'B and Kearny entered.

The place was warm and cosy and intimate, with mismatched hardwood tables, myriad hanging ferns, and handmade Tiffany-style lamps that cast a soft stained glow across the drinkers. Lying on the bar beside Ballard were two DKA report forms with typing on them. Ballard tapped them with a finger. Kearny scooped them up in passing.

Ballard murmured, apparently to Beverly, "Brunette by the jukebox. Tailed her last night."

The two detectives pulled out chairs on both sides of the generously endowed black-haired girl. She had a long upper lip that showed precise incisors. Those in the lower jar had a habit of worrying the protruding lip as she talked.

Her voice was sullen. "I'm waiting for someone."

"You weren't yesterday when Frankie Gallaway stopped at your table." Kearny had scanned Ballard's report for a few moments. "Your name is Rosario Renucci. You've been a maid for four years on Scenic Way." O'Bannon hadn't read Ballard's report, but he could follow Kearny's leads easily enough.

"*Married* name," said Kearny.

"What sort of scam is –" she began.

"Husband is Ermanno Renucci," said O'Bannon.

"Hard-working guy at a foundry on Brannan Street. Hot-tempered but a home-loving sort of person. Salt of the earth."

"If you think you can –"

"Two children, minors, ages four and two." O'B shook his head sadly. "Rosie, Rosie, what are we going to do with you? Ermanno finds out –" He shaped his lips in a *whew* position, shook one hand back and forth as if he'd caught it in a car door. "Comes home sometime, finds those two sweet little kids all alone –"

Her face seemed about to crumble, but she was still in there trying. "You guys don't beat it, I'll call the cops."

"And we'll call Ermanno." Kearny began reading in a low voice from Ballard's report. "Eight fifty-eight p.m., Wednesday, September twenty-ninth, subject met male Caucasian subsequently identified as Frankie Gallaway at Jacques Daniels', a bar at eighteen-forty-nine Lincoln Way."

He raised cold gray eyes to her defiant face, then read again.

"At twelve-o-seven a.m. subject and Gallaway left the bar and proceeded to the residence maintained by Gallaway at the rear of two-nine-eight Parnassus Street. This is a detached cottage reached by a passageway alongside the main building."

"Anybody who says Frankie and I –"

"Subject and Gallaway entered the bedroom at twelve forty-four a.m., switched out the lights at twelve fifty-eight. The lights remained off until two twenty-two a.m. Subject left Gallaway's residence at two forty a.m., after embracing with Gallaway in the open doorway."

She broke, abruptly, with a half-smothered sob.

"Damn you, you got any idea what it's like? The relatives drooling over the kids? Washing clothes? And dishes? And getting them up and off to school and –"

"'Tis far better to have loved and lost than to do thirty pounds of dirty laundry a week," observed O'Bannon.

"Look, what can I offer you not to tell Ermanno –"

"Tell us about your boss," suggested Kearny.

She seemed dazed by the abrupt switch. "My boss?"

"He ever make a pass at you?"

"Have other girls in there?"

"He's faking it, isn't he? The limp?"

"Doesn't limp once the shades are drawn, does he, Rosie?"

"How does he get the girls in and out without being seen?"

"How much extra does he give you to cover for him?"

"C'mon, Rosie. Give, girl. Give."

Ashen-faced and shaken, Rosie gave.

It was five a.m. on Saturday. O'Bannon stifled a vast yawn and shivered despite the car heater. He was on Seacliff Ave., a block from the subject's house – where, surprise, surprise, he'd found the specially equipped Cadillac street-parked when he'd arrived two hours before. And Colonel Sanders with that spacious three-car garage under the house!

It fit with what Rosie had overheard Sanders saying on the phone while making motel reservations. He'd be leaving the city around five a.m. on Saturday and would be there by midday at the latest. The clandestine nature of the departure, the fact that the motel was six or seven hours away from San Francisco – a probable five-to-seven bet, O'B thought, that a woman was involved.

He stiffened, crushing the paper cup which had contained his third coffee of the day. His rear-view mirror had seen a figure moving with the now-familiar crabwise shuffle. He used the radio.

"SF-2 to SF-3. Do you read me, Bart, over?"

"Loud and clear." Heslip was, by prearrangement, in his car a quarter block from the subject's house.

"He's just getting into the Caddy over here on Seacliff."

"He back-doored me! If he's tumbled to the stake –"

"Just being cautious. I've got him now. Out."

"10-4, cat. Good hunting. Over and out."

O'B already had his car in motion, backing and filling as the subject got the Caddy started. O'B was going to try a front tail, the most difficult but also the most difficult to spot. It meant making an educated guess in which direction Sanders would be going. O'B only knew for sure it wouldn't be west

– not unless the Caddy came equipped with water wings.

He pulled away ten seconds before Sanders did, took a left into the Presidio off 25th Avenue when he saw Sanders' left blinker go on. That made it easy. Golden Gate Bridge. North.

It was gloriously clear, going to be hot, with the not-yet-risen sun reddening strata of clouds above the Oakland hills before it burst out to make crinkled lead foil of the Bay through the whizzing orange handrails of the bridge. O'B sang with the radio while beating time on the steering wheel. He felt it: this was the day, this was the trip on which he was going to nail Sanders.

And then he almost lost him. Sanders abruptly veered across all four lanes into the old Blackpoint Cut-off which led across the tidal marshes to Vallejo. It took O'B twenty minutes to get turned around, pick him up, pass him, and drop into line an eighth of a mile ahead of him.

Tricky cat. Start out north, then go east. Actually, O'B liked it. Sanders *really* didn't want anyone tagging along.

O'B had assumed it would be northeast from Vallejo on Interstate 80, toward Sacramento, Tahoe, Reno, places like that. But instead it was 680 through Benicia to Concord, then down to turn east on 580 to Livermore, a hot dusty suburban sprawl supported by the nuclear research facility of the University of California.

"With *breakfast?*" exclaimed the dismayed waitress at the diner he'd chosen after Sanders had stopped at a more elaborate restaurant a block farther off the freeway.

"The sun is over the yardarm *somewhere* in this world, me lhove. So I'll be havin' a wee dram o' the Chablis wit' me eggs."

Stopping at Livermore for breakfast meant south on the new Interstate 5, which was unsullied by such namby-pamby things as restaurants, truck stops, gas stations, or roadside cafés. It was a freeway for the traveler in a rush. O'B was content to tag along behind now – Sanders surely would feel he'd shaken any possible tail by this time. Showed how wrong a man could be.

"Looks like it's Bakersfield," mused O'Bannon aloud.

Which again showed how wrong a man could be.

Fifty miles south on Interstate 5, Sanders turned west on California 152. *West?* Up through the Pacheco Pass? What the hell went on?

An hour later, when Sanders turned north

on U.S. 101 at Gilroy, O'Bannon knew. Tricky, indeed! The subject had in effect made a giant circle down through the great interior depressed valley which formed the heart of California between the Sierras and the Coast Range. Now he was headed up toward the Bay area again; if he kept going far enough, he'd be back in San Francisco.

He didn't go that far. At San Jose, 50 miles from the city, he cut over to Interstate 280 and left the freeway at Winchester Boulevard – in plenty of time to honor his motel reservation.

The Cozee-Up Motel was a U-shaped affair triple-tiered around a fiercely blue swimming pool masked from the street and the skyway by dense shrubbery. A motel designed for assignations. O'Bannon, his wrap-around dark glasses leaving little more than his teeth showing, was delving industriously in the trunk compartment of his Chevy Caprice when Sanders came from Registration in his crabwise shuffle. O'B watched him into the first-floor corner room farthest from the office, then went in himself.

"Something on the first floor," he told the iron-eyed woman behind the desk. "As far from the office as possible."

"The *very* end room was just rented, but –"

"How about the one next to it?"

"The maid hasn't gotten –"

"I'll have a cup of coffee while I wait."

A window booth in the coffee shop gave him an excellent view of the subject's dust-filmed Cadillac. The cups of coffee gave him heartburn in the two hours before the motel's senior-citizen maid had snailed her way in and out of his room. The temperature rose as the sun climbed a cloudless smoggy sky. O'B resisted the siren lure of a liquor store two blocks away; he didn't dare break surveillance. What the hell, his room would be air-conditioned.

As O'B was fumbling open his door, Sanders emerged from the adjacent one without a glance at the perspiring red-haired man. This gave O'B a chance to see that Sanders' bed was obligingly headed up against the partition between their two rooms.

He watched Sanders take a booth in the coffee shop, then got the necessary equipment from his suitcase. Using a quarter-inch cordless battery-powered drill and a long bit, O'B holed the wainscoting to come out under Sanders' bed. Through this hole he inserted a delicate high-resolution pencil mike, which he patched into a sound-activated Uher recorder. Fortunately the hum of the subject's air conditioner was not loud enough to activate the mike.

Sanders returned half an hour later, looking very drawn as he limped across the heat-softened blacktop. Probably that coffee, O'B thought. But what if the guy really *was* crippled? No, couldn't be. Otherwise, what was he doing in San Jose, a mere 50 miles from the city but arrived at by over 200 circuitous miles? Why back-door his own house at five in the ayem? Why street-park his car a block away?

O'B put the monitor plug in his ear. He heard the door opening. Bedsprings. A sigh of relief. Phone. Asking for a number. O'B realized he was holding his breath. Would it be a woman?

"Hello, Cassie? Just got in. That's right. Of *course* I made sure nobody saw me leave. Couldn't have anyone – what? Yes. What I thought, too. All right. Pick you up about six thirty. We'll eat early so nothing interferes with our night together."

Just what they had suspected! Sanders had a little thing going on the side down here in San Jose and had sneaked down to celebrate the end of his long charade with a shack-up in a motel. Well, kiss your two-seven-five thousand goodbye, baby. Say hello to them cold prison walls.

Cold. Shouldn't have thought of that. How good an icy beer would taste! Send out for a six-pack? No. Didn't want to pinpoint the fact that he was staying in his room.

Sanders was now in the shower, but O'B's, incredibly enough, didn't work. The opportunity had passed anyway, as Sanders was finished now. O'B couldn't chance being under the needle spray when the subject might suddenly decide to take off.

Pool, sparkling and inviting a few paces from his door? No. Same problem.

He tried again to make his air conditioner work. On the blink. Sweat was standing on O'B's face. At least he could get some ice. He found a pitcher and carried it down to the ice-making machine beside the office.

The ice machine was busted.

He drank tepid water from a styrofoam cup – the maid had forgotten to leave any glasses in his room. The water smelled of chemicals and tasted of fluorine. He kept on sweating.

He was rapidly coming to hate the guts of the man in the next room.

Thanks to the overheard phone conversation O'B was pouring sweat onto the sun-hot vinyl seat of his Caprice when Sanders limped out to the Caddy at six fifteen. Cassie, the girl on the phone, turned out to be a stunning blonde who lived in a ticky-tacky house off South Bascom Avenue that she'd probably gotten in a divorce settlement.

They ate supper at a very fancy place on East San Carlos near the San Jose State campus. From across the street it looked like cracked crab cocktails, rare roast beef washed down with a vintage burgundy, and chocolate mousse for dessert. O'B watched them through the restaurant window while choking down a foodchain's Quarter-Pounder made of a glutinous mass of chopped cow and soya meal. He ached for them to get back to the motel.

But they didn't go back to the motel. Instead they went south on Market Street, right out of the congested areas of San Jose into, surprisingly, traffic which got fiercer the farther from the center of town they went. Abruptly O'B realized he was buried in a crush of almost stationary autos with no idea of where the Caddy was. Left turn into Umbarger Road.

Which meant the Santa Clara County fairgrounds.

The traffic turned again, O'B willy-nilly with it. Dirt road now, a boy with a flashlight waving the Caprice into one of countless rows of parked cars. O'B got out. The Caddy was nowhere in sight. If Sanders had chosen this way to lose any possible tail, he'd sure succeeded. All O'B could do now was hope that the subject and his blonde had been headed wherever everybody else was going.

He was afoot in a field of sun-yellowed grass which had been trampled flat by thousands of feet. The crowd made no sense. Young and old, middle-aged and senior citizen, babes in arms, long-hairs and straights. A shirt-sleeve crowd, dogs yipping in the dust, transistor radios blaring country music.

Country music? He'd been shucked for sure. Sanders wouldn't be caught dead in this sort of hick crowd.

The mass was funneling down into a sluggish river of elbow-to-elbow humanity which flowed toward a central destination – a massive canvas tent pitched near the racetrack.

Carnival? No trucks or wagons, no midway, no barkers. But the other possibilities were almost endless. Rodeo? Boxing card? Tent revival? Country-western music show? Old-fashioned barn dance? Cattle auction or livestock judging? He seemed to be the only one in ignorance of which it was. Ah.

Posters. But the crush of people was so immense that O'B couldn't see what the posters said. Everyone except him was excited, up, hyper, full of anticipation.

Inside at last, and not even an admission charge collected. Nothing but a portable wooden stage set up at one end of the vast canvas structure and a sea of folding chairs rapidly filling with people. No trapezes slung high overhead. No center rings for performing dogs or horses. No pens, no judging blocks for cattle.

And no Colonel Sanders.

O'B prowled and looked. A group of youngsters in white gowns with gold collars took their place on the wooden risers to the rear of the stage. They started singing *That Old Time Religion*. He remembered, vividly and abruptly, sneaking under the canvas of revival tent shows as kid. The Holy Rollers one year.

One big roll and save your soul.

He'd clapped erasers for a week after school at Mission High for chanting *that* one in the hall.

Tonight it was a good old fundamentalist preacher all in black urging the sinful to save their souls, wash themselves free from all sin, find God, testify to the Power of The Word.

O'B turned to go. It had been a ploy on

Colonel Sanders' part to throw off any possible tail. Carefully skirting the traffic going to the tent revival, leaving O'B hopelessly mired in the jam-up. O'B's only edge was the pencil mike. Sanders wouldn't know about that. Once he and his blonde got going in that motel room –

The preacher had begun exhorting now, cajoling, arms thrust wide to gather in the sinful, his sweat flying, his voice hoarsening as it began to draw its inevitable emotional response.

"He hath filled the hungry with good things. Am I right?"

"You are right!" answered some voices from the crowd.

"He hath sent the rich away empty. Am I right?"

"You are *right!*"

O'B was working his way toward the exit to the parking lots.

"And I say to you, brethren, that The Shepherd rejoices more in the return of one lost sheep than he does in maintaining the whole flock. *Am I right?*"

"*You are right!*" With him now, a massive chorus.

"Then bring me your poor, and your maimed, and your halt, and your blind. And

I will make them whole again. So saith the Lord. Brethren, *am I right?*"

"*YOU ARE RIGHT!*"

Now O'Bannon was breasting a tide – the old and the crippled and the sinful, moving down the aisle to bear witness to the Lord. He paused, looked back, and was transfixed. There, among them, was the familiar silver hair, the pain-lined ascetic face, the bobbing crabwise movement. O'B gaped.

Colonel Buford Sanders, angle-player and game-player and insurance defrauder, going down the aisle of a tent preacher's –

That's when the images began to flick before O'Bannon's eyes, frame after frame like a slide show. Images created from a blazing, belated, but now total comprehension.

Sanders, hiring *his own* private eye. Not a second tail on Sanders that Wednesday – *a tail on O'B!* And, later, a tail on Ballard. Identifying them, clocking their movements, habits.

So Sanders could pay his maid to stage a seduction scene for Ballard, after she had hung around Jacques Daniels' to make sure he would notice her.

Sanders, street-parking his Caddy where he knew O'B would spot it, once O'B believed Sanders was sneaking out of town at five a.m.

Sanders deliberately being too difficult to tail for suspicion to be aroused, but never so difficult that the tail could be lost.

Sanders maybe even paying the management to gimmick the air conditioner and shower in the room whoever was tailing him would be sure to rent. Playing games, as usual.

And Sanders playing *more* games – the non-incriminating phone call to the blonde when he *knew* his room would be bugged.

And now Sanders, head bowed beneath the hands of the Healer in a revival tent at the Santa Clara County fairgrounds, under the watchful eyes of 20,000 people.

"*Oh, God!*" cried the Colonel in a loud voice. "*Oh, God, I am saved! Oh, God be praised! Oh, see me, a sinner, SAVED!*"

And he cavorted around on the stage, shouting the power of the Lord, and hurled up the aisle at a certain red-haired man the cane he would never need again – as 20,000 throats roared their hysterical approval.

Oh, yes, the cane he would never need again. Because Colonel Buford Sanders, USAF, Ret'd, was $275,000 richer with no possibility of ever being charged with fraud. Some 20,000 good souls, and a trained detective besides, had witnessed the miracle of his cure. A trained detective who, under oath, could only testify as to what he had seen and heard. Who, indeed, had been carefully lured there for that very purpose.

It was too much. It was all just too damned much.

The Colonel embraced the Healer with tears of joy running down his face. As O'B had no doubt, he soon would embrace his blonde – with no worries about what a pencil mike from the next room might pick up.

O'B started to curse. Aloud.

Then the king said to the attendants, Bind his hands and feet and cast him forth into the darkness outside...

Yes, O'B cursed. Loudly and bitterly and blasphemously, from the very core of his soul, at how thoroughly and totally he had been set up and taken in by the Colonel. O'Bannon, the Unbeliever, cursed.

...where there shall be weeping and gnashing of teeth.

And they threw O'B out. Bodily.

John Ball

One for Virgil Tibbs

We are happy to welcome John Ball to this anthology and especially happy to welcome detective Virgil Tibbs in his first short story. Through the medium of motion pictures Virgil Tibbs has become known round the world. The first movie about him was "In the Heat of the Night" (1967), in which Sidney Poitier played the role of Virgil, and played it superbly. The movie won five Academy Awards and was voted the best picture of the year by the New York Film Critics. Two sequels, "They Call Me Mr. Tibbs" and "The Organization," also starred Sidney Poitier.

Now join the famous black detective in his first short-story investigation – and we do mean investigation. Virgil Tibbs is the ranking homicide specialist of the Pasadena (California) Police Department – "at the top of the death-by-violence totem pole." He is a one-man procedural 'tec task force, and in his first short story he tackles a difficult and unusual case...

At 11:31 a.m. on an unusually fine morning in Pasadena, California, the operator of a power shovel swung a full load of soil over the top of a heavy truck and pulled the release. Since the truck was almost full, a small shower of stones rattled off the sides, some loose dirt, and one human skull.

Fortunately Harry Hubert, male, 31, was working close by. As he raised his arm to signal the truck driver to move on he looked down, then froze in his tracks. "Hold it!" he yelled.

He was not a superstitious man, but he did not want to handle the skull. He signaled the shovel operator to cease digging, pointed to what he had discovered, then waved his arms in the air to be sure that everyone understood that all work was to stop.

The shovel operator brought his machine to a halt and the truck driver shut off his engine.

Superintendent Angelo Morelli was sent for. Meanwhile, the truck driver got out of his cab and joined Hubert to find out what was wrong. He looked down at the object on the ground, bent over to examine it more closely, then spoke. "Alas, poor Yorick," he said.

He was an admirer of Sir Laurence Olivier.

Superintendent Morelli was a man accustomed to making decisions. It took him only seconds to assay the situation, then he sent for the police.

One of the all-white Pasadena patrol cars responded promptly. It arrived without lights or siren, and as the working officer driving it got out, Morelli wondered, What the hell. The officer was a woman and a comely one at that.

As soon as she was close enough, he read the nameplate over her right pocket. It said DIAZ.

Morelli checked her over. She was armed, of course; metal handcuffs were properly pouched on her belt, and there was even a small container of Mace visible.

The superintendent approached her. Although he was a rough-and-ready type, he also knew how to be diplomatic. "I certainly appreciate your quick response," he said. "However, I'm not sure this is suitable for a policewoman."

"I'm not a policewoman," she answered. "I'm a cop. Where's the fight?"

Morelli was amused. "No fight this time," he reassured her. "Do you get many of those?"

"I broke one up last night – knives in a bar. I have a suspect in custody."

"Then kindly step this way."

Officer Marilyn Diaz spent three minutes in a careful survey of the situation. Then, despite her immaculate uniform, which was the same as the ones worn by the male members of the department, she explored the fresh excavation and the approximate spot where the skull had been unearthed.

She had one question for the shovel operator. "Is there any way you can tell," she asked, "how deeply that skull was buried when you dug it up?"

"No, ma'am, because I started my pass at the bottom of the cut and came up. I would guess that it was somewhere near to the top."

"So would I," Diaz agreed. "Hold everything, will you?"

"Right."

Officer Marilyn Diaz, who is one of the particular prides of the Pasadena Police, returned to her car and picked up the radio mike. Socially she was an attractive and charming young woman; on the job she did not waste words. "I've got one for Virgil," she reported. "At the Foothill Freeway construction site, near Raymond."

"Paramedics wanted?"

"No, human remains, but so far bones only."

"Anything else?"

"Yes," Diaz answered. "I've seen the skull. Unless I'm very wrong, the victim was an eight-to-ten-year-old child."

On the wall of the small office he shared with his partner, Bob Nakamura, Virgil Tibbs had a small sign posted. It read: *Write, for the night is coming.* He was engaged in doing precisely that, presiding over a manual typewriter and punching out the words of a report that, by police tradition, would be hopelessly pedantic and at least twice the necessary length. He spent hours writing reports, as did practically everyone else in the department. It was the curse of the profession.

His phone rang. He took the call, listened, then got up and put on his coat. As the ranking homicide specialist of the Pasadena Police, the discovery of an unattached skull was referred to him automatically. Ray Heatherton could have handled it, but Ray was only too delighted to let Virgil Tibbs sit at the top of the death-by-violence totem pole. Virgil had earned the spot many times over.

Virgil picked up an unmarked car, drove

to the location, parked behind Marilyn Diaz' unit, then walked over to where the people were gathered.

Superintendent Morelli saw him coming, noted that he was black, and remembered what he had read in the papers. "Is that Virgil Tibbs?" he asked Diaz.

"It is," she answered.

"He's good, I understand."

"The best."

Seconds later she made the introductions. Morelli shook hands, then got down to business. "As soon as the skull showed up, we stopped everything immediately." He motioned to a hardhat who was waiting close by. "This is Harry Hubert, he was the first to spot it."

Virgil listened to the man's account, then talked to the truck driver and the shovel operator. After that he addressed himself once more to Morelli. "I don't want to hold you up," he said. "I know that tying up men and equipment is costing you money and job delay. If you need the shovel somewhere else, I don't see any reason why you shouldn't move it. I'll need the truck until we can check the load in detail. Also, I want to go over the spot where the dirt is being dumped."

"I thought of that," Morelli said. "I stopped the unloading immediately. I don't believe anything has been moved since Harry saw that skull come off the truck."

"For that I'll buy you your lunch," Tibbs said.

"You're on."

"Fine. While we're eating, there are a few questions you might be able to answer for me."

Sergeant Jerry Ferguson headed the investigation team that arrived almost immediately thereafter. Since there was obviously pick-and-shovel work to be done, Superintendent Morelli assigned a half dozen men to work under Ferguson's direction. With Agent Barry Rothberg three of them left for the fill area where the dirt from the excavation was being dumped. At a convenient spot the filled truck that had taken the last load from the power shovel spread out what it had on board as another police unit arrived headed by Lieutenant Ron Peron.

Under careful examination the load that had been on the truck yielded up three additional bones and part of a spinal column. That grisly discovery was made shortly before Captain Bill Wilson arrived to see how the investigation was progressing.

By nightfall a set of foot bones that was almost intact had been discovered *in situ*. Its position suggested that the body, which had presumably been buried not long after death, had lain approximately four feet, three inches below the surface of the ground, with the head in an easterly direction. After extensive photographs had been taken, and measurements made, the few recovered bones were turned over to the Los Angeles County coroner. Even careful sifting gave no hope of recovering the complete skeleton, a point that disturbed Virgil Tibbs.

Satisfied that for the moment no more evidence would be found at the location, he authorized Superintendent Morelli to resume the construction work. He did ask that careful watch be kept while the remaining digging was done in the immediate vicinity – unauthorized burials were not always single projects. After the amount of searching that had already been done, he did not feel he could halt the important and expensive project any further without something definite in the form of additional evidence.

In the morning Tibbs went to work with grim determination. From the real-estate maps he located the exact piece of property that had marked the spot where the remains had been uncovered. It had been a single-family dwelling on a medium-sized lot in a definitely lower-class neighborhood. There had been no basement.

By the time he had these facts, the coroner's office called: the bone specialist was on the line. Virgil talked to the doctor for several minutes and was not encouraged by the conversation. From the skull it had been determined that the deceased had been a child approximately eight years of age. But no information could be given either as to race or sex. "You mean you can't say whether it was a boy or a girl?" Tibbs asked.

"That's right. The indications simply aren't present at that age."

"Can you make an informed guess?"

"Not based on what I have here."

The black detective was patient. "What *can* you tell me?" he persisted.

"The individual is deceased. Beyond that, only what you already have."

"Any dental data?"

"I should have mentioned that, forgive me. So far as can be determined, and this is pretty definite, the deceased never had any dental work done. But this doesn't necessarily indicate neglect; the subject could have been seen by a dentist who found that no work was required."

"And the age of the remains?"

"Say from three years back. There are

several reasons why I can't be more definite."

"I think I know what they are," Virgil said. "Thanks, Doctor."

"You're most welcome."

Virgil turned to Bob Nakamura. "All I have to worry about now is a missing child, male or female, ethnic background unknown, who disappeared anytime from, say, three years ago to you-say-when. And the fact that all the bones were not located after very careful search suggests that the corpse may have been cut up and buried in various places."

Bob was sympathetic. "Tough case, but not impossible. You have the specific house to work with – that should tell you a lot. Better than that corpse in the nudist park."

"Hell, yes, that took weeks." And Virgil went back to work.

By noon he had the picture. The house had last been occupied by an elderly couple, Mr. and Mrs. Ajurian. Mrs. Ajurian was recently dead; her husband was in a nursing home in a senile condition. The Ajurians had no known living relatives. Before their occupancy the house had stood vacant for almost three years, tied up in litigation because the owner had been killed in a car accident.

Prior to that the house had been rented on a month-to-month basis, frequently to young people who had been required to pay in advance, and occasionally to transient farm labor. The house itself had been moved away when the area had been cleared for the freeway. It had been offered at auction, but no bids had been received.

Two hours after lunch the house itself was located. It stood, helpless and unwanted, in a row of similar derelicts that had been parked in an available open area. As Virgil explored it minutely, he could not escape a feeling of profound depression. It was in a wretched state of outside repair and, if possible, was even worse inside.

The single bathroom had been painted a particularly violent purple and despite long disuse, it still carried a faintly unpleasant odor indicative of bad sanitation. Where the telephone had been, the walls were covered with jottings in various hands; the smaller bedroom had children's crude drawings covering most of the wall space within their reach. None of the drawings revealed any talent either in art or draftsmanship.

The floor in one closet was missing; the rectangular opening had the remains of a ledge that had once, obviously, held an unattached trap door. There was, of course, nothing unusual in that – it was a conventional access hole – but something else about the house interested Tibbs. When he had spent the better part of an hour examining the structure, he thanked the employee of the house mover who was serving as his guide.

"Did you find out anything?" the man asked, walking outside with Virgil.

"Yes, I think so."

"What?"

Virgil nodded down the long row of empty shells, the tombstones of what had once been homes. "Did you notice anything different about this one?" he asked.

"Not particularly. Most of them were in pretty bad shape when they came out here."

"It's at least two feet higher off the ground than any of the others," Tibbs said. "A little more than five feet between the surface of the ground and the bottom of the floor joists. Room enough for a man to work in, if he had to."

Meanwhile, Bob Nakamura determined, by interviewing some of their one-time neighbors, that the Ajurians had been a quiet elderly couple who had never entertained and seldom went out. They were judged to have been capable of only the simplest physical tasks. No children had ever been seen on their premises. The only criticism that the Nisei detective turned up was that they frequently cooked food so heavily spiced that the odor was objectionable. A check of the records revealed that they had been on welfare.

During the time the house had stood vacant, it had been frequently used as a juvenile and young-adult rendezvous; several arrests had been made, but there had never been any indications of violence.

One former long-time resident of the street recalled a Mexican family that had lived in the house. There had been eight or nine children; he did not remember the family name, but he did recall how the kids were incessantly running in and out and slamming the door each time. He had been glad when they moved away. He also remembered a group of six young people, three long-haired males and three females, who had taken up residence, but who had been surprisingly quiet and peaceful.

By the time all this information had been gathered, another day had gone by.

Most of the next day went into a careful examination of all available missing-juvenile reports that fell within the proper time frame. They added up to a heartbreaking number. Dental charts ruled out most of them, but Tibbs was left with over fifty possibles and sixteen that offered the best prospects of a make. When that tedious task had at last been completed, he sat back in his chair and began to think.

Bob Nakamura had seen him like that before, his eyes open but unfocused, his body relaxed. After half an hour, Virgil stirred and Bob was prepared. "It's a damn tough case," Bob said.

Tibbs nodded slowly. "Yes," he agreed, "but if I can put one or two more things together, I may have it."

"Accidental death?" Bob asked.

Virgil shook his head. "No – murder."

"The evidence of that is in the remains?"

"No."

"What else do you need?"

"I want to go back and re-examine that house. But before I do that, I've got some other work to do." He got up and stretched. "I'll see you after a while," he said, and left.

The voter-registration lists gave him some information, much of it quite old. He went over the available data carefully, but found little to excite his interest. The Mexican family that had lived in the house had never registered anyone, a fact that suggested they might have been illegal immigrants – a major problem in Southern California. On the other hand, it could have been indifference or an inability to understand English.

The welfare rolls were more productive. From them Virgil learned that Emilio and Rosa De Fuentes, plus their nine children, had been publicly supported at that address for some time.

That was a breakthrough. Knowing that welfare recipients often retained that status for years, he sent out a message through the network in California to learn if the same family was now being carried on the rolls elsewhere. That accomplished, Virgil once more took refuge in his second-floor office in the old part of the Pasadena Police building, leaned back, and went into another session of concentrated thought.

When he finally came up for air, Bob Nakamura was back and ready to play straight man. "Are you any nearer?" he asked.

"Yes."

"Fill me in."

Tibbs stirred. "A lot of things are beginning to fit together. My chief problem at the moment is the lack of hard data to back up some of my conclusions."

"Let's hear the conclusions."

"All right. We begin with the Ajurians, the Armenian immigrants."

"You dug that far back?"

"No, but I know they were immigrants because of the way they cooked their food. People direct from the old country tend to continue life as they knew it, particularly where diet is concerned. Second- and third-generation offspring from that part of the world prefer less spicy food. The Armenian part is easy because the name ends in *i-a-n*, something almost wholly Armenian."

"Go on."

"The evidence supports the fact that they were relatively feeble, and did not entertain, particularly children. Also, I'm inclined to rule out the hippie sextet who lived in the house for a while. I learned a lot from the drawings I found on the walls of one of the rooms."

"Explain."

Tibbs swung around to face his partner. "Obviously they weren't made during the time the elderly Ajurians were occupying the house. Yet they didn't remove them. They were on the wall of what would have been the second bedroom. The inference, therefore, is that they didn't remove the drawings because a fresh paint job was beyond their physical resources, or financial means. I suspect they closed off that room and used it only for storage.

"The hippie sextet also left the drawings alone – perhaps they found them amusing. It wasn't their house, they were simply living in it, and they probably favored self-expression. They weren't made during that period since I have statements that no children were seen around the house while the hippies were there."

"The drawings could have been faked – done by an adult."

Tibbs shook his head. "The only idea that holds water along that line would be an adult making them to entertain a child who used that room – but again, there were no children reported on the premises."

He stopped suddenly. For a moment or two he stared off into space with his lips held tightly together, then a whole new expression took over his face. "It's a long shot, but worth checking out." He got up once more.

"Where are you going this time?"

"I need a social worker and a grocery store," Virgil answered.

The social worker proved to be unavailable. After tracking her down, Tibbs learned that she had gone to Europe and was somewhere in Spain studying the guitar. He made a note of her name and background, then began his canvas of the grocery stores. That proved a much easier job; he hit paydirt within an hour.

Sam Margolis had operated his small market and liquor store at the same location for many years. He knew most of his customers well, and he recalled the De Fuentes family. "Too damn many kids," he declared. "She usually brought a lot of them with her and they couldn't keep their hands off anything. They even swiped ice cubes and sucked on them."

"They were on welfare, I believe."

"Yeah, they were. But the old man usually found enough money for a bottle. He wasn't a drunk, but he hit the cheap stuff a lot."

"Have you got any idea where they went?"

Margolis shrugged. "Who knows? And to be honest, who cares? This is a cash business only – no checks except for welfare and payroll that I know. Two will get you five they were wetbacks, or whatever they call them now. And the woman –" He shook his head. "What he saw in her I'll never know. She was built like a pile of mashed potatoes."

"You've helped me a lot," Tibbs said. "More than you know. One thing more if you can remember. Were all the children that you saw normal, at least reasonably so?"

"All that I saw."

"And do you remember if they had a boy in his teen years, anywhere from about thirteen or fourteen up?"

Margolis was definite. "Sure, Felipe. He came to the store sometimes."

"What was he like?" Virgil asked.

"Another Mex kid," Margolis answered.

When Virgil Tibbs got back to his office, there was news for him: Mr. and Mrs. Emilio De Fuentes and their eleven children were on welfare in Modesto, California. In response Tibbs picked up his phone and called the police department there. When he had been put through to a detective sergeant, he made a request. He described the family and supplied the welfare case number to make things as easy as possible.

"What I need," Virgil said, "is some information on when they reached Modesto and precisely when they went on welfare. I'd like a copy of the original document accepting them as welfare clients. Then, if it isn't too much trouble, I'd like the birth records of any children added to their family since they arrived up there. Especially an evidence of twins."

"Can do," the Modesto sergeant said.

After he finished the conversation Virgil

left his office and went out for one more look at the abandoned house. He stayed inside it for more than an hour, making an almost microscopic examination of the drawings that had first attracted his attention. He satisfied himself that three children, apparently of different ages, had made them.

Child number one had been the oldest, but the drawings, eight of them, were also the simplest and the most repetitive. Child number two had had a less steady hand, but more imagination. Tibbs traced six of the drawings to his or her hand, and no two of them were similar. Child number three appeared to have been the youngest since the drawings he or she had made were the lowest on the wall. They were also the most varied and showed, on Tibbs' second examination, evidence of talent.

Despite the crudity of the draftsmanship, the third child had painstakingly tried to add background, drawing a horizontal line to suggest ground level in one instance and adding what was obviously the sun in another. A third drawing showed experimentation; when a first attempt to draw a symmetrical figure had failed, the child artist had added lines until there were many arms and legs, and even the torso had a multiplicity of wavy outlines.

Virgil returned late to his office to find two messages. One of them was a report that had come in from Modesto by teletype, the other was a penciled note from Diane Stone, the chief's secretary, that Chief McGowan would like to see him when he came in.

He put in a call to the chief's office, but McGowan had already left. Virgil was glad of that because there were still some loose ends to tie up before he went upstairs. Since the chief had sent for him personally, it did not require much deductive ability to know what was on the chief's mind.

A welfare report he had been waiting for was on his desk. From it he learned that the De Fuentes family had come from a small village in Mexico. That was a setback since it meant that his chances of getting accurate birthdates and related information were close to nil. Fortunately, there were other routes of inquiry.

Tibbs went home to his apartment and stretched out to rest. He wanted an expensive dinner, but it was his superstition to hold off splurging while he was still closing a case. There was still one very sticky fact to be established and while he was by that time reasonably confident, it still had to be rated as a long shot.

In the morning he visited the public school

where some of the De Fuentes children had been enrolled. He did not trouble the office for official records, interviewing instead some teachers who had been on the faculty when the De Fuentes children had attended the school. The first three he spoke with could not help him much; one was resentful that he was there at all. "You haven't got any business prying into those peoples' lives," she told him. "You ought to be ashamed; you're a black man yourself and here you're trying to put down other people who have been discriminated against all their lives."

The gymnasium instructor was the one who came through. "I do remember the De Fuentes children very well," he told Virgil. "I was interested in them because one of the boys, Felipe, had remarkable athletic ability and exceptional reflexes. I think he could have made it all the way to the big time if he had really worked at it. But he showed no interest in baseball or basketball."

"Do you remember if he had any particularly close friends at school?" Tibbs asked.

"Yes, he did – several, as a matter of fact."

"May I have some names?"

"Yes, and you can get the addresses in the office if you need them. Willie Fremont,

Cliff Di Santo, Trig Yamamoto, and – oh, yes, there was a girl too – Elena Morales."

By two in the afternoon Virgil Tibbs had determined that three of the families had moved away, but he had two forwarding addresses. He succeeded in locating the Yamamoto boy where he was working in the vegetable department of a supermarket. By a little after four he had found and also talked to the Morales girl who was a winsome little beauty and highly intelligent. She supplied him with the final data that he needed.

He went back to the office and called Mrs. Stone, to say that he was in if the chief still wanted to see him.

McGowan did. Virgil walked into the boss's office and sat down. When Diane handed him a cup of coffee, with cream and sugar exactly to his taste, he understood that he might be there for a little while.

"Virgil," the chief said, "I have a rather personal interest in the case you're working on – the child remains found during the freeway construction. Have you been able to make any progress?"

"I believe so, sir."

Captain Wilson arrived, and the chief filled him in.

"How much have you got, Virgil?" the captain asked.

"Since I'm not in court yet, and I don't have to provide absolute proof," Tibbs answered, "I can tell you that it's a case of premeditated murder. So far I can name the victim, give the time of death, and supply the motive. If all goes well, by tomorrow night I should have enough solid evidence for an indictment."

"Virgil," the chief said, "you never cease to amaze me. Instead of waiting for your report, suppose you bring us up to date now."

"All right, sir." Tibbs relaxed and enjoyed a little of his coffee.

"The preliminary work was quite simple," he began. "I located the plot, got the history of the dwelling that had been on it, and inspected the house itself. Fortunately it hadn't been destroyed, because there was quite a bit of evidence there, notably a series of children's drawings which were especially helpful."

"Children's drawings?" the chief queried.

"Yes, in fact they provided the essential clue when I finally had sense enough to see it. I completely missed it the first time."

"You must be slipping," the chief said.

"Undoubtedly, sir. Anyhow, without going into unnecessary details, I checked out the history of the house and satisfied myself that the most recent residents had all had one thing in common – no children were ever known to be on the premises during their tenure. There was a period of vacancy when children might have gone into the house to play, but I couldn't find any evidence to support that idea. It was also possible that someone could have taken a child there with criminal intent, but the available missing-persons reports tended to reduce the odds on that.

"So I focused my attention on a large Mexican family that had occupied the house about five years ago. There were nine children, ranging from a boy of fourteen to a one-year-old infant. I'm now satisfied that three of these children made the drawings I found on the walls of the second bedroom. Offhand I would fix their ages at about ten, nine, and eight, with the youngest the most talented of the three."

"That's interesting, I'm sure," Wilson said, "but where is it leading us?"

"Into proof of murder."

"You have my attention," the chief said.

"Consider first the fact that there were nineteen drawings and that they were done by three different children. There you have definite evidence of lack of family discipline. It was a rental property, but no regard was given to the rights of the owner – otherwise the children would have been restrained from drawing all over the walls of what was evidently their bedroom. And there was no indication of any effort whatever to remove the drawings when the family left. So we may conclude that the family in question was at the best irresponsible."

"I think I'm beginning to see something coming," Chief McGowan murmured.

"When this family lived in Pasadena, shortly before their departure, they had nine children. The family is now in Modesto and the latest head count is eleven."

"Which is not surprising," Captain Wilson commented.

"That's the key to the whole thing," Virgil said.

"Eleven children?"

"Exactly."

It was silent in the executive office for a few moments. Then Chief McGowan leaned forward in his chair. "I get it," he said.

Tibbs nodded. "In a neighborhood like that, sir, with all the constant comings and goings and the frequent turnover in residents, hardly anyone, even the children's playmates, can keep track of every child in a family. And I have now learned that since the family moved to Modesto, three more children have been delivered to them. The birth records are on file and I have copies coming in the mail."

"Three more children. Nine plus three are twelve. But you said the latest count was only eleven," Captain Wilson noted.

"Yes, sir. Now add to that these facts: we have a set of parents with a profusion of children. I'm not putting down large families, but the De Fuentes family may have been blessed with more than they actually wanted. They couldn't possibly support them – they were on welfare, and the mother was constantly pregnant.

"I was turning these thoughts over in my mind when an idea hit me. What if one of those children had been particularly unwanted, because of being retarded or otherwise afflicted? In most cases that wouldn't add up to murder, not by a wide margin, but here we are faced with the undisputable fact that a child of approximately eight years of age was buried under that house.

"If the child had died normally, since the family was already receiving assistance, some sort of funeral arrangements could have been made."

"Also," Captain Wilson added, "since they are Mexican, there is a good chance the family is Catholic. The obvious absence of birth-control measures would support that. If a child of theirs had died under acceptable circumstances, then they would want to have it buried in sanctified ground with the proper religious rites."

Tibbs nodded agreement. "When I re-examined the house itself," he continued, "I checked carefully for any evidence that might reveal an abnormal child. It was entirely possible, with all those children, such an unfortunate individual could be kept effectively hidden from the casual observation of the neighbors. If the child's condition was bad enough, that would have been almost automatic.

"I found what I was looking for in the drawings I described. One of them in particular. It had been done by the youngest of the three child artists and this child, as I mentioned earlier, had some artistic ability. He, or she, added touches of background and tried to make an actual picture. One of these efforts showed a child with what at first appeared to be multiple arms and legs, and a torso of wavy outlines, drawn in apparently to get the right proportions. Then I realized it wasn't that at all. First, the other drawings done by the same child exhibited no such difficulty, in fact the proportions were quite good. What the child was actually drawing was another child –"

"*Shaking!*" the chief interjected. "A spastic!"

"That's it, sir. Now I was confident that I knew why a large family might willfully dispose of one of its children. Even death by accident wouldn't call for the extreme measure of burying a child under the house. The answer was painfully apparent – a too large family with a problem child might make the terrible decision to simply get rid of it before moving on. A family leaves one location with a large brood of children; it arrives at the next one, still with a large brood – who is going to notice that one is missing?"

"There are institutions," the chief said. "Surely they must have known that."

"Perhaps they did, but there is some indication that despite the fact the family had been on welfare for some time, it may have come to this country illegally. Also, unfortunately, there are many people to whom any kind of institution is terrifying. I believe they thought that what they planned would be simpler. Anyhow, the social worker's report on the family, which I dug out and read, lists a boy who would have been eight and a half when the family moved away. His name was Alberto. I checked with Modesto where the family is receiving assistance now. There is no Alberto. That is hard evidence. I suspect that if we confront the father with the facts we now have, he will admit to what he probably has rationalized as a mercy killing."

"I can't understand," Captain Wilson said, "how they expected to get away with it. What did they tell their other children?"

"Probably that Alberto had been taken away, or some other excuse. The older children might have been cautioned never to speak of their spastic brother in case it might harm their own images. They would understand that."

Tibbs stopped for a moment and locked his fingers tightly together as he frequently did when he was under mental stress. Then he looked up once more. "You see, sir, they *did* get away with it. The missing child died years ago – we know that – he was buried, and there he lay. No one ever raised a question so far as I have been able to learn, and I strongly doubt if anyone ever would. It was pure accident that the burial site was excavated for the new freeway, and even that could well have passed unnoticed if the skull had not rolled off the top of the load. If that truck had been half full or less when the bones were loaded, the chances are good they would never have been noticed."

Chief McGowan had one more question. "Did the social worker make any mention of an abnormal child in her report?"

Tibbs nodded. "Yes, sir, she did. But she called him an 'exceptional child,' which was the term just coming into use at that time. If the family saw the report, or was shown it, that phrase would probably not register with them, particularly since English is not their native language. I don't think, gentlemen, that we will have too much trouble in obtaining a confession."

And in that, too, he was right.

Robert Bloch

A Most Unusual Murder

It all started outside an especially curious curiosity shop in London's Saxe-Coburg Square... and ended in a shabby lodging at 17 Dorcas Lane, the two friends drawn there by a famous mystery and themselves becoming part of the terrible legend...

Only the dead know Brooklyn.
 Thomas Wolfe said that, and he's dead now, so he ought to know.
 London, of course, is a different story.
 At least that's the way Hilary Kane thought of it. Not as a story, perhaps, but rather as an old-fashioned, outsize picaresque novel in which every street was a chapter crammed with characters and incidents of its own. Each block a page, each structure a separate paragraph unto itself within the sprawling, tangled plot – such was Hilary Kane's concept of the city, and he knew it well.

Over the years he strolled the pavements, reading the city sentence by sentence until every line was familiar; he'd learned London by heart.

And that's why he was so startled when, one bleak afternoon late in November, he discovered the shop in Saxe-Coburg Square.

"I'll be damned!" he said.

"Probably." Lester Woods, his companion, took the edge off the affirmation with an indulgent smile. "What's the problem?"

"This." Kane gestured towards the tiny window of the establishment nestled inconspicuously between two residential relics of Victoria's day.

"An antique place." Woods nodded. "At the rate they're springing up there must be at least one for every tourist in London."

"But not here." Kane frowned. "I happen to have come by this way less than a week ago, and I'd swear there was no shop in the Square."

"Then it must have opened since." The two men moved up to the entrance, glancing through the display window in passing.

Kane's frown deepened. "You call this new? Look at the dust on those goblets."

"Playing detective again, eh?" Woods shook his head. "Trouble with you, Hilary, is that you have too many hobbies." He glanced across the Square as a chill wind heralded the coming of twilight. "Getting late – we'd better move along."

"Not until I find out about this."

Kane was already opening the door and Woods sighed. "The game is afoot, I suppose. All right, let's get it over with."

The shop-bell tinkled and the two men stepped inside. The door closed, the tinkling stopped, and they stood in the shadows and the silence.

But one of the shadows was not silent. It rose from behind the single counter in the small space before the rear wall.

"Good afternoon, gentlemen," said the shadow. And switched on an overhead light. It cast a dim nimbus over the countertop and gave dimension to the shadow, revealing the substance of a diminutive figure with an unremarkable face beneath a balding brow.

Kane addressed the proprietor. "Mind if we have a look?"

"Is there any special area of interest?" The proprietor gestured toward the shelves lining the wall behind them. "Books, maps, china, crystal?"

"Not really," Kane said. "It's just that I'm always curious about a new shop of this sort –"

The proprietor shook his head. "Begging your pardon, but it's hardly new."

Woods glanced at his friend with a barely suppressed smile, but Kane ignored him.

"Odd," Kane said. "I've never noticed this place before."

"Quite so. I've been in business a good many years, but this *is* a new location."

Now it was Kane's turn to glance quickly at Woods, and his smile was not suppressed. But Woods was already eyeing the artifacts on display, and after a moment Kane began his own inspection.

Peering at the shelving beneath the glass counter, he made a rapid inventory. He noted a boudoir lamp with a beaded fringe, a lavaliere, a tray of pearly buttons, a durbar souvenir programme, and a framed and inscribed photograph of Matilda Alice Victoria Wood *aka* Bella Delmare *aka* Marie Lloyd. There was a miscellany of old jewelry, hunting-watches, pewter mugs, napkin rings, a toy bank in the shape of a miniature Crystal Palace, and a display poster of a formidably mustached Lord Kitchener with his gloved finger extended in a gesture of imperious command.

It was, he decided, the mixture as before. Nothing unusual, and most of it – like the Kitchener poster – not even properly antique but merely outmoded. Those fans on the bottom shelf, for example, and the silk toppers, the opera glasses, the black bag in the far corner covered with what was once called "American cloth."

Something about the phrase caused Kane to stoop and make a closer inspection. *American cloth.* Dusty now, but once shiny, like the tarnished silver nameplate identifying its owner. He read the inscription.

J. Ridley, M.D.

Kane looked up, striving to conceal his sudden surge of excitement.

Impossible! It couldn't be – and yet it was. Keeping his voice and gesture carefully casual, he indicated the bag to the proprietor.

"A medical kit?"

"Yes, I imagine so."

"Might I ask where you acquired it?"

The little man shrugged. "Hard to remember. In this line one picks up the odd item here and there over the years."

"Might I have a look at it, please?"

The elderly proprietor lifted the bag to the countertop. Woods stared at it, puzzled, but Kane ignored him, his gaze intent on the nameplate below the lock. "Would you mind opening it?" he said.

"I'm afraid I don't have a key."

Kane reached out and pressed the lock; it

was rusted, but firmly fixed. Frowning, he lifted the bag and shook it gently.

Something jiggled inside, and as he heard the click of metal against metal his elation peaked. Somehow he suppressed it as he spoke.

"How much are you asking?"

The proprietor was equally emotionless. "Not for sale."

"But –"

"Sorry, sir. It's against my policy to dispose of blind items. And since there's no telling what's inside –"

"Look, it's only an old medical bag. I hardly imagine it contains the Crown jewels."

In the background Woods snickered, but the proprietor ignored him. "Granted," he said. "But one can't be certain of the contents." Now the little man lifted the bag and once again there was a clicking sound. "Coins, perhaps."

"Probably just surgical instruments," Kane said impatiently. "Why don't you force the lock and settle the matter?"

"Oh, I couldn't do that. It would destroy its value."

"What value?" Kane's guard was down now; he knew he'd made a tactical error but he couldn't help himself.

The proprietor smiled. "I told you the bag is not for sale."

"Everything has its price."

Kane's statement was a challenge, and the proprietor's smile broadened as he met it. "One hundred pounds."

"A hundred pounds for *that?*" Woods grinned – then gaped at Kane's response.

"Done and done."

"But, sir –"

For answer Kane drew out his wallet and extracted five twenty-pound notes. Placing them on the countertop, he lifted the bag and moved toward the door. Woods followed hastily, turning to close the door behind him.

The proprietor gestured. "Wait – come back –"

But Kane was already hurrying down the street, clutching the black bag under his arm.

He was still clutching it half an hour later as Woods moved with him into the spacious study of Kane's flat overlooking the verdant vista of Cadogan Square. Dappled splotches of sunlight reflected from the gleaming oilcloth as Kane set the bag on the table and wiped away the dust. He smiled at Woods.

"Looks a bit better now, don't you think?"

"I don't think anything." Woods shook

his head. "A hundred pounds for an old medical kit –"

"A *very* old medical kit," said Kane. "Dates back to the Eighties, if I'm not mistaken."

"Even so, I hardly see –"

"Of course you wouldn't! I doubt if anyone besides myself would attach much significance to the name of J. Ridley, M.D."

"Never heard of him."

"That's understandable." Kane smiled. "He preferred to call himself Jack the Ripper."

"Jack the Ripper?"

"Surely you know the case. Whitechapel, 1888 – the savage slaying and mutilation of prostitutes by a cunning mass-murderer who taunted the police – a shadow, stalking his prey in the streets."

Woods frowned. "But he was never caught, was he? Not even identified."

"In that you're mistaken. No murderer has been identified quite as frequently as Red Jack. At the time of the crimes and over the years since, a score of suspects were named. A prime candidate was the Pole, Klosowski, alias George Chapman, who killed several wives – but poison was his method and gain his motive whereas the Ripper's victims were all penniless prostitutes who died under the knife. Another convicted murderer, Neil Cream, even openly proclaimed he was the Ripper —"

"Wouldn't that be the answer, then?"

Kane shrugged. "Unfortunately, Cream happened to be in America at the time of the Ripper murders. Egomania prompted his false confession." He shook his head. "Then there was John Pizer, a bookbinder known by the nickname of 'Leather Apron' — he was actually arrested, but quickly cleared and released. Some think the killings were the work of a Russian called Konovalov who also went by the name of Pedachenko and worked as a barber's surgeon; supposedly he was a Tsarist secret agent who perpetrated the slayings to discredit the British police."

"Sounds pretty far-fetched if you ask me."

"Exactly." Kane smiled. "But there are other candidates, equally improbable. Montague John Druitt for one, a barrister of unsound mind who drowned himself in the Thames shortly after the last Ripper murder. Unfortunately, it has been established that he was living in Bournemouth, and on the days before and after the final slaying he was there, playing cricket. Then there was the Duke of Clarence —"

"Who?"

"Queen Victoria's grandson in direct line of succession to the throne."

"Surely you're not serious?"

"No, but others are. It has been asserted that Clarence was a known deviate who suffered from insanity as the result of venereal infection, and that his death in 1892 was actually due to the ravages of his disease."

"But that doesn't prove him to be the Ripper."

"Quite so. It hardly seems possible that he could write the letters filled with American slang and crude errors in grammar and spelling which the Ripper sent to the authorities; letters containing information which could be known only by the murderer and the police. More to the point, Clarence was in Scotland at the time of one of the killings and at Sandringham when others took place. And there are equally firm reasons for exonerating suggested suspects close to him – his friend James Stephen and his physician, Sir William Gull."

"You've really studied up on this," Woods murmured. "I'd no idea you were so keen on it."

"And for good reason. I wasn't about to make a fool of myself by advancing an untenable notion. I don't believe the Ripper was a seaman, as some surmise, for there's not a scintilla of evidence to back the theory. Nor do I think the Ripper was a slaughter-house worker, a midwife, a man disguised as a woman, or a London bobby. And I doubt the very existence of a mysterious physician named Dr. Stanley, out to avenge himself against the woman who had infected him, or his son."

"But there do seem to be a great number of medical men amongst the suspects," Woods said.

"Right you are, and for good reason. Consider the nature of the crimes – the swift and skillful removal of vital organs, accomplished in the darkness of the streets under constant danger of imminent discovery. All this implies the discipline of someone versed in anatomy, someone with the cool nerves of a practising surgeon. Then too there's the matter of escaping detection. The Ripper obviously knew the alleys and byways of the East End so thoroughly that he could slip through police cordons and patrols without discovery. But if seen, who would have a better alibi than a respectable physician, carrying a medical bag on an emergency call late at night?

"With that in mind, I set about my search, examining the rolls of London Hospital in

Whitechapel Road. I went over the names of physicians and surgeons listed in the Medical Registry for that period."

"All of them?"

"It wasn't necessary. I knew what I was looking for – a surgeon who lived and practised in the immediate Whitechapel area. Whenever possible, I followed up with a further investigation of my suspects' histories – researching hospital and clinic affiliations, even hobbies and background activities from medical journals, press reports, and family records. Of course, all this takes a great deal of time and patience. I must have been tilting at this windmill for a good five years before I found my man."

Woods glanced at the nameplate on the bag. "J. Ridley, M.D.?"

"John Ridley. *Jack*, to his friends – if he had any." Kane paused, thoughtful. "But that's just the point. Ridley appears to have had no friends, and no family. An orphan, he received his degree from Edinburgh in 1878, ten years before the date of the murders. He set up private practise here in London, but there is no office address listed. Nor is there any further information to be found concerning him; it's as though he took particular care to suppress every detail of his personal and private life. This, of course, is what roused my suspicions. For an entire decade J. Ridley lived and practised in the East End without a single mention of his name anywhere in print, except for his Registry listing. And after 1888, even *that* disappeared."

"Suppose he died?"

"There's no obituary on record."

Woods shrugged. "Perhaps he moved, emigrated, took sick, abandoned practise?"

"Then why the secrecy? Why conceal his whereabouts? Don't you see – it's the very lack of such ordinary details which leads me to suspect the extraordinary."

"But that's not evidence. There's no proof that your Dr. Ridley was the Ripper."

"That's why this is so important." Kane indicated the bag on the tabletop. "If we knew its history, where it came from –"

As he spoke, Kane reached down and picked up a brass letter-opener from the table, then moved to the bag.

"Wait." Woods put a restraining hand on Kane's shoulder. "That may not be necessary."

"What do you mean?"

"I think the shopkeeper was lying. He knew what the bag contains – he had to, or else why did he fix such a ridiculous price? He never dreamed you'd take him up on it, of course. But there's no need for you to force the lock any more than there was for him to do so. My guess is that he has a key."

"You're right." Kane set the letter-opener down. "I should have realized, if I'd taken the time to consider his reluctance. He must have the key." He lifted the shiny bag and turned. "Come along – let's get back to him before the shop closes. And this time we won't be put off by any excuses."

Dusk had descended as Kane and his companion hastened through the streets, and darkness was creeping across the deserted silence of Saxe-Coburg Square when they arrived.

They halted then, staring into the shadows, seeking the spot where the shop nestled between the residences looming on either side. The shadows were deeper here and they moved closer, only to stare again at the empty gap between the two buildings.

The shop was gone.

Woods blinked, then turned and gestured to Kane. "But we were here – we saw it –"

Kane didn't reply. He was staring at the dusty, rubble-strewn surface of the space between the structures; at the weeds which sprouted from the bare ground beneath. A chill night wind echoed through the emptiness. Kane stooped and sifted a pinch of dust between his fingers. The dust was cold, like the wind that whirled the fine grains from his hand and blew them away into the darkness.

"What happened?" Woods was murmuring. "Could we both have dreamed –"

Kane stood erect, facing his friend. "This isn't a dream," he said, gripping the black bag.

"Then what's the answer?"

"I don't know." Kane frowned thoughtfully. "But there's only one place where we can possibly find it."

"Where?"

"The 1888 Medical Registry lists the address of John Ridley as Number 17 Dorcas Lane."

The cab which brought them to Dorcas Lane could not enter its narrow accessway. The dim alley beyond was silent and empty, but Kane plunged into it without hesitation, moving along the dark passage between solid rows of grimy brick. Treading over the cobblestone, it seemed to Woods that he was being led into another era, yet Kane's progress was swift and unfaltering.

"You've been here before?" Woods said.

"Of course." Kane halted before the

unlighted entrance to Number 17, then knocked.

The door opened – not fully, but just enough to permit the figure behind it to peer out at them. Both glance and greeting were guarded.

"Whatcher want?"

Kane stepped into the fan of light from the partial opening. "Good evening. Remember me?"

"Yes." The door opened wider and Woods could see the squat shadow of the middle-aged woman who nodded up at his companion. "Yer the one what rented the back vacancy last Bank 'oliday, ain'tcher?"

"Right. I was wondering if I might have it again."

"I dunno." The woman glanced at Woods.

"Only for a few hours." Kane reached for his wallet. "My friend and I have a business matter to discuss."

"Business, eh?" Woods felt the unflattering appraisal of the landlady's beady eyes. "Cost you a fiver."

"Here you are."

A hand extended to grasp the note. Then the door opened fully, revealing the dingy hall and the stairs beyond.

"Mind the steps now," the landlady said.

The stairs were steep and the woman was

puffing as they reached the upper landing. She led them along the creaking corridor to the door at the rear, fumbling for the keys in her apron.

" 'Ere we are."

The door opened on musty darkness, scarcely dispelled by the faint illumination of the overhead fixture as she switched it on. The landlady nodded at Kane. "I don't rent this for lodgings no more – it ain't properly made up."

"Quite all right." Kane smiled, his hand on the door.

"If there's anything you'll be needing, best tell me now. I've got to run over to the neighbor for a bit – she's been took ill."

"I'm sure we'll manage." Kane closed the door, then listened for a moment as the landlady's footsteps receded down the hall.

"Well," he said. "What do you think?"

Woods surveyed the shabby room with its single window framed by yellowing curtains. He noted the faded carpet with its pattern wellnigh worn away, the marred and chipped surfaces of the massive old bureau and heavy morris-chair, the brass bed covered with a much-mended spread, the ancient gas-log in the fireplace framed by a cracked marble mantelpiece, and the equally-cracked washstand fixture in the corner.

77

"I think you're out of your mind," Woods said. "Did I understand correctly that you've been here before?"

"Exactly. I came several months ago, as soon as I found the address in the Registry. I wanted a look around."

Woods wrinkled his nose. "More to smell than there is to see."

"Use your imagination, man! Doesn't it mean anything to you that you're in the very room once occupied by Jack the Ripper?"

Woods shook his head. "There must be a dozen rooms to let in this old barn. What makes you think this is the right one?"

"The Registry entry specified 'rear'. And there are no rear accommodations downstairs – that's where the kitchen is located. So this had to be the place."

Kane gestured. "Think of it – you may be looking at the very sink where the Ripper washed away the traces of his butchery, the bed in which he slept after his dark deeds were performed! Who knows what sights this room has seen and heard – the voice crying out in a tormented nightmare –"

"Come off it, Hilary!" Woods grimaced impatiently. "It's one thing to use your imagination, but quite another to let your imagination use you."

"Look." Kane pointed to the far corner

of the room. "Do you see those indentations in the carpet? I noticed them when I examined this room on my previous visit. What do they suggest to you?"

Woods peered dutifully at the worn surface of the carpet, noting the four round, evenly spaced marks. "Must have been another piece of furniture in that corner. Something heavy, I'd say."

"But what sort of furniture?"

"Well –" Woods considered. "Judging from the space, it wasn't a sofa or chair. Could have been a cabinet, perhaps a large desk –"

"Exactly. A rolltop desk. Every doctor had one in those days." Kane sighed. "I'd give a pretty penny to know what became of that item. It might have held the answer to all our questions."

"After all these years? Not bloody likely." Woods glanced away. "Didn't find anything else, did you?"

"I'm afraid not. As you say, it's been a long time since the Ripper stayed here."

"I didn't say that." Woods shook his head. "You may be right about the desk. And no doubt the Medical Registry gives a correct address. But all it means is that this room may once have been rented by a Dr. John

Ridley. You've already inspected it once – why bother to come back?"

"Because now I have this." Kane placed the black bag on the bed. "And this." He produced a pocket-knife.

"You intend to force the lock after all?"

"In the absence of a key I have no alternative." Kane wedged the blade under the metal guard and began to pry upwards. "It's important that the bag be opened here. Something it contains may very well be associated with this room. If we recognize the connection we might have an additional clue, a conclusive link –"

The lock snapped.

As the bag sprang open, the two men stared down at its contents – the jumble of vials and pillboxes, the clumsy old-style stethescope, the probes and tweezers, the roll of gauze. And, resting atop it, the scalpel with the steel-tipped surface encrusted with brownish stains.

They were still staring as the door opened quietly behind them and the balding, elderly little man entered the room.

"I see my guess is correct, gentlemen. You too have read the Medical Registry." He nodded. "I was hoping I'd find you here."

Kane frowned. "What do you want?"

"I'm afraid I must trouble you for my bag."

"But it's my property now – I bought it."

The little man sighed. "Yes, and I was a fool to permit it. I thought putting on that price would dissuade you. How was I to know you were a collector like myself?"

"Collector?"

"Of curiosa pertaining to murder." The little man smiled. "A pity you cannot see some of the memorabilia I've acquired. Not the commonplace items associated with your so-called Black Museum in Scotland Yard, but true rarities with historical significance." He gestured. "The silver jar in which the notorious French sorceress, La Voisin, kept her poisonous ointments, the actual dirks which dispatched the unfortunate nephews of Richard III in the Tower – yes, even the poker responsible for the atrocious demise of Edward II at Berkeley Castle on the night of September 21st, 1327. I had quite a bit of trouble locating it until I realized the date was reckoned according to the old Julian calendar."

Kane frowned impatiently. "Who are you? What happened to that shop of yours?"

"My name would mean nothing to you. As for the shop, let us say that it exists spatially and temporally as I do – when and where necessary for my purposes. By your current and limited understanding, you might call it a sort of time-machine."

Woods shook his head. "You're not making sense."

"Ah, but I am, and very good sense too. How else do you think I could pursue my interests so successfully unless I were free to travel in time? It is my particular pleasure to return to certain eras in this primitive past of yours, visiting the scenes of famous and infamous crimes and locating trophies for my collection.

"The shop, of course, is just something I used as a blind for this particular mission. It's gone now, and I shall be going too, just as soon as I retrieve my property. It happens to be the souvenir of a most unusual murder."

"You see?" Kane nodded at Woods. "I told you this bag belonged to the Ripper!"

"Not so," said the little man. "I already have the Ripper's murder weapon, which I retrieved directly after the slaying of his final victim on November 9th, 1888. And I can assure you that your Dr. Ridley was not Jack the Ripper but merely and simply an eccentric surgeon –" As he spoke, he edged toward the bed.

"No you don't!" Kane turned to intercept

him, but he was already reaching for the bag. "Let go of that!" Kane shouted.

The little man tried to pull away, but Kane's hand swooped down frantically into the open bag and clawed. Then it rose, gripping the scalpel.

The little man yanked the bag away. Clutching it, he retreated as Kane bore down upon him furiously.

"Stop!" Woods cried. Hurling himself forward, he stepped between the two men, directly into the orbit of the descending blade.

There was a gurgle, then a thud, as he fell.

The scalpel clattered to the floor, slipping from Kane's nerveless fingers and coming to rest in the spreading crimson stain.

The little man stooped and picked up the scalpel. "Thank you," he said softly. "You have given me what I came for." He dropped the weapon into the bag.

Then he shimmered. Shimmered – and disappeared.

But Woods' body didn't disappear. Kane stared down at it – at the throat ripped open from ear to ear.

He was still staring when they came and took him away.

The trial, of course, was a sensation. It

wasn't so much the crazy story Kane told as the fact that nobody could ever find the fatal weapon.
It was a most unusual murder...

Barbara Callahan

Lavender Lady

Barbara Callahan's first story, "The Sin Painter," appeared in the August 1974 issue of Ellery Queen's Mystery Magazine. We described it as an unusual and interesting mystery debut.
   Mrs. Callahan's second story is a long step forward in her writing career. The second story is also unusual and interesting, but it is more; it is a sensitive and moving story, deeply felt by the author – so deeply felt that it will touch your heart...

It was always the same request wherever I played. College audiences, park audiences, concert-hall audiences – they listened and waited. Would I play it in the beginning of a set? Would I wait till the end of a performance? When would I play *Lavender Lady?*
   Once I tried to trick them into forgetting that song. I sang four new songs, good songs

with intricate chords and compelling lyrics. They listened politely as if each work were merely the flip side of the song they really wanted to hear.

That night I left the stage without playing it. I went straight to my dressing room and put my guitar in the closet. I heard them chanting *"Lavender Lady, Lavender Lady."* The chant began as a joyful summons which I hoped would drift into silence like a nursery rhyme a child tires of repeating. It didn't. The chant became an ugly command accompanied by stamping feet. I fled to safety.

Milo, my manager, found me in the closet with my guitar. His dark eyes, reproving and cold, told me I would be without him if I did not go back onstage. I couldn't bear the thought of facing the night alone.

I stood in the wings and listened to him lie. "Miranda will be right back. She broke a string. She loves to sing *Lavender Lady* as much as you love to hear it."

The chanters applauded wildly. Milo slipped offstage and grabbed my arm.

"They'll forgive you this time," he snapped. "Now go out there."

"And you, Milo, you'll forgive me?"

"Yes, yes, but only this time."

Now I must play *Lavender Lady* at the end

of every concert. I used to cry when I sang it but now I am drained so by it that Milo has to come onstage and carry me off. I slump over my guitar in a faint. I've been told that audiences love my finale.

I don't know exactly what happens to me when I play that song. I can remember only the introduction to it. After that the song takes over and tells me what to do.

It tells me to stare at a blankness over the heads of the audiences. In a review of my concert in Philadelphia a critic wrote: "Miranda Smith focuses on a fragment of space that becomes quite real to her. Perhaps lavender-colored ectoplasm materializes somewhere below the first balcony. The golden-haired folksinger becomes a medium for the expression of love offered and then terror unleashed. She begins *Lavender Lady* with a radiant smile and ends it with a sadness so overwhelming that it annihilates her. The last note of the song is like the final beat of her heart. Her arms slide limply over her guitar, her golden hair tumbles over the cold surface of the instrument. She becomes still, terribly still. Then the dark-haired prince, her manager, Milo McGee, comes to carry his Sleeping Beauty away.

"Once more the *Lavender Lady* has

triumphed by pushing the frail musician into a trance from which, according to McGee, she awakens the following morning. Who is this Lavender Lady and why does she exert such power over the millionairess-singer? McGee has hinted that she is Miranda's mother, the lovely socialite who abandoned the child when she was eight years old."

Milo is such a liar. He knows she isn't Mother, yet he told a magazine writer that the last time I saw Mother she was wearing a lavender gown. She was wearing a brown fur coat.

The women hired by my father to care for me were old and irritable. I was horrible to all of them. When Father interviewed the young woman with the long blonde hair, I knew I would like her. As soon as we were introduced, she hugged me. The lavender scent she wore tickled my nose and made me sneeze. She told me she wouldn't use it any more, but I wanted her to. The lavender was a lovely clue to her presence. I could always find her.

Lavender Lady, so young and so dear,
Lavender Lady, I know when you're near.

She taught me my lessons at home. We worked hard. Afterward we went down to the pond or to the grape arbor. We played wonderful games until I became tired. Then she put me on her lap and sang to me. At dusk I took her hand. We ran all the way home because we were two princesses being pursued by the Fiend of the Fields who wanted to change us into mushrooms.

Sometimes we tired of the arbor and the pond. We went outside the estate, across the road, and down to the rock pile. The rock pile was the moon and we climbed all over it. It was fun being a Moon Maiden until we met the Moon Monster.

The Lavender Lady never called him the Moon Monster. She called him Jim. She told me Jim was our secret friend whom we had met in a secret place. I was never to tell anyone about Jim who sat with his arm around her while I scrambled on the rocks. I never told anyone our secret.

Lavender Lady, the secrets we shared,
Lavender Lady, I never was scared.

Milo keeps secrets well, I think. His lies please him more than the truth. He knows about the Lavender Lady and the Moon Monster. He's the only one I ever talk to about them. He knows how I begged her to send Jim away. He spoiled our games so finally she did.

I told Milo about our journey too. The Lavender Lady asked my father if she could take me to visit her mother. Father wanted the chauffeur to drive us, but the Lavender Lady refused. Her mother would be embarrassed, she told Father, if such a magnificent car pulled up in front of her shabby house.

    The Lavender Lady and I took a bus. It was the first time I had ever been on one. "You poor little rich girl," the Lavender Lady said as she helped me onto the bus. After a while I didn't care much for the gaseous odor. I put my head on her shoulder and breathed in her lovely lavender scent until I fell asleep.

She shook me gently at our stop. I looked up and down the street but I didn't see a shabby house. We walked around the block and waited for another bus. As we sat on the bench the Lavender Lady reached into her large handbag. "Surprise," she said, "we're going to surprise my mother. She thinks you are a little blonde-haired girl. We'll fool her. I'll put this on you."

    I laughed and laughed when I looked into the mirror of her compact. I had become a red-haired little girl with pigtails. And I laughed again when she put the red bandanna with black bangs on it over her head.

Lavender Lady, so pretty and wise,
Lavender Lady, you loved to surprise.

Milo is cruel sometimes. I wish I had never told him about the wig. When I wanted to avoid recognition on a flight to Los Angeles, he put a red wig with pigtails on me. After I threw it on the floor, Milo refused to fend off passengers who came to me for my autograph.

I took off the red wig when we left the bus. The walk was long and hot. The Lavender Lady wanted to run but I told her that the Fiend of the Fields didn't live around there.

Her mother's house was so ugly. The paint was peeling off and the porch was falling apart. We walked up two rickety steps when the door was opened by the Moon Monster.

"Where is her mother?" I asked him.

"She went away," Jim said.

"Like my mother did?" I asked.

"I guess so," he answered.

I hugged the Lavender Lady tightly. Poor beautiful thing. I knew exactly how sad she must have felt.

Lavender Lady, such sadness you've known,
Lavender Lady, you won't be alone.

Jim pulled me away from her and kissed her. I didn't like that so I kicked him. He raised his arm to hit me but the Lavender Lady blocked him. She took me into the kitchen and heated some soup. It was chicken noodle but it tasted odd. I fell asleep at the table.

When I woke up I was lying on a dirty cot in a bedroom. Jim was sitting on a chair next to me.

"Where did she go?" I cried.

"To make a phone call. Now go back to sleep."

I tried to get up but Jim pushed me down. The room was so smelly. When she returned she would wrap me in her lavender scent and everything would be all right again. When I heard her footsteps downstairs I ran to the door. Jim picked me up and dumped me on that terrible cot, then locked the bedroom door when he left. I pounded and pounded but she must not have heard.

The next morning she brought me oatmeal. Then she washed my tear-stained face. When she rocked me back and forth in her arms I began to feel better. "Take me away from here," I begged.

"He won't let me do that," she said. "We'll just have to do what he says until we get our chance to escape. This is like one of our games by the pond. We're two princesses but we'll get away."

The Lavender Lady took me outside the awful house. We walked to a field where Stars of Bethlehem curtsied in the wind. She sat down and I made a garland for her hair. After I tired of picking flowers I wondered why we didn't walk through the fields into the woods, away from the ugly house and away from him.

"Now," I told her, "let's go now. He'll never know."

She shook her head. "He's upstairs in the house. He is looking at us through binoculars. He'll overtake us."

"But his car is gone. He drove away."

"No, little rich girl, that's the trick. He drove it around the back of the house. He's still there."

When he came walking through the field, smashing the flowers under his feet, she smiled at him. She could pretend so well. She jumped up and hugged him. Together they opened a suitcase filled with money. She tossed some of it into the air.

"Green snow," she sang, "green snow, the loveliest snow."

Her garland fell off as she danced around with Jim. I picked it up and pulled it apart.

In fields full of flowers, we spent happy hours, Beneath trees dark and shady, dear Lavender Lady

Milo is talking now to someone outside my bedroom door. He's saying, "She didn't care a hoot for her, you know, but the crazy kid thought she did."

"Miranda's naive," a voice answers.

It's my secretary. Milo is talking to her about me. He must be telling her about my mother. Milo is lying again. I always knew mother never cared a hoot for me.

When I was back on that filthy cot I could hear the Moon Monster and the Lavender Lady talking, just as I can hear Milo and my secretary now. The Moon Monster was saying something about getting rid of me because I would recognize him later. I became frightened until I heard her say that she would take care of me. Everything would be all right. She would take care of me.

The next morning he sat sullenly at the table while she made breakfast for us.

"Why feed her? Hurry up, will you?"

She flashed him a stern look that silenced him. She winked at me. I winked back. I knew we would be leaving him that day.

We walked slowly to the field of Stars of Bethlehem. When we were down the hill I grabbed her hand. I touched something in it that was cold and hard. It fell to the ground into the flowers. The sunlight hit it while it was falling and it glistened like silver."

"My watch," she cried, "I dropped my watch."

She began to push aside the flowers but I pulled at her.

"Father will get you another one, come on."

She continued clawing at the flowers. I wanted her to leave. A game would do it. She loved games. I spread my arms and fluttered them.

"I'm a butterfly, a yellow butterfly. I'm flying. I'm flying. You're the Lavender Locust and you must catch me."

I flew away. I turned back once and saw her starting to get up. I flew up and down hills. I came to a stream. It was a good place to wait for her. I took off my shoes to wade for a bit.

"Butterfly, butterfly, where are you?" she called.

She was coming. I was so happy.

"You can't catch a butterfly," I shouted. It was nice that she was playing the game. When she came closer I saw that there was something shiny in her hand. She had found her watch. She stopped by a tree to catch her breath. Then she started to run toward me.

But I liked being a butterfly. I liked having her chase me. I didn't want the game to end. I giggled when I saw the stepping stones a few yards from me. I ran in the water to the first one and then to the second. I jumped across on all of them, skidding only once on the green slime that covered them. I sat down across the stream to wait for her.

Her golden hair flying, she skipped from the first to the second stone. And to the third. But on the fourth stone her foot slipped on the green slime. I screamed as she fell backward and hit the side of her face on the third stepping stone. When her head rolled over I saw the reddish-purple bruise on her fair skin. She tried to get up but she fell back again, back on that hard terrible rock. The stream water next to her turned red.

*Lavender Lady, clear water runs red,
Lavender Lady, you cannot be dead.*

I cannot sleep tonight as I usually do after a concert. My eyelids have become reddish purple curtains. They are the same color as the bruise on the Lavender Lady's face. They are the same color as that ghastly shirt Milo is wearing tonight. I've asked him not to wear it, but he told me my secretary likes it.

They're still talking outside my door. Milo is not talking about my mother. He is talking about the Lavender Lady and he is telling my secretary a vicious lie about her. I can bear his other lies, but not this one. He is saying that the silver thing I saw in the Lavender Lady's hand was not a watch, but a knife. He's saying, "She had a silver pocketknife with her to kill a kid who was born with a silver spoon in her mouth."

I'll have to prove to Milo it was a watch. I'll take him to that stream. Perhaps the watch is still there, rusted and buried under the stepping stone. When I take him, I'll ask him to wear the reddish-purple shirt. It will go well with his face if he happens to slip.

Reddish-purple, reddish-purple. What was the word printed on that colored pencil I had when I was a child? Magenta, yes, that's it, magenta.

Such a lyrical word. It should be in a song. I need a new song, a new song that will captivate me just as *Lavender Lady* did. I'm getting a melody in my head right now. It is so sad it makes me cry. This song will be better than *Lavender Lady*. It will be a better ending for my concerts. It will thrill my audiences. It will overwhelm me.

I've got the first two lines. They go like this:

Magenta man, once kind and strong,
Magenta man, you've done me wrong.

Editorial Postscript

The story you have just read was nominated by MWA (Mystery Writers of America) as one of the five best new mystery short stories published in American magazines and books during 1976.

Joyce Harrington

Blue Monday

She wore a different color every day. One day she was all in pink – pink dress, pink shoes, pink handbag, pink scarf. The day before she was all in lavender. The next day all in red. Then brown. Green... A study in depth by one of the most talented of the newer writers...

She was dressed all in pink. As I boarded the bus behind her, I couldn't stop looking at her pink shoes. Up the high grimy steps they went. Cheap shoes. Flimsy sandals made to last for one summer, if that long. The feet inside them were long and lumpy, as if too many years of ill-fitting shoes had caused them to break out in bumps of protest.

   I followed her into the bus, dropped my fare into the change box, and watched her walk up the aisle. The skirt of her pink dress was wrinkled. I tried to imagine where she had spent her day, all her days, the kind of office she worked in, the chair she sat in that had pressed wrinkles into the skirts of all her dresses.

Yesterday she had been all in lavender.

She sat in a window seat in the middle of the bus. As she slid into the seat her pink handbag, a long pouchy thing, swung and thumped against her hip. I walked past her, carefully averting my eyes so that she wouldn't notice that I had been watching her, and chose a seat two rows behind her. From there I could see her shoulders, her neck and the back of her head. I opened my newspaper and settled down for the ride.

On her head she wore a scarf of some filmy material, probably nylon. It was folded into a triangle and tied under her chin. Pink. Through it her hair, arranged in some intricate and unfashionable manner, was visible as a series of knobby clusters of curls. The scarf was evidently intended to keep the knobs in place.

The bus started on its long haul to the suburbs. Normally I read the paper a little, doze a little, look out the window and take note of the small changes that occur along the familiar route and the things that remain the same.

But lately I find my eyes drifting away from the newspaper and from the window and fastening on the back of her head. I no longer doze. Each day the scarf is a different color.

She was talking to her seat companion. I couldn't hear what she was saying. Her head was turned slightly so I could see her lips moving. She wore a pink lipstick and her teeth protruded just enough to give her mouth a somewhat pouting appearance. Against her sallow skin, her mouth seemed to be a separate living organism. She spoke rapidly, interspersing her words with quick half-hearted smiles. When she did this, the side of her face creased into concentric curved lines which would one day be permanent wrinkles. I guessed her age to be about 40.

The bus rattled on through the outlying part of town where ramshackle frame houses lean discouraged against each other down the slope toward the river. Normally I like to look out the window along this stretch of the ride. I was born in this part of town, although the house I grew up in was torn down long ago to make room for a new section of highway. If I feel a bit self-congratulatory as the bus carries me by this decayed remnant of my childhood, I feel I've earned it. I've worked long and hard to give my family a decent place to live.

Lately I have been distracted from even

this pleasant satisfaction. I don't quite understand why it should be so, but somehow her presence on the bus produces in me a vague irritability. She is a source of discomfort, and I wish she would take a different bus. I find myself watching for her at the bus stop each evening, waiting to see what her day's color will be, and then, unconsciously at first, but quite deliberately now, taking a seat somewhere behind her so that she is never out of sight.

Let me explain that in 25 years of marriage I have never looked at another woman. My wife is small, quiet, and kind. She has never demanded more of me than I could give. I have worked for the same company all my life. I started as a messenger boy and now I am a division manager. A few years ago I realized that I would rise no higher in the company. But I am content.

My division runs smoothly. The typists come to me with their problems and my wife and I attend their weddings. The young men regard me as an old fogey, but they are eager to take advantage of my long experience. Some of them will rise above me in the company; others will leave. It no longer matters. In due time I will retire on full pension.

My life, like my division, has also run

smoothly. My children, a boy and a girl, grew up respectful and well-mannered. My son is a science teacher in a high school on the other side of town, and my daughter is married and lives nearby. She is expecting her second child. My wife makes dresses for our three-year-old granddaughter. We have never been plagued with accident or illness, although my wife occasionally suffers from arthritis when the weather is damp.

Why, then, should I be irritated by this woman on the bus? She is nothing to me. If she chooses to dress one day entirely in pink and the next entirely in orange, and so on through the rainbow, surely that's her affair. It needn't concern me. Why do my thoughts persist in speculating on the probable contents of her closet? Particularly on the rows of shoes it must contain, neatly ranked in pairs of every conceivable color. I wonder if she's married, and what her husband thinks of this color mania of hers.

The bus rolled through the belt of light industry that serves as a boundary between town and suburb. My newspaper lay forgotten in my lap. Soon she would be getting off. My own stop lay a half mile farther on. In a way we were neighbors, although I had never seen her anywhere but on the bus.

Suddenly I yearned to know where she lived. I folded my newspaper – my wife likes to read it in the evening after dinner – and felt an unaccustomed quickening of my heartbeat.

She always pulled the signal cord for the bus to stop – even if someone else had pulled it before her, even though the bus always stopped at her corner. Perhaps she was afraid that if she personally did not pull the cord, the bus would go on and on forever and she would never be able to change into her next day's outfit, red or gray or purple, whatever it might be. Five or six people stood and lurched down the aisle while the bus was still moving. I was among them.

On the corner the people fanned out in all directions. She crossed the main road in front of the bus and headed north. I stood on the corner feeling slightly displaced and watched the bus drive away. I instantly regretted having gotten off. There was nothing for me to do but walk. I could follow the bus down the road to my usual stop. Or I could follow her.

At the first gap in the stream of traffic I hurried across the road. She was about half a long block ahead of me. She walked with a stiff-legged jouncy stride and the pink handbag swung rhythmically from her arm.

Her pink dress had some kind of ruffled collar and this flapped up and down as she walked. The tail of the pink scarf fluttered and at one point flew up, exposing the back of her head. I could not distinguish the exact color of her hair, although it seemed to be dark, a kind of dusty brown.

She turned the corner and I hurried to catch up. My heart pounded and I was having trouble drawing breath. My legs were trembling from the effort not to run. When I reached the corner, she was nowhere in sight but the door of the third house from the corner was just closing. There was no one else on the street.

I walked on casually, taking in as much of the house as I could without stopping. It was a small house, as most of the houses were in this area, and it sat back from the street on a small plot of lawn. It was painted pale green with darker green trim. There was a wide front window with green drapes hanging open at the sides, and in the middle a green ceramic lamp with a green shade. I could see no more without stopping to stare. It was a house like all the others on the block, unrelenting in its greenness, but in no way out of the ordinary. With one exception.

The house was surrounded with flower beds. The flowers tumbled against each other with no regard for order: orange marigolds, purple petunias, stiff zinnias of many colors, daisies and delphinium, nasturtium and portulaca, all thrown in together in heaps and huddles of every kind and color. It was a surprise.

   I walked on down the block. My eyes still tingled with the shock of those tumultuous flower beds. My heart slowed to its normal steady pace and I breathed more freely. My legs, however, were extremely tired and I longed for a place to sit down and rest.

   Could she be the gardener? The creator of that flamboyant atrocity? Indeed, I suppose she could, although I would have expected something else. A garden of many kinds of flowers all chosen for a uniformity of color would have been my guess.

   It became more and more necessary for me to sit down and pull myself together before going home. My way took me through the small shopping area of the village: a few shops, a beauty salon, the post office, and a small cocktail lounge. I had never been inside the cocktail lounge. I knew that some of the bus riders stopped off there occasionally before going home. I hoped that none would be there to see me – or at least none with whom I had a nodding acquaintance. I was not in the mood for conversation.

I found myself standing at the bar before my eyes had accustomed themselves to the gloom. The bartender was attentive. I have never been much of a drinker and ordered the first thing that came into my head.

"A whiskey sour, please."

I laid my newspaper on the bar and noticed that my hands were stained with ink. The paper was damp where I had clutched it.

"The men's room?" I murmured.

The bartender pointed to a glowing sign at the rear of the long room.

As I made my way down the room I became aware that my hands were not the only part of me that had been sweating. My clothes felt limp and sodden, and in the air-conditioned chill I began to shiver uncontrollably. It had been warm outdoors, but not uncomfortably hot. I wondered if I were coming down with something, a summer cold or a touch of the flu.

I let the hot water run over my hands until the shivering stopped, then washed with the gritty powdered soap from the dispenser. As the ink ran away down the drain, I glanced into the mirror. I was shocked by what I saw.

Instantly I blamed it on the distortion of the glass, the fact that the mirror was old and flaked. But for a split second the face I saw was not my own – or rather it was my own, but with a subtle difference. The features were those I'd known for many years, the face I shaved each morning, the face whose lines and pouches and discolorations I'd accepted as badges of respectable seniority. But the mouth had an unpleasant downward quirk, the nose was pinched, and the eyes – the eyes were worst of all.

I dried my hands on the roller towel. Imagination, I thought. No sense in feeling guilty over stopping for a quick drink, even though I'd never done it before. Nothing wrong in taking a walk through the quiet suburban streets. I would have to come up with some reason for getting home late, but there would be no need to lie. I had never lied to my wife.

"It was such a nice evening, I took a walk and then stopped off for a drink."

Back at the bar my whiskey sour was sitting in a circle of wetness. I sat on the barstool and glanced around the room. It was a pleasant enough place, running heavily to wood paneling and beamed ceiling. There were perhaps five or six other customers. A man and a woman sat at a table lost in an earnest whispered conversation. The others were congregated at the end of the bar chatting raucously with the bartender.

Politics or baseball, most likely. I sipped my drink. Oh, it tasted good. It was just what I needed. Strength flowed back into my legs, and the evil vision in the men's-room mirror faded from my mind.

My wife accepted my explanation without question, but she was a little disappointed that I had forgotten to bring her the newspaper. I had left it on the bar. I offered to walk down to the stationery store after dinner to get her one. I detoured past the green house with the flower beds, but saw no one.

The next evening I left the office a few minutes early and hurried to the bus stop. I wanted to get there before she did, so that I could determine from which direction she came. Things had gone badly in my division. A report that was due in the president's office the following morning had been badly botched by a new typist. She came to me in tears, claiming she had not been given adequate instructions and she couldn't read Mr. Pfister's handwriting anyway and there was no need for him to be insulting.

"He called me a dumb little idiot," she sobbed.

Normally I can settle these upheavals with a few words. Mr. Pfister was ambitious, ingratiating with those above him and overbearing with those below. The girl probably had some justification. But as she poured out her woes, I found my eyes wandering to her thin summer blouse. It had no sleeves and its round neck was cut low. It quivered with her sobs. As she bent into her handkerchief I could see that she wore no brassiere.

My thighs trembled in the kneehole of my desk. Beneath my jacket my shirt grew suddenly clammy. I wondered if my face had changed into the face I had seen in the men's-room mirror the night before. I swung my chair around to face the window.

"Go back to your desk," I said. "Do the report over and see that you get it right, even if it takes you all night."

I heard her gasp and mumble, "Yes, sir." Her soft footsteps receded. Before she reached the door, I said, "Miss – um," I couldn't remember her name. "In the future see that you dress more suitably."

She ran down the hall. A few minutes later I left and went to the bus stop.

The sky was the color of tarnished brass. The air was hot and heavy, and little whirlpools of wind lifted bits of scrap paper from the gutter, flapped them about, and dropped them abruptly. We would have rain. I stood on the corner and tried to look in all directions at once. I wanted to see where she came from, to find out, if I could, which building she worked in. There was still five minutes before the bus was due.

I was watching the entrance to the new glass-fronted office building across the street and might have missed her had not a screaming siren called my attention back down the street to the entrance of my own building. The police car sped past me bound for some emergency or other, but my eyes remained riveted on the high arched doorway of the building where I had invested all the working years of my life. She stood just outside the revolving doors, scanning the livid skies. Then she turned and walked with her stiff jouncing stride toward the bus stop.

I faded back into the doorway of a shop. Could it be possible she worked for my company? I had never seen her in the elevators or in the lobby. The company employed hundreds of people. It occupied the entire building. There were many divisions and sections. I suppose there were many people working there whom I didn't know. That she should be one of them seemed a bad joke on me.

As she neared the bus stop, I saw that she carried a red umbrella. Had she worn red today because she knew it would rain and she wanted her costume to match her umbrella? Or had she an umbrella as well as scarf, shoes, and handbag to match every dress in her wardrobe?

Today's red dress was tightly cinched with a red plastic belt. I had not noticed before how small her waist was, nor that she was very tall. Below the gleaming belt her haunches flared and filled the red cloth. The red shoes seemed even more hurtful than yesterday's pink ones. I was impatient for the bus to appear.

At last it came, and she was among the first to get on. Have I said that the riders of this bus are extremely well-mannered? That among this small crowd of homeward-bound suburbanites, it is customary for the gentlemen to stand back and allow the ladies to board first? I consciously violated that rule. Pretending absorption in some deep mental problem, I elbowed my way to the door of the bus and chose a seat immediately behind her. There were a few shocked murmurs, but I ignored them. She was joined by the same woman who had shared her seat before.

It is truly amazing how much you can learn about a person simply by listening in on fragments of conversation. For instance, I learned that she was a widow.

"...when poor Raymond was alive..."

That she didn't sleep well.

"...and those pills didn't help a bit..."

That she lived with her invalid sister.

"...so I said, my sister needs that ramp for her wheel chair, so it'll just have to stay..."

That she didn't have a dog.

"...I'd like to, but she's allergic to animal dander..."

And that she would be alone in the house over the weekend.

"...I have to take her back to the hospital on Saturday for another series of tests. It may take a week..."

And all the while I watched her red mouth swimming in the placid pudding of her face. Yes, she had changed her lipstick from pink to red. I noticed, too, that at close range her cheeks were covered with a fine down and there were patches of skin where the pores had coarsened. I wondered how she failed to notice my scrutiny, but she seemed oblivious.

About halfway home the rain started. It fell straight down at first, heavy blinding sheets of water. Lightning flickered on the hilltops and the streets were quickly swamped. The bus ground slowly on, its windshield wipers barely able to cope with the deluge. She scarcely noticed the storm, but continued chatting with her neighbor. Her voice, now that I was close enough to hear it, was jarring and nasal. She was so very different from my wife.

The rain had slackened off before we reached her stop, but it was still coming down in a fine slanting spray when we got off. She was safe beneath her red umbrella. I had no protection but my newspaper. It seemed ridiculous to hold it over my head. However I held it, the paper would be soaked before I got home. I tossed it into a trash can and followed her from the bus stop.

This time I followed quite close behind her. She was engrossed in managing her umbrella, her large red handbag, and a shopping bag from a downtown department store. (Had she shopped in that store today because its shopping bags were red?) Besides, it seemed to me that she was one of those semiconscious people, only becoming aware of others when they had a direct effect on herself. I had no meaning in her life.

I saw her go to the door of the green house, search in her red bag for a key. I passed by as she was struggling to close her umbrella, then heard the door slam shut as I walked on. By the time I reached the cocktail lounge I was drenched and shivering.

"Whiskey," I said to the bartender and went straight to the men's room. I toweled my head on the roller towel and then quite deliberately stood before the mirror. This time I did not look away, but examined my reflection closely as if by doing so I could force my features back into their usual aspect of gentleness and benevolence. I was able to manage a compromise – a mask of bland indifference.

A shot glass was waiting for me on the bar, with a water chaser. I drained it and gestured for another. Tonight I would not have the excuse of taking a walk on a fine evening.

"The bus was delayed. I got soaked, so I stopped for a drink."

No use lying. My wife would smell the whiskey on my breath. When I left the cocktail lounge, I remembered to stop at the stationery store to buy another paper. The rain was only a fine mist now, but I tucked the paper under my jacket and went home.

After dinner, while my wife read the newspaper and I pretended to watch television, I thought about the woman on the bus. Why was it I never saw her in the mornings? Perhaps she took an earlier bus and had breakfast in a coffee shop downtown. Or maybe she took as late a bus as she could so as to spend more time with her invalid sister. How long had she been widowed? Did she have men friends? Did she perhaps go off on weekends with them? Did she have drawers full of underwear of many colors to match her dresses?

"Don't you feel well? You look a bit off-color."

"No, fine. I'm fine. I think I'll go to bed."

My wife had accepted my excuse, only frowned a little over my drinking, and had made me change out of my wet clothes.

"Would you like some hot tea with lemon?"

"Nothing. I'm just tired."

The next evening was Friday. She wore brown, a sad color and one that made her look unhealthy. I'd had a bad day. The vice-president in charge of marketing had named my division as one suffering from antiquated methods, and I had been called on to justify my procedures. Business was bad all over and my results did not look good. Rumors flew in and out of cubicles all afternoon.

I still had not been able to find out where in the company she worked. I didn't even know her name. When I followed her from the bus stop it was without the usual excitement, and my two drinks at the cocktail lounge seemed more a matter of habit than of need. I didn't go into the men's room. As I sat at the bar I thought about my retirement plans.

Years ago I had bought an old farmhouse on an isolated lake in the southeastern part of the state. We always spent our vacations there and many weekends, and I had tinkered it into passably modern condition. When I thought about the time when I would finally leave the company, it was always with the farmhouse in mind. There would be time to read – I had always promised myself that I would one day make up for my lack of a college education by reading all the world's great literature. The fishing was good, and my wife could grow a vegetable garden.

When I got home I didn't bother to make an excuse for my lateness. My wife didn't demand any.

"Would you like to go to the farm this weekend?" she asked.

"No, I don't think so. Maybe next week."

On Saturday I took a walk. There didn't seem to be anyone at home in the green house. No doubt she was with her sister at the hospital.

On Sunday I took the car. I drove past the house twice in the early afternoon. On my third circuit of the block I saw her coming down the drive with her hands full of gardening tools. She wore faded green slacks and a green smock. Her gardening gloves were green and her head was covered with a green scarf. I couldn't see her shoes.

I parked the car around the corner and walked back. The street was deserted except for the two of us.

"What a lovely garden," I called out, hovering on the sidewalk and hoping that my face was safely keeping to its usual unremarkable lines.

"Oh," she said. "Why, thank you. It's a lot of hard work."

"Must be. I never have much luck with flowers. I guess I must be lazy."

"Oh, now," she tittered. "It's not *that* difficult. But people do say I have a green thumb."

"Now, tell me," I said, taking the liberty of crossing the lawn to where she stood. "How do you get such good results with carnations? Mine are always so spindly and have hardly any blooms at all."

I listened to a long harangue on fertilizers, bone meal, and the efficacy of good drainage, nodding wisely all the while, my eyes fixed on her green sneakers. At the conclusion she giggled girlishly and said, "Well, I've talked your ear off and myself into a fine thirst. Would you care for a glass of iced tea?"

"That's very kind of you. It's pretty hot out here in the sun."

"Well, come on inside. It's always nice to meet a fellow gardener. Someone who understands."

I understood. I'd seen her sharp glance at the third finger of my left hand. I've never worn a wedding band.

We went round to the back door. Across half of the back steps lay a sturdily braced wooden ramp.

"My sister," she explained. "She's confined to a wheel chair. She'd be much happier in a nursing home, but after my husband died she insisted on living with me. To keep me company, she says. To keep an eye on me, I say. But don't worry. She's not here today."

We entered the kitchen. It was yellow. Yellow wallpaper, yellow cabinets, yellow cloth on the table. Even a yellow refrigerator. She poured tea into tall yellow glasses.

"Do you live around here?" she asked.

"Not far. I have to confess, I saw your flowers a few days ago and came back in the hope of meeting the person responsible."

"You must be married." She certainly believed in coming to the point.

"I have been." Sometimes a little lie is unavoidable.

"Come into the living room. We can be comfortable there."

The house was small. I stood in the kitchen doorway and looked into the green living room, the magenta dining room, a rose-colored bedroom. On the other door of a closet in the bedroom hung a blue dress. On the floor a pair of blue shoes stood ready. Tomorrow was Monday.

"May I trouble you for another napkin? I've slopped my tea a little."

She obligingly went across the kitchen to a cupboard. I picked up her green gardening gloves. She had large hands. I picked up the knife with which she had sliced a lemon for the tea...

Afterward I was really thirsty. I drank the tea. It was slightly warm. My clothes were damp. I left the green gardening gloves on the yellow counter. I went out by the back door and drove home.

On Monday morning the office was agog. One of the telephone operators had been brutally murdered in her home. The police came and interviewed everyone who had known her. They ignored my division. The rumor that went the rounds had it that she had been stabbed 27 times. It seemed a bit exaggerated to me. My division ran smoothly that day.

In the evening I went to the bus stop. I looked for her in her blue dress, but she didn't come. Maybe she had taken an earlier bus. Or perhaps she was working late. She could even be on vacation.

I settled down on the bus and opened my newspaper. The woman sitting in front of me had the most irritating way of shaking her head as she talked to her seat companion. She wore long dangling earrings and they distracted me from my newspaper, from the view out the bus window.

Perhaps I'll take the early retirement option.

R. L. Stevens

Five Rings in Reno

There is a new trend in current literature – fiction involving real-life persons. Sometimes the events narrated actually occurred; sometimes the events might *have occurred. In R. L. Stevens' story we go back in history to Reno, Nevada, on July 4, 1910. There you will meet Jack Johnson, Jim Jeffries, Jack London, and – how easily it* might *have happened! – Dr. Arthur Conan Doyle, creator of Sherlock Holmes, playing a strange double role – prizefight referee and champion detective!...*

In his excellent biography, *The Life of Sir Arthur Conan Doyle,* John Dickson Carr tells us that Doyle was invited to act as referee for the heavyweight championship fight between Jack Johnson and Jim Jeffries in Reno, Nevada, on July 4, 1910. Doyle tentatively accepted, with great pleasure, but changed his mind a week later and sent his regrets.
    Now what if Doyle had gone to Reno...?

Arthur Conan Doyle stepped off the train at the Reno depot looking a bit bewildered. After traveling across an ocean and a continent to reach the small city near the foot of the Sierra Nevada mountains, he had at least expected someone to meet him.

"Sir Arthur!" a voice called suddenly, and he turned to see a slim blond young man striding toward him. "Didn't expect the train to be on time. They never are!"

"These are my bags," Doyle said, indicating two well-traveled Gladstones. "You would be Mr. Summons?"

"Charlie Summons, at your service, Sir Arthur."

"The title I value most is that of 'Doctor,' if you don't mind."

"Oh – certainly, Dr. Doyle! This way, please."

"Somehow I expected Reno would be larger."

Charlie Summons turned with a trace of apology. "Well, it's not London, Sir – Dr. Doyle – but we like to think of ourselves as the biggest little city in the west. And this fight is really goin' to put us on the map!"

"It's certainly a lengthy journey by train," Doyle remarked. "I've written occasionally about the American west, but this is my first personal view of it. When I visited the States in '94 I never came further west than Chicago and Milwaukee."

"I read what you wrote about the Mormons of Utah in *A Study in Scarlet*. Could have sworn you'd actually been there!"

Doyle smiled at the compliment. "I read a great deal about your country before coming here."

They had reached the street outside the depot, and Summons was loading the bags into the back seat of an elegant black motorcar with polished brass trim. "This is a 1908 Packard," Summons explained. "You don't see many cars out west yet, but we have a few of 'em available for special visitors like yourself."

"It is quite a handsome vehicle," Doyle conceded, climbing up into the passenger's seat. "I suppose the motorcar is the coming thing in London too, though I do hate to see them replacing the hansom cabs."

Charlie Summons cranked the engine and then jumped in as the car coughed into life. "Times are changing, Dr. Doyle. Last month a biplane took off from a street in Washington right next to the White House."

"I'll remain on the ground, thank you," Doyle said with a smile.

"We've got you a fine room at the Reno Hotel. Everyone important is staying there. There's another writer too – Jack London. He's covering the fight for the San Francisco *Chronicle* and the New York *Herald*."

Doyle's face lit up. "I'll be interested in meeting Jack London. Some people have detected minor evidences of us in each other's stories. When I toured America last time I met Rudyard Kipling in Vermont and we became good friends."

Summons pulled the car up in front of the hotel. "Oh, oh! There's Monica Malone – that means trouble!"

Doyle found himself mildly amused by the man. "And what trouble might such a comely young woman offer?"

"She read how you helped solve that mystery in England a few years back, and she imagines you're Sherlock Holmes himself. She'll be wanting your help."

"Holmes! Is that name going to haunt me here too?"

But he climbed down from the car and went to meet the young lady. "Dr. Conan Doyle?" she asked. "I must speak with you on a most urgent matter."

"Nothing is so urgent right now as the fight that will take place in two days. I am not here in my capacity as an author – or as a doctor – but as a referee." Though he was 51 years old and only recently married to his charming second wife, Doyle still had an eye for a beautiful woman. Miss Malone's cameo face reminded him of a girl he had known long ago, during his university days.

"I realize I'm intruding on your time," she said apologetically, "but if you could only listen to my story –"

"My dear young lady, I have only just arrived in your city. I have important meetings with the principals in this prize-fight, and you understand I must attend to that business first. But should you chance to be in the neighborhood early this evening, I will try to find time to speak with you."

"That's most kind," she said.

Then, before Doyle could say more, he was whisked away by Charlie Summons. "We're running a bit late, Dr. Doyle. They're waiting for us."

Summons settled him into a front room with windows overlooking South Virginia Street. The hotel was crowded with guests, and even in the halls Doyle was aware of money changing hands. Obviously the fight was attracting a great deal of betting interest.

After a half hour in which Doyle unpacked and washed up, Summons escorted him to a first-floor meeting room where a number of men were awaiting him. Doyle's first impression was that the sporting classes were much the same in America as in England. Colonel Raff Grayson, who seemed to be one of the fight's promoters, could easily have acted a role in Doyle's prizefighting drama, *The House of Temperley*, which was playing at London's Adelphi Theatre.

"So good of you to make the journey, Dr. Doyle," he said, rising to shake hands. "The problem of selecting a referee acceptable to both sides in this fight has been immense. The color question – black versus white – has raised needless tensions on all sides. Frankly, you were the only person acceptable to both managers."

Doyle bowed slightly. "I consider that a sincere compliment, especially since I know so little of American boxing."

"The rules are much the same as in your British sport," Colonel Grayson assured him. "The Marquis of Queensberry is well known here. But our main problem was finding a referee whom both sides trusted. As you know, Jeffries has come out of retirement to win back his heavyweight title from this black man, Jack Johnson. Feelings are running high, and there is even talk of race riots in some American cities."

"All seems peaceful here," Doyle observed.

"Don't be deceived. A man was knifed to death near the depot two nights ago – a reporter out here to cover the fight. His killer has not yet been found."

"I know enough about the American west," Doyle said, "to realize that the price of human life is not high out here. A wrong word spoken during a poker game, I understand, can lead to a stabbing or shooting."

Grayson exchanged glances with the other men, whom he had not yet introduced. "Come, Dr. Doyle, we feel ourselves far more civilized than that! The west of 1910 is far removed from the west of 1890."

"Perhaps," Doyle admitted. "Even passing through New York I read of a recent diamond robbery and killing. Crime is certainly not confined to the western states."

"In any event, precautions have been taken for Monday's fight. As one of the promoters I can assure you the crowd will be under complete control."

A large man of indeterminate middle age spoke up. "I was a fighter myself, Dr. Doyle. I know what it's like to stand in the center of a ring and hear the crowd shouting for blood after an unpopular decision."

The Colonel made the belated introductions. "This is Nevada Wade, Dr. Conan Doyle."

Doyle smiled. "Sounds like a cowboy's name."

"Cowboys and boxers aren't much different," Wade agreed. "I was a heavyweight contender in my fighting days, but I never had a crack at the championship."

He looked like a man who could still hold his own in the prize ring, and Doyle wondered why he had retired. From the looks of the large diamond ring on his little finger he might well have come into money. "When will I see the site of Monday's battle?" Doyle asked, shifting his attention back to the Colonel.

"We'll go out to the fairgrounds tomorrow morning. The ring and the seating are already in place, but the workmen are still adding the finishing touches." He looked up at the ornate wall clock. "Only forty-eight hours to fight time, Dr. Doyle. Less than that, really."

He made an effort to introduce the others in the room – backers and managers and promoters – but Doyle found himself quickly engaged in more conversation with Nevada Wade. "I understand there's a new Sherlock Holmes play in the Strand this summer."

Doyle nodded. "*The Speckled Band* opened last month, and it's been quite successful."

"One of my favorite stories – the one with the snake."

Americans never failed to amaze him. This man with a cowboy's name and callused fists had actually read his stories! "That is the one. We tried using a real snake on stage – nonpoisonous, of course – but it didn't work out. Now we have an ingeniously jointed dummy manipulated with black thread like a puppet. It is most effective."

"I should like to see the play sometime," Wade said.

"Perhaps we will have an American production."

Charlie Summons appeared at Doyle's side and whispered, "If you want to scram out of here, I'll help you."

"Scram –?"

"On the weekend of a big fight this crowd'll be drinking all night. I already told the Colonel you needed to rest after your long trip out here."

"Thank you," Doyle said, and he was genuinely grateful.

He ate with Summons in the hotel restaurant, listening to the slim young man's tales of Reno's sporting life. At one point he asked, "Just what is your connection with Colonel Grayson?"

"Oh, the Colonel pays me. I run errands for him – things like that."

Doyle had earlier noticed the bulge under the other man's coat, and now he commented upon it. "Are you his bodyguard too?"

"What? Oh, you mean the gun? This is still the west, Dr. Doyle. You'll find a good many men carrying weapons."

"Interesting."

"I guess they don't carry guns in London."

"No, not in London. Not even our police-officers."

Charlie Summons took a sip of the wine Doyle had ordered with the meal. "Say, this isn't bad."

"My tastes run more to French than to California wines, I'm afraid. But as you say, isn't bad." He was beginning to like the young man for some reason, perhaps because he was so typically American.

"You going to see Monica Malone?" Summons asked suddenly.

"Who?"

"The girl outside the hotel when you arrived."

"I'd completely forgotten about her."

"She'll prob'ly come around tonight to see you."

As Doyle was to discover within the hour, the young man's prediction proved accurate. He had barely left Summons and started up to his room when Monica Malone intercepted him. She clutched a folded newspaper in one hand, and as she spoke there were tears in her eyes. "I must see you, Dr. Doyle. You said you would talk with me."

"And I will. But I can hardly invite you up to my room. Let us sit in that corner of the lobby where we won't be disturbed."

She followed him to a red plush sofa partly hidden by a tall fern in an ornate jardinière. "Thank you so much, Dr. Doyle. These last days have been a nightmare for me."

He sat down beside her. "I assume you are referring to the brutal murder of your fiancé near the railway station two nights ago."

"Someone has told you who I am!"

"No, not really, Miss Malone. But I noticed your agitated state, and the fact that you are carrying a copy of yesterday's newspaper folded so that an account of the killing is visible. You also wear an engagement ring, which you twist nervously with your fingers, as if you were considering removing it. The conclusion seems a likely one."

"You sound like Sherlock Holmes himself!"

"Please!" He held up a hand to silence her. "I pretend no special powers to solve this mystery. But tell me what happened."

"Tom – my fiancé, Tom Andrews – came out here last month to cover preparations for the fight. He was a reporter for *Ring & Turf*, an eastern sporting weekly. I arrived yesterday to join him and discovered he'd been murdered."

"I understand the fight has touched off some scattered violence because of the racial aspects."

"No one would have killed Tom for that reason – he was completely fair to both men! They'd more likely have stabbed Jack London – he's been wondering aloud about the Negro having a yellow streak."

"What about one of the other reporters? Had your fiancé been on bad terms with any of them?"

She shook her head, fighting back the tears, and he wanted to comfort her somehow. To give her a few moments to compose herself, he took the folded newspaper from her hand and read the brief account of the murder. There had been no witnesses, and the young reporter's wallet was found intact. So robbery could not have been the motive. The fatal stabbing near the railroad station must have had another cause.

"Could he have gone there to meet someone arriving by train?" Doyle asked.

"But who? I wan't due until yesterday and he knew that."

"Still, a great many persons are arriving daily for the fight. He might have gone to meet one of them."

"I think he knew he might be killed, Dr. Doyle."

"Why do you say that?"

"He left a message for me at his hotel. Just a brief note – I have it here." She opened her purse and produced an envelope with a folded piece of paper inside.

Doyle read it aloud. "*Dearest Monica: If anything should happen to me before you arrive, remember the fifth day of Christmas. All my love, Tom.*" He studied the note with a deepening frown. "The fifth day of Christmas? What could that mean?"

"That's why I want your help, Dr. Doyle – I don't know! I tried to talk with the police about it, but they paid no attention. They're too busy keeping things calm before Monday's fight."

He continued to study the note, the only

message from a man he'd never known, a man now dead. "Did you know Tom last Christmas?"

"Certainly. He gave me this ring then."

Doyle was instantly alert. "Just one ring?"

"Of course. Why do you ask?"

"In the old carol, *The Twelve Days of Christmas,* there is a line that goes, '*The fifth day of Christmas, my true love sent to me five gold rings.*'"

"Of course! We always sang that at Christmas-time! Tom was sending me a message about five gold rings. But what rings?"

"I don't know," Doyle admitted.

"Engagement rings?"

"One other possibility presents itself. This weekend in Reno the word *ring* has another meaning."

"A prizefighting ring!"

"Perhaps." He folded the note and returned it to its envelope. "He left this at the hotel for you?"

"Yes, at the desk."

"Let me keep it for a time. Something might occur to me."

"Thank you, Dr. Doyle. If you can find the person who killed Tom –"

"We won't go quite that far yet." He rose. "Please excuse me now. I have had a tiring train trip, and I'm anxious to get some sleep."

"I'll look for you tomorrow."

He smiled at her. "Tomorrow I must go to the fairgrounds to inspect the scene of the action and meet the participants. But I will try to help you in any way that I can."

"Thank you, Mr. Holmes – I mean, Dr. Doyle."

He watched as she crossed the lobby to the street, and then went up to his room. Once more that confounded Sherlock Holmes had intruded on his life.

On Sunday morning he walked down to the Reno railway station using the newspaper account of the tragedy to seek out the scene of the crime. He thought that he had found it, and was bending to examine a stain on the sidewalk, when a familiar voice hailed him.

"Dr. Conan Doyle! What brings you out this early?"

It was Colonel Raff Grayson, just alighting from his motorcar. He seemed to be alone. "Good morning, Colonel. I'm just exploring a bit of your city."

"Nothing to see down at the depot. But if you'll wait while I pick up some freight I'll drive you out to the fairgrounds."

His freight proved to be a wooden cage of

pheasants, which Doyle helped him carry to the back seat of the motorcar. "Will you be having a pheasant shoot after the fight?" he asked the Colonel.

"No, just a pheasant roast. These birds are only two to three pounds each, but at two servings a bird I have enough here for ten of us. I figure my wife and me, Nevada Wade and his lady, both fighters and their women, yourself, and Mr. Jack London. I hope you'll be able to join us."

"I'd be pleased," Doyle said, "though I don't know whether Mr. Johnson and Mr. Jeffries will feel up to roast pheasant after fighting fifteen rounds."

Colonel Grayson smiled. "Oh, I think Jeffries will finish the black boy much quicker than that. Just off the record, of course."

Doyle was silent, avoiding any hint of favoritism on the day before he was to referee the event. He waited until they were on the road, heading for the fairgrounds, before he spoke. "Did you know the reporter who was murdered the other night?"

Colonel Grayson turned to smile at him. "The old detective instinct getting you, Dr. Doyle? I didn't know him, but Charlie Summons had played cards with him a few times these past weeks. Charlie says he was a nice fellow."

"Who do you think stabbed him?"

"The fight is attracting a certain criminal element to Reno, Dr. Doyle. It's unfortunate but true."

The Reno fairgrounds was at the northeast edge of the city. Today, under a warm July sun, it was a beehive of activity. Motorcars and wagons were parked everywhere in a haphazard fashion, while workers climbed over the grandstand puting the finishing touches on the seats and refreshment stands.

As they approached after parking the automobile, Charlie Summons hurried forward to meet them. "You'd better come quick, Colonel! Johnson and Jeffries are both here, and I'm afraid they'll start fighting a day early!"

They found the two heavyweights at the center of a growing circle of partisan supporters. Jack Johnson, his gleaming black head catching the noonday sun, was taunting the grizzly Jim Jeffries. Johnson never lost his smile, not even when one of the crowd called out, "What about the yellow streak, Johnson?"

"I will show you tomorrow who has the yellow streak." And still smiling he turned his back on Jeffries.

Colonel Grayson quickly interrupted to introduce the fighters to Conan Doyle. Jim Jeffries shook his hand vigorously. "I been reading those Sherlock Holmes stories – he's a great one, he is!"

And Johnson was no less enthusiastic. Doyle was amazed they would welcome an Englishman so warmly to referee their fight. He was really beginning to enjoy himself for the first time since his arrival when Nevada Wade approached with a short, light-haired man in his mid-thirties. At the sight of them Jack Johnson stalked away.

"Dr. Arthur Conan Doyle, this here's a greater admirer of yours – Mr. Jack London."

London shook Doyle's hand with as much vigor as Jeffries had. "A pleasure to meet you, Dr. Doyle – or Sir Arthur."

"Dr. Doyle suits me fine. I read your book *The People of the Abyss* with a great deal of interest, Mr. London."

"I wrote it while living in London for some months in 1901. My funds had run out and I actually lived with those poor East End people." London smiled. "Later I rented a room in the home of a London detective. It wasn't 221B Baker Street, though."

"I should hope not," Doyle replied with a chuckle. Summons and the Colonel went off to unload the pheasants, while Nevada Wade continued to stroll with the two authors. Doyle was anxious to see the ring itself, and to get the feel of the place. When they reached it he went up the steps and climbed between the ropes, closely followed by London.

"There is nothing quite so invigorating as the prize ring," the American said. "I've been here ten days writing up the training camps and the fight preliminaries."

Doyle bent to examine London's eye. "As a physician skilled in such matters, I could not help noticing the fading after-effects of a black eye. Have you been engaging in some fisticuffs yourself, Mr. London?"

"That happened two weeks ago, in an Oakland bar. It was in all the papers, I'm afraid. A drunken brawl, they called it."

"Was it?"

London sighed, gazing out at the empty rows of seats, and changed the subject. "My wife gave birth to a daughter on June 19th. The baby only lived three days."

"I am sorry," Doyle said.

Nevada Wade joined them in the ring, "Which of you chaps has published the most?" he asked, flashing his diamond ring.

Doyle laughed. "Oh, Mr. London is far ahead of me. How many books is it now?"

"Twenty-four," London answered almost mechanically. "Though I hardly have your fame."

"Tell me something," Doyle pursued. "In *The People of the Abyss* you showed a real compassion for the poor and downtrodden of London's East End. Yet your writings thus far about the fight have shown a decided racist slant. How do you explain this seeming contradiction?"

Jack London shrugged. "I am what I am, Dr. Doyle. And we will see tomorrow who the better fighter is."

"Jeffries can't come back," Nevada Wade said. "Once they've retired they never come back."

"We'll see." London gave a slight bow in Doyle's direction. "Until tomorrow."

Doyle watched the younger writer climb out of the ring, then turned to Wade. "An odd sort of chap – a real contradiction."

"He's had some hard times, Dr. Doyle."

"He mentioned his daughter's death."

"That's only part of it."

Doyle was reminded of the other death in recent days, and of the message Tom Andrews had left for Monica. "Tell me, Mr. Wade, is this the only prize ring brought in for the fight?"

"Brought in?" Wade didn't grasp the question.

"I mean, are there any other boxing rings in Reno?"

"Well, sure." He removed his western hat and scratched at his balding head. "The Athletic Club has one, and the Boxing Club. And right now each of the two training camps has a ring."

"Counting this one, that would make five in all."

"Well, I guess so," Nevada Wade conceded. "What about it?"

Doyle shrugged. "Now tell me about yourself. You say you boxed professionally?"

"That was a good many years ago, but the sport was my life then."

"Why did you give it up?"

"In the west a man has to live the best way he can. Some gamblers wanted me to take a dive and when I won instead, they broke my hands. I decided it was better to be a gambler than a fighter."

"Are you betting on tomorrow's fight?"

"Sure thing."

"Which way?"

"Like I said, Jeffries can't come back. If there's to be a Great White Hope, it isn't Jim Jeffries."

"Which side is the Colonel on?"

"The other side," Wade answered with a dry chuckle. "He's always on the other side."

Doyle stood for a moment in the center of the ring, turning first one way, then the other, imagining himself as he would be the following day. He touched his mustache, smoothing the ends with their long waxed points. "They say Johnson is something of a clown in the ring, constantly taunting his opponent."

"He play-acts a lot, it's true," Wade agreed. "But it'll be a Jeffries crowd here tomorrow."

"It should be an interesting fight."

Doyle dined again that evening with Charlie Summons, finding himself increasingly taken with the little man. But before they'd had time to relax over coffee and cigars, Monica Malone rushed up to the table. "Dr. Doyle, I must see you! Will you be long? I've been looking everywhere for you."

Doyle excused himself and followed her out to the hotel lobby. "What agitates you so, my dear girl?"

"I didn't want to speak in front of that man."

"Summons? He was a friend of your fiancé."

"I doubt that," she said. "But what I have to tell you is that I recognized someone Tom did know – a man named Draco. He's connected with the rackets back east. Tom wrote an exposé about him – how he doped a race horse."

"Giving him a motive for wanting to kill your fiancé. Where can I find this man?"

"I just saw him entering a bar down the block."

"Did he recognize you?"

"I don't think so. He wouldn't remember me."

Doyle made his regrets to Charlie Summons and set off down the block to the bar Monica had indicated. She pointed out a tall, dark-haired man lounging against a corner of the bar, and Doyle approached him.

"Mr. Draco, I presume?"

The face that turned to him was scarred and ugly. It was plain to see how Monica had recognized him so easily. Doyle remembered Jack London's black eye from the barroom brawl, and prayed the writer would never end up like this. "What do you want?" Draco asked.

"Just to talk. My name is Arthur Conan Doyle."

The name obviously meant nothing to the man. "You a Limey?"

"I'm from England, yes. I am over here to referee the fight tomorrow."

"Yeah?" This interested him.

"I believe you know a man named Tom Andrews."

Draco muttered an obscenity.

"He was murdered here in Reno three nights ago. Did you know that?"

"If I'd been in town I'd of done the job myself."

"But you weren't in town?"

"Just got in today. Come for the fight."

Doyle was inclined to believe the man. Besides, his statement could be easily checked. "I have been told you drug race horses. Wouldn't think of trying your skill on a prizefighter, would you?"

"Not a chance! Listen, I'll tell you about your friend Tom Andrews, in case you still think he's some sorta saint." The man stepped a bit closer, and Doyle could smell gin on his breath. "Sure, I doped a horse or two in my day. Andrews found out about it and wrote his story. But he didn't turn it in to his editor right away. Oh, no. He came to me first and showed it to me. Said he'd tear it up if I'd give him five thousand dollars."

"Interesting. What did you do?"

"Told him I wouldn't be blackmailed and kicked his butt outa my office." He smiled at the memory. "I didn't have no five grand anyhow."

"So he printed the article?"

"Damned right! Ruined my racing career."

"What are you doing now?"

"Picking up a buck any way I can."

"Do five rings mean anything to you? Five rings in Reno?"

Draco looked blank. "Not a thing."

Doyle put down money for another gin and left the man there. In the street, fighting to keep her place on the crowded sidewalk, Monica was waiting. "What did you find out?" she demanded.

"Nothing. Draco only just arrived in Reno."

"So he says!"

"Let me escort you back to your hotel, Miss Malone. The city is growing more crowded by the hour, and the streets may not be safe for a young woman."

"I can take care of myself."

"I am sure you can. But the person who killed Tom might find it very easy to knife you in a crowd. Your inquiries could be worrying him."

She paled at his words. "Perhaps you're right."

"Come along."

"I was foolish to think of you as Sherlock Holmes. There's nothing you can do for me or Tom."

"I never pretended to be Holmes," he insisted. But was it true?

Five gold rings...

He started humming it to himself as they walked. *Seven swans a-swimming, six geese a-laying, five gold rings, four colly birds, three French horns, two turtle doves, and a partridge in a pear tree.*

Ahead of them a boy set off a string of firecrackers in the gutter. It was the eve of America's Independence Day, an odd time to be humming Christmas carols to oneself.

Five gold rings...

"You're right," he told her at the door of the hotel. "I'm not Holmes."

She turned to gaze into his eyes. "I only wish that you were."

The morning dawned warm and sunny. There would be a shirtsleeve crowd at the fight in a few hours. Doyle hoped the decision would be clean-cut. Any uncertainty as to the outcome could only carry over into the streets of Reno.

Charlie Summons called for him promptly at nine, escorting him out to the motorcar. "Beautiful day for it, Dr. Doyle."

"That it is, Charlie."

"The Colonel has a tent up on the fairgrounds, for his celebration dinner afterwards."

"Too bad you're not included on the guest list."

Charlie snickered. "Colonel Grayson said he might include me, if one of the fighters doesn't feel up to eating."

Though the fight was still some hours off, people were already streaming into the grandstand. Many carried picnic lunches and bottles of beverage. And the crackle of fireworks had become almost constant. "Is this how they celebrate your Fourth of July?" Doyle asked.

"You'll get used to the noise," Summons assured him.

In the striped tent set off beyond the parking lot they found Colonel Raff Grayson making last-minute preparations. "I will have chefs to prepare dinner after the main event," he told Doyle. "By that time I'm sure you'll have worked up an appetite."

Doyle nodded.

Nevada Wade came in with a young woman clinging to his arm. "The press is searching for you, Dr. Doyle. They want an interview with Sherlock Holmes!"

"I'm not –" Doyle began, then fell silent. What difference did it make? He could be Sherlock Holmes if they wanted him to be.

Outside, heading toward the press tent, he came upon Monica Malone. "Here for the fight?" he asked.

"I'm here to settle with Tom's killer."

"What?"

"One of the reporters told me Tom was on Draco's trail. He was sure Draco was heading for Reno to close some sort of crooked deal. I have a gun in this handbag, Dr. Doyle, and when I see Draco –"

"My dear, don't even talk such foolishness!" He grasped at the purse, feeling the metallic weight of it. "I'd better take that."

He slipped the small weapon out of the purse and dropped it in his pocket.

"That won't stop me," she insisted. "If you can't do anything, I will!"

The crowd was thickening around them. Spectators mingled with souvenir vendors, and at that moment Doyle's eyes were caught by a gold American eagle on the cover of an Independence Day program. "Birds," he muttered to himself.

"What did you say?" Monica asked.

"Of course! They were all birds! I remember now!"

"What are you talking about?"

The excitement welled within him. "Hurry, woman! Find some police-officers and bring them to Colonel Grayson's tent!"

Then he was on his way. The first person he saw as he burst into the tent was Draco. The ugly man turned from his task, surprised at the sudden intrusion. "You again!"

And then Colonel Grayson came forward. "Can I be of service, Dr. Doyle?"

"On the contrary, Colonel. I came to assist you in dressing those birds for dinner."

Grayson shot a glance at the table behind him. "You needn't concern yourself—"

Doyle felt the hardness of Monica Malone's gun in his pocket, and he drew it out. "Just stand there, both of you. Police-officers will be here soon enough."

"Police? For what?"

"To arrest you for murder, Colonel. You killed Tom Andrews when he tried to blackmail you."

"That's insane!"

"Is it? Andrews was killed near the railway station, because that is where he found you awaiting your delivery. Just as I found you yesterday morning. He left a message for Monica Malone, telling her to remember the fifth day of Christmas. In the old carol the fifth day's gift was five gold rings. Not wedding rings, or prize rings. I finally remembered something I read long ago. In the carol the gifts of the first seven days are all birds. The five gold rings referred to five ring-necked pheasants – like those on the table behind you. I didn't count the birds at the station yesterday, but I remembered you had enough to feed ten guests, at two servings per bird. Therefore, five birds – five ring-necked pheasants."

Grayson started to move then, but Monica lifted the tent flap and entered with the police. "What's all this?" one detective asked. "Aren't you Arthur Conan Doyle?"

Doyle handed over his weapon and picked up a carving knife instead. "If you'll cover the Colonel, we'll see what's in these five birds."

He slit them open, one after another, and carefully extracted a number of small hard objects. "Wash them off and you will find they are diamonds – no doubt from that New York robbery a few weeks back. Colonel Grayson was acting as a fence for the loot, and probably planning to resell it to Draco here. Somehow Andrews found out about Draco's involvement and tried to blackmail the Colonel. That's when he was killed. I should have known those birds were valuable. Grayson sent Charlie Summons to meet me at the station, but he went himself – and alone – to pick up a heavy cage of pheasants."

"But how did you know there were jewels in the birds?" Monica asked.

Arthur Conan Doyle smiled. "The diamonds? Well, you see Sherlock Holmes once solved a case in which a carbuncle was hidden inside a Christmas goose. But come, it is almost fight time and I must be in the ring."

Jack Johnson stopped Jim Jeffries in the fifteenth round, thus retaining the heavyweight championship of the world. And Jack London wrote, "Jeff today disposed of one question. He could not come back. Johnson, in turn, answered another question. He has not the yellow streak."

His article made no mention of Sir Arthur Conan Doyle.

Etta Revesz

Like a Terrible Scream

This is the 443rd "first story" published by Ellery Queen's Mystery Magazine... a first story with great emotional impact...
  Excerpts from the author's letter to your editor will give you an insight into the special quality of Etta Revesz's first story. She wrote: "Perhaps the best way to describe myself is to say that there are many skins in my closet, and many stories in my heart. That my hands have fashioned fabrics into garments of many moods, and that my dreams crowd the stars in the heavens... To be more mundane, I have roamed the woods of Maine, peered at the New York skyline from Brooklyn, been frightened by violence in Chicago schools, fallen in love in Iowa, gone seining in East Texas streams, lived widowhood in Connecticut, become a writer in California, worked as a dress designer in New York and Dallas, turned catatonics into actors when I put on plays in a state mental hospital, 'rapped' with female felons while working in

a state prison system, discovered the essence of misery while working for a welfare department"...

Me, I just sit here and wait until the man outside push the little button and the door open with a small click and the Father walk out. The Father, I know him since I be five, which is now eight years. I bet he never think he come to see me in lockup. Kid lockup they call it, but look like real grown-up jail to me.

I look out the little window for two days now. All I see is sky and maybe a airplane go by. The bed is clean but the floor is cement stone and hard on my leg. It is the door that I hate with much feeling. It is gray and iron, like the brace I wear on my leg. The little square window is high and I am yet too little to see out it and down the hall. I know a man sits there by a high desk and pushes buttons for many doors like I have to my cell. Yesterday I push up tight against the door because I am afraid. I think maybe I am the only one left here. But all I see is the ceiling of the hall and it is gray and not so clean.

It is hard to sit here and see the Father leave. He try. He try hard to make me tell why I do it.

"Confess, my son," Father Diaz say. "Tell me why did you do that terrible thing? You could not have realized. You were not thinking right!"

The good Father he lean his head way down and I think he cry, but I shake my head. How can I tell him? If I tell him the reason why I have done this it would be all for nothing. So I let him put his hand on my head and I say nothing.

"Kneel, my son," the Father say. "If you cannot tell me, tell God. It will help."

"No, Father," I say. "I cannot kneel."

He look very unhappy then, almost I think he will slap me when he take his hand away from my head. But he does not.

"A boy that cannot kneel and ask forgiveness from God is lost," he say and then go to my iron door and punch the little black button that tell the man at the desk to open up.

Now I sit here on my cot and wait for the Father to leave. My leg is out straight with my iron brace beginning to hurt me. Always at this time when night sounds start, Rita come home and take it off for me and rub my leg. Her hands, always so soft, rub away the stiffness. She talk to me about things outside. Always she ask to see my picture that I make that day. It was Rita that buy the paper and black crayon for me to draw. And last Christmas she bring me a box of paints! How much I do not guess it cost, but I know it cost much.

I feel in my eyes the water begin, but I want not to cry. I look again at Father Diaz's black suit. Like a crow he looks, standing with his arms folded close to his side like wings. I cannot stop my eyes from making tears. I pretend it is because my leg hurts and I try not to think of Rita.

I decide to tell Father Diaz that I cannot kneel because my iron brace does not bend. Then he would not think that all his teaching about God and the Blessed Virgin was for nothing. But it is too late. I hear the click and the door pop open and I am alone again.

Soon they will bring me food. I do not like noodles and cheese. Cheese should be on enchiladas. Noodles and cheese and maybe wheat bread with edges curled up like a dried leaf. Next to it a spoonful of peanut butter which I hate. It glues my tongue to my teeth. I think back to what Rita always bring to me.

Every night before she go to her job she come by the house with a surprise. First she take off my iron brace and rub my leg and then she put the brown bag in my lap and we stick both our heads close to see what big pleasure is there. Sometimes I look up and see her eyes big on me and smiling when I find a bag of candy or a pomegranate or even a new paint brush. At such time I feel a big pain over my heart and my jaw hurt from not crying. Rita she hate for me to cry. How can she know that it is for love of her that I cry?

Sometimes when only Mama and I are home I stop my painting and look out the window. We are high, two stairs up, but I can see the branches of the tree growing from the brown square of land in our sidewalk. It is not very healthy this poor tree, and has dry brown limbs with no leaves much. But still I watch the sun on what leaves are still there. It is when the sun is low and shines even with my tree that I like it best. Long fingers of white light run sharp from the center and when the wind blows everything shoots gold and shining. It is like a sign from God that the day is gone and Rita will run soon into the room and call out.

"Pepito," she calls, "I am here again. Your ugly old sister is here again!"

I pretend I do not hear her and then she come and put her hands around to cover my eyes from behind.

"Guess who it is?" she ask in make-believe man voice.

"My ugly old sister!" I say and then we both laugh. My sister Rita is not ugly. Sometimes she have a day off and she let me draw her picture. She sit by the window quiet while I look at her and put my markings on my paper. Sometimes I forget to move my hand when I look at her. Rita have long black hair and she tie it back so her neck looks very thin. Her mouth is still but when she think I am not watching, her lips move a little and I think she is telling secrets to herself. It is her eyes that I cannot draw so well.

When I look once they are laughing and show a joke ready to be said, but when I look again, I feel I must weep. Once I really start to cry at least a year ago when I was only twelve. Rita rush over and hug me.

"My little Pepito." She touch my cheek. "Does your leg hurt? I will work hard and save – oh, I will save so and will take you to a big hospital where the finest doctors will make a miracle on your leg."

"No," I tell her. I can never lie to Rita even when I want pity. "It is my love for you that make me cry. You are like Sunday music."

"She just laugh then and the next day when she come she say, "Here is your Sunday music for your ears to hear on Wednesday!"

I love my Mama and Papa almost as much as I love Rita. But Mama sigh often as she count her beads and wears black instead of colors bright and gay like Rita. I remember long time before, when we first come to city, Mama sing always. Sometimes she dance with Papa when Papa say about the big job he going to get.

"No more driving the junk truck for me," says Papa. "Lucerno family will be on easy street soon."

When Papa finish driving truck for Mr. George Hemfield he go to night school. When I wake up at night from the couch where I sleep because my leg hurt, I see Papa sitting at the kitchen table with books. All is quiet. Only sleeping sounds and the tick-ting of the wake-up clock and the hush sound of the books when Papa close them. Then I hear him push the chair and walk to his bed.

Carlos and Mikos, my big brothers, sleep in the bedroom. They have the big bed and Rita sleep with little Rosa in the little bed. Rosa is very small, only three years, and Rita call her Little Plum. Mama and Papa have the back porch for them. Papa fix it up and when Mama say, "What about the heat, my husband, when the winter come?" Papa he laugh and grab Mama as she pass him to the stove and say, "I will keep you warm – like always!"

"You crazy fellow, not before the children!" And Mama push his hand away like she is mad but I see her lips smile. Mama think I know nothing about life because I stay at home, because I do not run the streets and only walk outside for special days like Easter and Christmas and Cinco de Mayo when the world is spinning to guitar music.

At first when we come to city I go to school but after a while the stairs and long walk is too much. Rita try to carry me but the iron prison on my leg make her tired and once she drop me and the iron bend and cut into my leg. I learn, but not very much. It is hard for me to read the words and the teacher do not call my name very often.

Rita try to help. She is in the high school and she show me to make my letters. But I cannot do well. At my desk I draw pictures of what I want to say. It is much easier and soon the school hall show them on the walls.

One day the Principal give Rita a note for Mama to come and talk with him. Papa he go instead and after a long time in the Principal's office he come out and we walk home. Papa walk very small steps and not even holds my hand from sidewalk to car street. When we get to house Papa pick me up and carry me up to Mama. He hold me very tight and push my face to look behind him but I know he angry, sad angry. He tell Mama that a special teacher is going to teach me at home because they have no place for me at my school.

The teacher come but not for long. After a while another lady come to talk to Mama about budget and say that if Mama bring me to Down-Town I go to special school. Papa get mad and go Down-Town but come back soon. He say nothing and now I stay home and draw much.

I hear the pop of my iron door and a kid like me come in. He is an old one in experience at this place and they let him bring the food. He push open my door with a foot and carry in the tray. I watch him look where to put it.

"Here's your supper, Crip," he say. "Where d'ya want it?"

I sit up and look at what there is to eat, but all I see is red jello and two pieces of brown bread poked into a sauce of broken meat. I take off the square paper box of milk and tell him to take the tray. He looks worried at me.

"Look, Mex," he speak low. "Not eating won't help."

I shake my head and lean back on my cot and he leaves. It is almost dark now in my little gray room. I can put on a light. It is held away from me in a wire basket like a muzzle for a dog, but I have nothing to look at anyway.

So I stand and press against the stone wall so I see up and out the window into the soon night.

In the sky is fuzzy lines of color, like the cotton when you pull it out of the box and it spread fine in your hand. Somewhere I hear a noise and the red and green light of a airplane pass my eyes. So small it is, like a ladybug. So far away and such a small spot, much bigger looks the bird that flies closer to my window, not knowing that night is close and he should be in his nest. I am all alone now in my darkness.

It is like the darkness that came to our house the day Papa come home from new job hunting. For long days Papa try for new job, after he come home from school and hold high his beautiful piece of paper with gold words saying he is a educated man.

"This is just the beginning," say Papa. "I am just the number one to bring home the High School Certificate. Look, kids," say Papa, "this little piece of paper will be our passport to a new life."

We have a good dinner that night and Mama make a toast. "My man, with all this education, will be *presidente* yet!" Papa kiss Mama then and she let us all watch. Rita dance that day. She was 15 and the next one who would bring home such a paper. But it was not to be.

Papa's paper was only words and no one pull Papa in by the arm and give him a good job. Each day it was harder and harder to see his face at night and each night he have more and more red wine. At last Papa go back to his old job. It was a big truck and Papa was very tired at night after filling it with broken cars and iron and rusty pipes. Soon Mama cry all the time and then Rita stop her school. She come home one day and say she have a fine job that pay much money but she have to work at night. Papa ask who boss is, but Rita say he is Up-Town man and that Papa would not know him.

Rita sleep late now every morning and sometimes she look sad at me when she say goodbye to go for job. Always she look tired and one day she and Mama have big fight. Rita say she move out nearer her job and Mama say, "No," but Rita go anyway. She tell Mama she come every day to see me and bring money every week. The house seem so still now and Mama sit long times with little Rosa on her lap and I hear her say, "Little Plum" over and over.

Now for me the day begins when Rita come, for Rita keep her promise. One day she come and after we eat the caramel corn she bring, Rita tell me of a secret she and I will have. It is a plan to make me walk straight without iron brace.

"Pepito," Rita say and put three dollars in my hand, "I want you to hide this and every week I will give you more until there is enough and then we will visit the doctor who fixes legs."

We find empty box that oatmeal come in and cut a hole in the round top big enough to fold money into. It is our secret hiding place and I push the box under the couch where I sleep. Each week Rita add more money, sometimes even more at one time.

Our home is not very happy now. With Rita the smiles have gone. Carlos and Mikos are big now. Carlos is in the high school but want to stop and he and Papa fight now. Carlos say to Papa. "Old man, you live on your daughter's hustling!"

I watch as he pull himself up and like a bear try to squeeze the words back into Carlos' mouth. Papa's big hand slaps out at Carlos but he is quick and runs out and down the steps to the street. For the first time I see Papa cry, and when Mama come in and ask, he will not tell her what hurts him.

I cannot sleep that night. I know what hustling is. It is the walking of the streets that a woman does to offer her body to any man who will pay. I have hear Carlos and Mikos talk when they think I sleep. I hear the names of some girls and then rough words and then small swallowed laughter. I am much older than the pain in my legs. I am as old as the new leaves on my poor tree on the sidewalk.

My pillow is hard that night and I close my eyes against my fear. It is then that Rita's face come before my mind. I see her smooth skin and the quick way her body moves and the softness of her breast. I have watched her grow more beautiful in form as in heart. I have made the curve of her with my crayon on white paper. Do not think I look upon her with more than a brother should. But is it wrong to see beauty when it grows before your eyes? Her name is really Margarita, like the white flower with the golden center.

I cannot bear the evil pictures that pass before my eyes, and I cross myself and insist to my mind that Carlos spoke in anger and said a lie. I prefer it so.

When Rita come that next evening I want to tell her what Carlos say so we could laugh about it together and she could slap his face. But I keep silent. When she ask me why I do not smile I tell her a lie. I say my foot hurt.

"Come," she say, "get our box and let us count the money."

We open the top and count it in her lap. "We need more," Rita say. "I will work overtime."

I nod for I am afraid to ask and afraid not to ask. For the first time I want Rita to leave.

It is weeks before I sleep well and I blame it on my leg but I know it is Rita that worry me. Now I look at her more closely as if I expect to see a sign that all was a lie. Once I start to say something.

"A woman that sells her body." I stutter over the words. "What would one call her?"

Rita look at me quick and pulls her lips tight, then smiles. "Don't tell me that my little Pepito is growing up!"

She put her hand on my head and push my hair off my face.

"You do not answer me," I say.

"A prostitute." She turn away from me and her hand drop.

"That is an evil thing for a woman to do, isn't it?" I say.

"It all depends."

She turns and picks up a big bag. "Look what I brought you."

After we eat the big oranges she lean her head against mine and speaks into the room.

"You must not concern yourself with ugly things. You must see only beauty and put it on paper. I do not know any prostitutes and neither do you."

She leave soon after and before I sleep that night I curse my brother Carlos and his vile tongue.

It goes on as before now with Rita and me. Soon it is her birthday. She is to be 18 in a week and I decide to buy her a present. Mama has said that 18 is a special age for a girl and I want to make it fine for her birthday. The only money I have is under my couch in the oatmeal box. I decide within myself that it would not be wrong to use some of it for Rita's birthday present.

Mama is surprised when I tell her I will go down the stairs and on the street until I explain to her what I want to do. I tell her I have saved some money and I show her the $20 I have in my pocket. She helps me down the first steps and watches me as I walk down the street to where the stores are.

The stores are filled with fine things and I move slowly from one window to the other. Before one I stop a long time and almost decide to buy a small radio. But I think maybe a pretty dress would be better for Rita. A white dress to make her hair blacker than the midnight and the white like snow against her golden skin.

Now I look for a dress shop. Across the

street is a large store with dresses like a flower garden. At the corner I stand waiting for the street light to change when I hear voices behind me. It is what they say that makes me turn and follow them instead of crossing the street.

I do not know all of them but one boy is Luis. He is older than Rita but was in school with her and sometimes Carlos bring him to the house. It is when I hear him say the name Rita that I decide to follow them.

"Yeah, that damn Rita," one boy say. "Since she move Up Town into the big time, you can't even touch her any more."

"I hear she's hooked up with some pimp who is really rolling in clover." They all laugh.

My blood! I feel it leave my body and sink to the sidewalk. Surely the earth will open up and these boys will fall into hell! I cannot walk any more. They turn the corner and disappear. My heart is dead inside of me. No longer can I doubt what I feared. No longer can I doubt.

I feel people shove at me as they pass me and still I cannot move. Long later I take steps, slowly down the sidewalk. All the time in the center of my throat is a sore spot I cannot swallow away. Like a terrible scream that has no sound.

It was when my leg hurt so much that I stop and lean my face against the smooth glass of a store window. Cool it feels on my hot cheeks. My eyes I close tight – so tight it hurt. Colors dance in my head and run to stab my heart. My leg beats out the music of pain.

No longer can I stand the ache so I open my eyes again. There, under my look, I see the guns. Like soldiers ready to march when the general shout out a command. They wait quietly, these black snails that carry death inside a shell.

For a long time I look at these guns. Has not a Father Diaz said that death is only another life? And a better one?

I move to the store door. It is glass with a wire across it, like the knitting Mama does, all looped together. I put two hands on the door handle. It is stiff and cold like a gun, I think. Down I push and shove open the door. I stumble on a mat and my iron brace rips at the rubber as I pull my leg free. A small bell shakes and makes a ringing. I walk in.

When the police ask me I shake my head and when Mama and Papa cry in the courtroom for children and the judge ask me why I kill my sister on her birthday I still am quiet.

They would not understand how hard a thing it was to do. To lose your star when you are thirteen is to walk blind on the earth. Better this way than to see your star fall from the heavens and end in mud. Always to me Margarita will be like her name, pure white on the outside and golden in the center.

And that is why I lie here on this cot with the black of my little room hiding me from the night of nothingness and I am called a murderer.

Editorial Postscript

The story you have just read was awarded the coveted Edgar by MWA (Mystery Writers of America) as the best new mystery short story published in American magazines and books during 1976.

S. S. Rafferty

The Pennsylvania Thimblerig

This story concerns events that took place in Philadelphia, Pennsylvania, on July 4, 1776. Some of the events are matters of history, some might be termed "unrecorded." The historical facts changed the course of this country, and of the world. The "previously unchronicled" events contributed to that momentous change, and are food for historical conjecture. Here, then, is the account of the most important detective performance in Captain Jeremy Cork's career – a case before the Second Continental Congress on July 4, 1776, in emergency secret session – a case in which you will meet, among others, Benjamin Franklin, Thomas Jefferson, John Hancock, Samuel Adams, John Jay, and a Philadelphia Thimblerig...

The oppressive blanket of heat that plagued the colonial seaboard in the summer of 1776 well matched the revolutionary fever in the body politic, and Captain Jeremy Cork's own seething indignation.

His choler arose from his failure to be elected a Connecticut delegate to the Second Continental Congress, despite the fact that he had given his ship, *The Hawkers,* to the rebel navy. It seemed the past events of Lexington and Concord had unleashed a civic unrest from which my employer was not immune. *The Hawkers* is, or was, the mainbrace of the financial empire I had constructed for him with patient yeomanry.

Ostensibly, his reason for coming to Philadelphia in late June was to observe the ship's transfer to Commodore Hopkins, but I was not taken in by that ruse. Cork wanted a place of importance in these revolutionary doings, and, finding no opening, had decided to be as close to the hive as possible.

Thus, in addition to the swelter and recurring thunderstorms, I had to sustain the brooding and silent Cork. My evenings were made bearable by his absence from our rooms at Morby's in Spring Garden Street. He would spend the dark hours at the City Tavern with the various delegates and would come home cheered. But by daylight he became morose again.

It was mid-morning of 4 July when the

first breeze in days rose up from the bay and wafted through the windows of our sitting room. I looked up from my reading of the *Gazette* to enjoy the zephyrs.

"The wind's up. It's a shame we don't have a ship to take advantage of it," I chided him.

"Consider her on loan," he said, dishing up another helping of oysters from the sea bucket in the corner. It was his third plateful of the day; since our arrival, shellfish had been the mainstay of his diet.

"A loan without collateral is often uncollectable," I said. This was our first interchange since dawn, and I feared I had now ended all conversation for the rest of the day.

"Oaks," he said, shucking a shell and sprinkling the oyster meat with Madeira and a pinch of dillweed, "you always manage to sound dangerously like a Tory."

Now there you have it! The main difference between us was this damnable war. I well realised the injustices of the King, and the possible need to rectify them with arms, but I am a man of commerce, a man who must protect an investment. Reconciliation on better terms was my thinking, not revolution and separation, which could destroy us all.

You will mark well I said the war was our *main* difference. There is another that has plagued me for years, and that is his excursions into the solutions of crime and skulduggery, which he calls "social puzzles." Yet, despite my previous misgivings about these puzzles, I found myself wishing that one would turn up, if only to occupy that fertile mind that was now so fallow.

Not wanting to sit in silence, I said, "I see your friend Dr. Franklin has lost his dog, and from the reward in this advertisement, he seems to value the animal highly."

"Are you suggesting that I become a dogcatcher?" He glared at me.

"Just making conversation, Captain. Might I ask, how long are we going to sit here doing nothing?"

He didn't answer, for a knock came to our door, and Morby himself entered. The portly innkeeper had a military man with him. The officer's blue coat, criss-crossed at the breast with white belting, and his bucktailed, cockaded hat bespoke him to be a Major of the Philadelphia Associators, a militia company of tradesmen. Yet the part-time soldier did not have the demeanour of a tradesman any more than he did of a military man. He was pale and thin, and his hands were milky white like those of a gentleman. Morby's introduction clarified the matter.

"Beg pardon, Cappin, sor, but Dr. Church would like a word with ye."

"Yes, Captain," the middle-aged soldier said, stepping forward. "I was at drill with the company at the State House Yard when Morby summoned me. I know of your reputation in such cases and would appreciate your help with Mr. Custis."

"By all means, Doctor. What seems to be Mr. Custis' problem?"

"He's dead, Captain. Dead by foul means, if I know arsenic poisoning when I see it."

I looked at Cork, who, for the first time in days, had a glint in his eye.

Morby clutched his pudgy hands. "I would sorely like ye help, Cappin. A man dying of pie-son makes the house look bad."

"Ah, then he's a guest here at the inn. Well, where away, man. What room?"

We followed our callers down the hall and up a landing to the third-floor attic.

"Came in two days ago, he did," Morby said, opening the door and showing us into a simple bedchamber. "Paid a week's advance."

It was a typical second-class room with a writing table, chair, and small cot upon which lay the corpse. The Captain examined the body and smelled the mouth.

"Arsenic, to be sure, Doctor," he said, testing the flexibility of the dead man's hand and arm. "Would you say he died not more than an hour ago?"

"Undoubtedly. I was about to summon the sheriff when Morby here mentioned your name."

"He should be summoned in any case. Have you been through his effects?"

"We thought it best to have other witnesses," Dr. Church said.

"Yes," Cork said, walking to the writing table. "Did he take breakfast this morning, Morby?"

"No, sor, just asked for hot water, he did."

"To make himself some tea, no doubt." The Captain picked up a travelling cup and smelled it. "A deadly cup at that." He handed the container to the doctor, who sniffed it.

"Arsenic, Doctor. Look here. A box of green tea on the table, along with some orange peels. I think our Mr. Custis would have been better off to have availed himself of the pleasure of Morby's dining room below this morning. Well, who is he? Where is he from? And why was he poisoned? Morby!"

"Lor's be, Cappin, all I know, he was a gentleman in travel of some kind. From New York, I think he said."

"Yes," Cork said, returning to the bed, "a gentleman by clothing, but with the hands of a workman, and living in a second-class accommodations. It is certainly strange."

I had been too busy watching Cork to fully take in the body. Cork was, as always, quick to observe minute points. The man's linen was expensive, yet somehow it did not go with the sunburnt face and rough hands, or the queue tied back with a fine silk ribbon.

"A bit incongruous," I said.

"Incongruity is often the nub of a puzzle, Oaks," Cork said, opening a travelling case he had drawn from under the cot. He dumped the contents onto the bare floor.

"Incongruity, indeed," he frowned. "Our Mr. Custis lies in death in a fine brocade suit, yet his satchel yields raw buckskin breeches and vest, worn boots, and rather despicable hose." The box also contained a quill, a small slate, an hourglass, a book of Common Prayers, and a sharp dagger.

Dr. Church, who had been going through the table drawer, held up some strips of paper. "Could this have any meaning, I wonder?"

Cork came across the room, took the seven

strips, and examined them. They were white, thin, and no more than a quarter of an inch in width by about twelve inches in length. He mused over them for a few moments and then took them to the window, where he held each one up to the sunlight.

"Most interesting," he said, after a careful study. "Doctor, I trust that you can handle the details here as far as the corpse is concerned, and Morby, I leave you to deal with the sheriff."

"But, sor, sor," the innkeeper pleaded, "the suspicion on the house!"

"As likely not, Morby. He brought his death in with him in the tea. You only supplied the water. Come, Oaks."

We started to leave when the good doctor called after us. "Begging your pardon, Captain, but you are taking those strips with you. If they are important, and you seem to think they are, shouldn't you leave them here for the sheriff?"

"Under the rules of evidence in the Commonwealth of Pennsylvania I would agree, Doctor, but this transcends boundaries. Pay my respects to the sheriff and tell him I will be in touch with him."

"Well, this leaves me in a rather precarious position. After all, I am only a physician. Where can you be reached?"

"On Bristol Road at the home of Dr. Benjamin Franklin," he said, turning towards the door with myself in tow and, as usual, in the dark.

The haste with which Cork moved bespoke the pent-up energy that had been building within him the past fortnight. He no sooner had left the death chamber when he entered our rooms, slipped into a coat, and was off down the stairwell to the common rooms below. He paused to send Josh, the boy of all work, to tell Tyngs to have the calash ready.

The calash, driven by its owner, Falcor Tyngs, is one of the many luxuries Cork allows himself in Philadelphia. It galls me to pay out good monies for the carriage, horse, and driver when we rarely use them, but the Captain insists. Within minutes all was ready and we were away.

"If you don't mind my asking," I said as we clattered over the scorching cobbles into Broad Street, "why all this rush to Dr. Franklin's?"

"We have here a perplexity of no mean proportions, Oaks." He leaned back into the breeze that our locomotion created. "Consider the facts at hand. A workman disguised as a gentleman is poisoned. In his possession are curious strips of paper. Who, then, is the best paper expert in Philadelphia to confront them with than Poor Richard, the master printer himself?"

"You think the paper had some bearing on Custis's death then?"

"Of course. Put all the points together. How did this poor devil die? By poison, mixed with tea. When was the last time you ate an orange, Oaks? Don't you see?"

"Tea and oranges," I mused aloud. Then it struck me. "He's British. The only oranges are on the Redcoats' tables."

"And tea, too, for that matter. Then there is the sun-parched skin to be considered. West Indies, if I make it right."

"That is reasonable. But the paper? That confounds me."

He reached into his pocket and drew out the seven strips. "Note that they are similar in shape and size. But there the similarities end. The quality of each piece of paper is different. All are of top grade, but different."

"Samples of some kind," I said.

"Yes, that could be, but the oblong shapes suggest another function. Paper samples are usually square or triangular. Paper is too expensive to waste so much on a sample. Well, let us see what Dr. Franklin has to say."

The appointments of the house on Bristol

Road mirrored its owner's eclectic taste. Amid the sturdy native furniture were beautifully shaped pieces from Europe, as well as lush draperies and fine oil paintings.

He sat in an armchair of red brocade, his foot resting gingerly on a low stool. Here was a man who had met three kings and had visited with numerous lesser royalty, and yet he chose the brown frock of the Quakers as his garb. His grey hair was cut to the length of his collar, and his face was remarkably unlined for a man of 70. He looked up from a sheaf of documents in his lap as we entered, his blue-grey eyes peeping over his eyeglasses.

"Forgive me for remaining seated, gentlemen. The gout again, my dear Jeremy," he said, offering some port from the table beside him. I was surprised to hear Dr. Franklin call the Captain "Jeremy." Few people ever do.

After Cork had explained the Custis affair, he turned over the paper strips, and the venerable doctor examined them closely.

"You are right about all the pieces being of good quality, Jeremy," he said, holding them up to the light.

"Three of them have a portion of a watermark, Doctor."

"Yes, I see that. Now this one with the cloverleaf is from the Rittenhouse Shop here in Philadelphia. And if I read the bead and chain lines correctly in this one, it is from DeWees's Shop in Virginia. I have sold Gerald DeWees rags in the past for use in his papermaking process."

"Excellent," Cork said, picking one of the strips. "The watermark here appears to be a C and an L, which I immediately recognized as the product of Chris Leffingwell of Connecticut. Now we have something more to go on. Three different papers from three different colonies, and if I guess right, the remaining four are from still other colonies."

"Jeremy," the doctor laughed, "you will have to erase the word 'colony' from your speech, my boy."

Cork dropped the paper strip he was holding. "Then it's done," he said, the surprise showing in his voice.

"This very afternoon. The Declaration of Independence was approved by the Congress, so you will have to start calling these colonies states."

"But I've had no word of it. Do you have a copy?"

"The document is at Dunlap's, the printer. Our courier took it there this afternoon. Copies will be struck off and carried by post-riders to all the states to-night."

I sank back into my chair. So it was done. These shores were now independent and vulnerable.

"Well, well," Cork beamed, "that is good news, but I'm afraid it will do Mr. Custis no good. Have you any notions, Dr. Franklin?"

The old man heaved a sigh. "Jeremy, I would like to be of more assistance, but at the moment I am heavily involved in Congressional work. I have to find factories for flint and gun production, and there's food to be raised for the army. I'm afraid I haven't time to spend on trifles."

I truly felt sorry for Cork. The word "trifles" went through him like a rusty blade. But I could sympathise with Franklin, an aged, overburdened man being pestered with a minor crime. Yet he was sensitive enough to see that he had hurt the Captain.

"Trifle was a poor choice of word, Jeremy. A person's death is no trifle. You'll have to forgive me. I am a bit out of sorts to-day. My gout is acting up, my son has decided to remain with the Royalists, and some scoundrel has slain my dog."

"Slain?" Cork asked. "I thought it was merely lost?"

"And so it seemed when I placed a notice for his return, but the old fellow was found just two hours ago out in the brush with its throat cut."

"Perhaps he attacked someone," I suggested. "In this heat, dogs often become angry at the slightest agitation."

"The cur, like his master, was old and beyond agitation, Mr. Oaks. No, it was an act of malice – probably by a Tory seeking some petty revenge against me. I fear this division between Tory and Whig will be a greater problem than General Howe's army. Perhaps the Declaration of Separation will change some minds. Ah!" he said to a visitor who had just been shown into the room, "here's its author now."

The caller was strikingly handsome and straight as a gun barrel. He was over six-foot-three and in his mid-thirties. Despite the heat of the day, his high forehead was dry, his reddish brown hair unrumpled.

"After eighty-six changes by others, I could hardly call it original authorship," the man said. He was introduced as Thomas Jefferson.

"I warned you that is the hazard of preparing a document that must be approved by a body of men. It is a risk I have always avoided," Dr. Franklin said impishly, but Jefferson didn't appreciate the jest.

Cork must have felt we were intruding,

and got ready to leave, when Dr. Franklin stopped him.

"You might explain your problems to Tom while you're here, Jeremy. He enjoys solving problems as much as you do."

Cork obliged and gave him all the details, as well as the paper strips.

"So," Jefferson said after examining the strips, "you believe these samples are from seven different places, yet they are all exactly the same length and width. The measurements intrigue me. Have you a measuring stick about, Ben?"

One was forthcoming and Jefferson measured the pieces of paper with great care.

"Twelve and three-quarters by one-quarter." The Virginian stroked his jaw. "Ben, you are familiar with such matters. What is the usual size of a paper mould?"

"These strips are from American wooden moulds. You can tell by the deckle. They are usually, if not always, twelve and three-quarter inches by sixteen and three-eighths inches."

"So these were trimmed from the lengths of single sheets. But why always in quarter-inch widths?" Cork asked.

"Trimmed – that's your answer, Jeremy," Dr. Franklin said with a wince as he moved his painful foot. "The quarter-inch width is a trimming, and if the trimming is the same in seven different parts of the country, it has to be a universal item."

"Like shinbucks! Money!" Cork cried, getting to his feet. "Now it all makes sense. Our Mr. Custis has somehow obtained samples of bank-note stock used in the printing of money in seven colonies – I mean, states. He was English, or pro-English, which means only one thing."

"A counterfeit scheme, of course," I said.

"To be sure, Oaks," Cork said, turning to Franklin. "With the proper stock and copper plates, the British could flood the land with worthless money, further compounding our troubles."

"Jeremy," Dr. Franklin smiled, "you have my deepest apology for calling this case a trifle."

"Think nothing of it. If it weren't for an alert medical officer, the plot would have worked. We will have to find out who this mysterious Mr. Custis really is, and how he planned to execute his foul deed."

Dr. Franklin got to his feet with another wince of pain and leaned gingerly on his cane. "I leave Custis to you, Jeremy. I have a more urgent task. Tom, we must send a message to Hancock to convene the Congress in emergency session. Details will have to be forwarded to all the state committees for safety and a countermine developed to block the British plot. If we work through the night, we can use the same post-riders who carry the Declaration."

The place was astir like a toppled nest of yellowjackets, with servants being called, notes being written and dispatched. Having no place in it, Cork motioned me with his head and we left.

"Captain, you have my congratulations," I said, as the carriage headed back to the city. "You not only have uncovered a plot, but you have protected your own estate. You realise how much of your cash is in Continental bank-notes?"

He grunted and took on his brooding again.

"Good Lord, man," I said. "You are not offended because you weren't invited to the emergency meeting, are you? As I understand it, they are held in secret session."

"No, I doubt that I could do much there, Oaks," he said. "What does concern me is our new country's naivete in political subterfuge. We are helplessly new at what the Italians call *spione*. It is not in our nature to be deft in the double-deal, but I fear we will have to develop the black arts of Europe quickly and effectively. Well, now to Mr. Custis."

Dusk had fallen when we alighted at Morby's door to find Dr. Church waiting for us. We repaired to the taproom and took a table. The doctor was still in his Major's militia uniform, and was greatly agitated.

"Captain Cork," he said, looking furtively around the room, "I have made a very disturbing discovery. For my own curiosity I performed a necropsy on Custis's body after the sheriff had released it. In the victim's gullet I found this."

From his pocket he withdrew a piece of white linen and carefully unfolded it to reveal a small metallic ball about the size of a pea or rifle pellet. He also produced small bits of felt which, he said, he found under Custis's fingernails.

"I didn't notice any neck wound," I said, thinking the doctor was implying that Custis had been shot.

"I don't think that's the doctor's inference, Oaks." Cork rolled the ball in his palm and then smelled it. "It looks like silver, but it could be antimony."

"Aha, so it wasn't arsenic, then," I said. "And it wasn't murder, either. Custis committed suicide by swallowing a poisonous metal ball." I was quite proud of myself, for, though I have been against our involvement in crime, I had been around it long enough to learn something.

"I'm sorry, Mr. Oaks." The doctor gave me a weak, almost painful, smile. "The ball is of silver, which would have no effect on the body chemistry. Death was by arsenic, and it was in the tea. My tests proved that beyond question."

"I see what you are aiming at," Cork said, still playing with the ball. "You found it in the gullet..."

The doctor looked embarrassed. "Forgive my rude speech, Captain. My old masters at Edinburgh would be appalled. It was lodged in the esophagus, to be exact, midway in the *pars thoracica* area."

"Gullet will do me fine, Doctor," Cork went on. "Then if he was unconscious within minutes from arsenic, the ball had to be swallowed before his death trance."

"Precisely." The doctor knocked the table with his knuckles for emphasis. "But why would a man, with the clutch of death on him, try to swallow a silver bullet?"

Cork thought for a moment, then said matter-of-factly, "To conceal it, of course."

"Well, I see no rhyme or reason to it." Dr. Church rubbed his chin. "Any more than I can understand the bits of felt under his fingernails. At first I thought he might have grabbed at a material made of felt in his death agony, but I re-examined his room just before you returned, and can find nothing made of felt in the place."

"Well done, Doctor. You have proved a first-class investigator. The felt ties it all together, although the silver ball is still a mystery." Cork went on and explained the counterfeiting conspiracy and the significance of the paper samples. "Custis was posing as a coucher in various paper shops throughout the country. A coucher, gentlemen, is the worker who takes the wet sheets of paper from the mould and places them between pieces of felt to absorb the water. What better role could you adopt to gain inside knowledge of which paper was to be used for money printing? A man's occupation often clings to him unnoticed. No, perhaps this little ball will unlock some more information."

"My, oh, my." Dr. Church's eyebrows went up. "Little did I know when I summoned you this morning that I would be involved in a matter of such magnitude. The Congress in secret evening session, a plot abroad in the states – my, oh, my."

"The smallest of us may have to make

large contributions, Doctor. Is there a good jeweller in the neighbourhood?"

Church said yes, that a Martin Whitlow kept a shop in the next street.

"Well, Doctor, since he is probably closed for the day, might I rely on your official uniform as a Major of the militia company to fetch him here? Ask him to bring a jeweller's glass, a scale, and the sharpest cutting tool he has."

The doctor left, and Cork pushed his chair back to the wall and stretched out his long legs. For the first time in days he had a relaxed, if not a jubilant, look on his face.

"Well," he said, signalling to Morby, "we might as well enjoy our free moments. Morby, bring some Apple Knock, and send over the thimblerig for a few games."

Thimblerigging is something he never gets to play in our Connecticut homeport, gambling being frowned on there. But in the larger cities he indulges himself, and, I must say, he is rather lucky at it. But, considering the import of the problem at hand, I considered it frivolous to bet on which of the three shells hid the pea.

The thimblerig, a jaunty stout fellow, came up to the table and tipped his hat. His wide grin was catlike as he greeted what he assumed to be another pigeon.

"Evening, sirs," he said, spreading out the tools of his trade – a soft cloth, a hard pea, and the three shells. "Name your limit, but I only deal in gold or silver. No paper, thank you."

Cork threw his head back and laughed deeply. "Perhaps our efforts *are* futile, Oaks. Play on for a half-joe, my man."

The pea was placed under the center shell and the thimblerig's hands flew in a whirl, moving the shells in a complex choreography. When he stopped, Cork tapped the center shell, and the gambler looked annoyed. The pea was under it, and Cork collected his coin.

They were in the middle of the sixth game when the doctor-Major returned with an elderly, disgruntled man at his elbow. "I never saw such luck," the thimblerig said in disgust, paying off for the sixth time and leaving us.

"These fellows tickle me," the Captain said, pointing to a chair for the jeweller. "They use their clever hands to misdirect you, but the trick is to keep your eye on the pea. Well, sir, Mr. Whitlow, is it? We seem to have gotten you out of bed."

The old man had dressed hurriedly, and had not combed his hair, which fell over his eyes in a white thatch. "I retire at sunset, as

God intended all His creatures to do. This bluejay came slamming at my door like the thunder of hell itself. What's this land coming to, I'd like to know? Toy soldiers disturbing a man's sleep, goods in short supply, and annihilation riding to us in British men-of-war. I tell you, sir, we are being cajoled by madmen –"

Cork cut off his tirade with an upraised hand. "We will take only a few minutes of your time, Mr. Whitlow, and then you can return to the safety of your bed. Would you examine this article?"

The jeweller took the silver ball, hefted it in his hand, and looked as if something were wrong. He took a glass instrument from his pocket and studied the ball's surface, then placed the ball on the scale.

"Just as I thought," he grumbled, "it's hollow. Its size doesn't match its weight. If it's a bullet, it's not heavy enough to kill anyone. Good Lord" – a sudden thought occurred to him – "these Continentals aren't going to use silver bullets, are they?"

Cork ignored the question and asked if there were any markings on the surface.

"Just the seam where it was sealed. It's very good work, no doubt about that.

"Very good," Cork said. "Now can you cut it open very carefully?"

The old man looked deeply insulted and picked up a small blade with a fine sawtooth edge. "Been doing delicate work for over fifty years," he muttered as he cut slowly through the metal. "The hands and eyes are as good now as they ever were. Here you are. Is that all?"

"Yes, Mr. Whitlow," Cork said, pushing his thimblerig winnings across to the man. "Thank you. And my best to Mrs. Whitlow and your large brood."

The jeweller shot him a quizzical look. "Now how did you know I have many children?"

The Captain smiled and bid him good evening. "It seems that Dr. Franklin's advice about early to bed and early to rise produces more than wealth and wisdom." He chuckled.

"Isn't there something inside this?" the doctor pointed to the now split ball. Stuffed into one of the hemispheres was a white object. Cork probed it delicately with a knife point until it came loose. It was a tiny wad of material which, when unrolled, proved to be a square of the finest silk, of incredible thinness. Cork spread it out on the table and smoothed its surface.

"Why, yes, there is a message of some kind written on it," I said.

Cork read it through twice and then made room at the table for me to read over his shoulder.

> "King H has approved. Plates ready 1 August. Will deliver after word from B. that payment made.
>
> Dor. Q."

I could make no sense of it, and the doctor-Major said, "What is it, Captain?"

"I'm afraid I will have to ask you to refrain from reading this," Cork said, folding the silk material. "I hope you won't be insulted, but this is a highly confidential matter."

"Of course," Church said with a hurt smile, "I am sure that the Congress can vouch for my trustworthiness since I serve as their courier."

He bid us good night and left, and I said to Cork, "You may have hurt his feelings, Captain. After all, he has helped us quite a bit. What's so secret, anyway? Is it a code of some sort?"

"That's what bothers me most, my boy. It is not a code, as I expected. Fetch me Falcor Tyngs, will you?"

"We are going out again?"

"Not at the moment. I will have to study this a bit further. Send Tyngs to our rooms and then have the ostler prepare two mounts."

When I returned from the stable to our rooms, Cork had finished giving Tyngs instructions of some sort, and sent him off.

"You're acting rather curiously, Captain," I said, sitting down opposite him at the table. He had taken out the silk material and was reading it anew. He knitted his brows for a long minute and then blinked his eyes wide open in surprise. "Of course!" he cried.

"You have decoded it, then."

"I told you it wasn't a code. It is just that I don't keep up with the social notes. Weren't you telling me that John Hancock has a new bride?"

"Yes, a Miss Dorothy Quincy. Quite a piece of friggery, I gather. Wait, Dorothy Quincy, Dor Q. Do you mean that the wife of the president of the Congress wrote that message?"

"The reference to King H would make it appear so. He is called 'King Hancock' by his detractors, is he not?"

"Well," I chuckled, "you can hardly blame people, the way he parades through the streets with all sorts of liveried servants in his train. Could we have intercepted a Congressional message?"

"Hardly, under the circumstances. We suspect the late Mr. Custis of having been a counterfeiter."

"And the message mentions payment for plates," I cried. "Bank-note plates! My God, I can hardly believe it. Hancock is one of the richest men in America. He's reportedly a snob –"

"And a smuggler," Cork added.

"I see your point, Captain. But King George has put a £500 reward on Hancock's head. But then a young new bride can turn a man's direction. Shouldn't we report this?"

"Yes, and as quickly as you can."

"As I can?"

"Oaks, I am depending on you, for I have other matters to attend to. Take this to Dr. Franklin at the State House and tell him all you know."

I started to protest, but he would have none of it, and rushed me to the stable and had me ahorse in minutes. My last objection was met with a slap of Cork's hand on my mount's hindquarters, and I found myself flying towards Chestnut Street.

I entered the courtyard and, while dismounting, could hear voices from the centre rooms of the first floor – the Congress was in heated argument. The doorkeeper's lodgings were in the west wing, and when I pounded on his entry, I was greeted by a gentlewoman. My frantic pounding had alarmed her.

"Sir, you scared me out of my wits. I thought the Indians in the upper east wing had finally burned us down."

I looked at her. "Indians?"

"Visitors. They are very careless with fire. What do you want, sir?"

I told her of the urgency of my talking to Dr. Franklin, and she took me to the centre hall, where I repeated my need to the doorkeeper of the Congressional chamber. It took me about ten minutes to persuade him to take my message to Dr. Franklin. I was surprised when Thomas Jefferson, and not the doctor, returned with him.

"Mr. Oaks," he said in an irritated tone, "Dr. Franklin's gout prevents him from coming out. He suggests that you talk to me."

Well, Cork had specifically said Dr. Franklin and no one else, but I took it upon myself to explain how we had come by the message and handed him the silk cloth. He read it slowly, as all lawyers do, and said nothing for several seconds.

"This is either preposterous or else the most dangerous charge ever. Wait here."

Jefferson was gone for quite a while, and I could hear the room within fall silent. Then Jefferson reappeared and beckoned me in.

All eyes were on me as I entered the large

chamber. My heart was pounding with anxiety. Why, I asked myself, had Cork left this unpleasant task to me? The delegates' chairs were comfortably arranged in an informal manner, and I noticed the familiar, but not friendly, face of Roger Sherman from Connecticut, a man I admired for he had risen from a shoemaker to a prosperous land dealer. Sherman's glare told me that great gravity had settled over the body of men.

I walked forward towards the double brass-fitted fireplaces that faced the door. They were, of course, unlit, but the unbearable heat of the room made it seem as if they were both ablaze. The closeness of the room was further abetted by the pungent wafting that came through the narrow openings of the window tops from the stable across the street. I turned towards the back wall, where there was a panoply consisting of a drum, swords and banners. They were the trophies of the capture of Fort Ticonderoga, a place to which I wished I could be transported that instant.

Below the panoply was the President's desk, with the official mace on it. Behind it sat John Hancock, a look of black anger on his face. I found myself appealing to Jehovah.

"Sir," Hancock's voice roared at me, "you

have brought a charge into this chamber that is both absurd and treasonous!"

"Mr. President," a shortish delegate began.

Hancock looked his way, still angry. "The chair recognizes Mr. Samuel Adams of Massachusetts."

"I move that we become a committee of the whole while we hear this man."

Someone seconded the proposal. Hancock called for a voice vote and all said "Aye." Hancock then rose from his chair and stepped down to sit with the other delegates. I have long heard of Samuel Adams's parliamentary ability, and this was a shrewd example of it. By moving for a committee of the whole, he had automatically made anything said unofficial.

"Mr. Oaks," Dr. Franklin said from his chair, "this is most disturbing. Can you give us all the details of the affair?"

My throat was parched as if from sand, my arms wouldn't move. I opened my mouth to speak and found salvation. I heard Cork's voice boom from the doorway.

"Gentlemen," he said, "forgive my intrusion, but I don't think Mr. Oaks's recitation will be necessary. The case has been solved to your advantage, Mr. Hancock."

Well, by jing, there he was, strutting into

this august assembly like a peacock, a smile of self-satisfaction on his face. Dr. Franklin asked him to explain, and Cork raised the curtain on the most important performance of his life.

"Good sirs," he said, "and particularly you, Mr. President, have my heartfelt apology for being a jackanapes. Here I have been following false trails when the real problem lay under my nose. A traveller's mysterious death set off a chain of circumstances that led me to a counterfeit plot. And that, ironically, is what it was. A counterfeit, a fake. There was no plot – not against our money, at least. The plot was deeper and infinitely more dangerous."

Every man in the room leaned forward in anticipation.

"Mr. Thompson," Cork said to the secretary of the Congress, "is this the document you sent to Dunlap the printer late this afternoon?" He handed him a paper and the man looked at it quickly. From my vantage point I could see that it was in holograph with many corrections on it.

The man looked at it quickly. "Yes," he said, returning it to Cork, "I recognize it as such."

"Good. Now, I give it to Mr. Jefferson, its original author."

Jefferson took the paper and read it with the same slow exactness he had used on the silk material. He looked puzzled and then reached down and took another paper from the lawyer's bag at his feet and compared the two papers.

"Why, the copy sent to the printer has been changed! I have here my own fair copy, which incorporates all the additions and deletions passed on this afternoon. The printer's copy has been altered. Here, where we originally said 'life, liberty, and the pursuit of happiness,' this copy deletes 'happiness' and says 'property.' And there are other changes. We took out the mention of slaves to appease the Southern delegation, and here it is back in again. This is dreadful. If printed copies have left for the states –"

"Take your ease, sir," Cork said. "But if that document had gone out to the people, you would have crushed any faith in this Congress, and possibly in the revolution effort as well. Just a few simple changes and a few additions would have pointed up the differences in regional attitudes, and set the northern states against the southern, the townsman against the farmer, the landed against the poor. Thus the document meant to unite would have served to divide. It was a simple thing to do. The copy sent to

Dunlap's is indeed a calligraphic mess. Eighty-six changes and deletions. Words crossed over. A few more would not have been noticed."

"But unless it were one of *us* –" Hancock began. "I don't see how any outsider could have done it."

"And why not, Mr. President?" Cork shook a finger. "I would suggest better security measures in the future. There are troops in the State House yard each day. Perhaps not everything can be heard through the window, but the gist of things can be. Besides, our culprit didn't need to eavesdrop. He had seen the document after Mr. Jefferson wrote it."

"Why, no one saw it prior to submission but John Adams, Dr. Franklin, and myself," Jefferson said.

"Precisely. Did you leave it with them?"

"With Dr. Franklin, yes."

"And Dr. Franklin's dog was destroyed and the body hidden. Doesn't that suggest that someone broke into the house on Bristol Road, silenced the dog so his entry would not be discovered, and then read the document?"

"But why all this nonsense about counterfeiting," Dr. Franklin grumbled, "and this secret-message business?"

"The first was to create a crisis, which

would bring you into session on the night the Declaration of Independence was to be dispatched. The second was to make sure you stayed in session until the post-riders had left. The next time you use your courier to take things to a printer, don't trust him simply because he is a medical man and a Major in the Associators."

It was after midnight when we reached Morby's and, as usual after a triumph, Cork was famished. Despite the late hour, the hearths were relit and a feast was in preparation. Cork eschewed fish since it had been his main diet, and ordered roast kid, ducklings in bing sauce, and a huge bowl of broccola laced with lemon butter.

"How did you get on to Dr. Church?" I asked him as we ate our snapper stew. "He certainly was convincing."

"Not really," he said. "Just up to a point. When he conveniently gave us the silver bullet with the message inside, I became suspicious. You will recall I was annoyed that it wasn't in code. Why would anyone go to such trouble to conceal a message and then write it out in plain language? That is bad *spione*."

"Then why didn't he encode it?"

"Because he could not be sure that I would

be able to decode it in time to warn the Congress. But his telling us that he had found felt under Custis's fingernails was sheer poppycock. He wanted to strengthen the evidence that Custis had worked as a coucher in paper shops. A coucher works with his hands in water all day, and certainly would not have the callused and tanned hands that our corpse did."

"And what of Custis? Who was he?"

"We'll never know. Probably a seaman whom Dr. Church had duped into playing the role of a traveller. A little poison in his tea, and he became the perfect player."

"But, Captain, how could this lead you to the Declaration plot?"

"I had Tyngs check on Church, and he found that Church had been away from the city on trips at frequent intervals. Once my suspicions were aroused, I asked myself why he was doing this. It came to me when I thought of the thimblerig. Of course he was doing one thing to cover another, and the Declaration was the most important thing in Philadelphia this day. I went to Dunlap's and learned that it was Church, as an official courier, who had delivered the document from the State House, and there you have it."

We were just slicing into the ducklings

when John Hancock entered the room with Mr. Jefferson and a third man.

"May I present Mr. John Jay," Hancock said. We shook hands and they sat down.

"Captain Cork," Mr. Jay said, "we were all very impressed by your ingenuity in solving this problem, and the Congress would not like to lose such a talent. At the moment I am in charge of covert activities against the enemy, but I would like you to take over my operational branch."

Well, that explained it. Now I knew why I was sent to the State House to give Dr. Franklin the silk cloth and bear John Hancock's ire. Captain Cork's gall is unspeakably enormous. Having detected the plot, he could have quickly reported it – but not Cork. He had to involve the entire Congress in his victory. And this new appointment told me he had worked a smart bit of thimblerig himself.

Later that night in our rooms I noticed that Cork had kept the copy of the Declaration that Dr. Church had changed.

"Isn't that the property of the government?"

"A gift from Mr. Hancock," he said.

Well, at least for once, we received something for our services, even if it was only a scrap of paper.

AUTHOR'S NOTE: The original Declaration that was sent to Dunlap's was, in reality, lost and never recovered. The document on view in Washington, D.C. is an engrossed copy on parchment, which was signed by the members of Congress on August 2, 1776. There were no signatures on the Dunlap copy.

Harold Q. Masur

Murder Never Solves Anything

The first time Albert Osborn needed Scott Jordan's services it was strictly in Jordan's capacity as a lawyer. The second time was different. Osborn needed more than legal work – he needed Scott Jordan's detective ability. And it was the kind of case that needed a tough-minded, no-nonsense legal beagle...

Albert Osborn was an ambitious young man, volatile, brash, self-confident. But all these characteristics quickly dissolved under the pressure of calamitous events. I found him sitting disconsolately in his cell at the 19th Precinct, subdued and chastened.

"Thank God," he said fervently, clasping his hands in supplication. "Thank God you're here, Mr. Jordan."

"I heard the news, Albert. Did you kill her?"

He swallowed and shook his head.

I had first met Albert two years ago when he'd bought a junior partnership in a Wall Street brokerage firm, using money borrowed from a doting aunt, Mrs. Agnes Mahler, a fluttery, powder-haired lady, the childless widow of a wealthy scrap-metal dealer. Albert had retained me to handle the legal details. And until this morning, apparently, he'd had no further need for a lawyer.

Now Aunt Agnes was dead. Someone had banged an ancient Grecian urn against the base of her skull. And within 24 hours New York's finest had put the arm on Albert Osborn, the victim's only living relative and sole legatee under her last will and testament.

"How come they nominated you, Albert?" I asked.

"We had a terrible fight, Aunt Agnes and I," he said miserably. "One of her neighbors heard us and told the police."

"A fight about what?"

"I needed some money and Aunt Agnes lent it to me, but her check bounced."

"How much money?"

"Eighty thousand dollars."

I lifted an eyebrow. "I thought that all the partners in your firm, Zachary and Company, were making a bundle. What happened?"

He sighed. "Do you know about the two-thousand percent rule?"

"Vaguely. Refresh my recollection."

"Brokers operate on borrowed money, mostly lent by banks. The Stock Exchange prohibits us from raising more than twenty times our net capital. Zachary and Company exceeded the limit."

"Using what as collateral?"

"Unregistered stock."

"That's against the law, Albert."

"I know. I know. And when the bank caught on, they called in the loan immediately and notified the Exchange. The Board of Governors gave us an ultimatum: raise enough cash within a week to take us out of violation or suffer a suspension. So Mr. Zachary laid an assessment on every partner for his proportionate share. My contribution was the smallest, eighty thousand dollars. I was strapped, Mr. Jordan. Like everyone else I'd taken a bath when the market got clobbered."

"So you appealed to Aunt Agnes."

"I had no choice. If I couldn't raise the money, I'd lose my interest in the firm."

"And your aunt agreed?"

"Willingly. She'd just returned from a long Caribbean cruise and was in a good mood. She drew a check to my order, I deposited it and gave one of my own to Mr. Zachary."

"They bounced?"

"Like rubber balls. Both marked INSUFFICIENT FUNDS. Here." He took Mrs. Mahler's check from his pocket and proffered it. "Mr. Zachary," he continued, "was very chilly. He gave me forty-eight hours to make good or clear out my desk." Albert's chin went out of control. "My future, everything, all down the drain."

"Take it easy," I said. "What happened next?"

"I was wild. I went storming over to my aunt's apartment. I ranted and berated her and called her all sorts of names. I have a terrible temper, Mr. Jordan. I'm not proud of myself."

"Did she offer an explanation?"

"She kept shaking her head. She said the bank must have made a mistake. But banks don't make mistakes like that, Mr. Jordan." He blinked. "I admit I made a lot of noise – but I didn't kill her."

"Did she have any enemies?"

"I don't think so."

"Close friends?"

"The lady next door. Mrs. Stewart – Claire Stewart. They visit back and forth all the time. It was Mrs. Stewart who told the cops about our fight. Listen, this is an awful place. Can't you get me out of here on bail?"

"Not likely, if you're indicted for homicide. But I'll see what I can do."

He sat, deflated and forlorn, watching dismally as the turnkey let me out. Over at Homicide the cops were disgorging information with all the prodigality of a slot machine. So I appealed to Detective Lieutenant John Nola and got little more than consideration.

"Counselor," he told me, "this time you've got a loser. The accused needed money. He was slated to inherit the victim's estate. He was angry at her and he threatened her. There was no sign of a forced entry. Nothing missing. His fingerprints were on the murder weapon. All of which gives us that unholy trinity – means, motive, and opportunity. The Grand Jury will vote a true bill and we're going to process your client into the slammer for life plus forty. You'll never prove him innocent."

"I don't have to, Lieutenant. That's a legal presumption in his favor. You fellows have to prove him guilty."

He simply smiled and shifted one of those thin Schimmelpenninck cigars to the other side of his mouth. I walked out, flagged a cab, and drove to the site of the crime – an old dowager of a building on Park Avenue operated now by an economy-minded landlord. Self-service elevator and no doorman. Claire Stewart's apartment was listed on the directory. I identified myself and she buzzed me in.

I had been expecting one of the victim's contemporaries, someone's ancestor, shrunken, wrinkled, arthritic. Instead I was greeted by a tall abundant redhead in her early forties, vital and vivid, totally feminine, and given to bravura flourishes. I sat in her sumptuous living room and listened.

"I really don't know whether Albert killed his aunt or not," she said. "I merely told the police what I heard. This building is one of the old ones, you know, solid, with very thick walls, and we don't usually hear our neighbors. But oh, my, Albert was in a state. Turned up to several hundred decibels. And the language! I haven't heard words like that since I divorced my first husband."

"For example?"

"I will not repeat such obscenities."

"If it goes to trial the prosecutor may insist."

"In open court? Why, that's disgusting!"

"Did Albert threaten his aunt?"

"Not in so many words. He told her she was a deceitful, stingy old woman who had outlived her usefulness. I just hope he remembers those words when he's in a wheel chair in some nursing home. Did you know they found his fingerprints on the murder weapon? A Sixteenth Century urn that Agnes' dear departed husband had smuggled out of one of those Greek islands. It was Mr. Mahler's most prized possession and after he was cremated, Agnes kept his ashes in it. Isn't that touching? And then because it was used in such a terrible way all the ashes spilled out and were trampled into the carpet by the police. I think that's sacrilegious. Agnes simply venerated those ashes."

"Would Mrs. Mahler open the door for anyone who rang?"

"Are you kidding? This city is a jungle. People are being mugged and killed all over the place. Agnes was super-cautious. She would never have admitted a stranger. But she would certainly have opened the door for Albert, especially if she thought he had returned to apologize."

"Did you speak to her after he left?"

"She came here straightaway and confided in me. She was terribly upset. She simply could not understand why the bank had refused to honor the check. And she used my phone to call the bank and tell them they had made a very costly error and that she was going to hold the bank responsible. She said she would be down there first thing in the morning for a full explanation. But of course she never did go. Poor dear."

"Who found the body?"

"A cleaning lady who came every morning. When nobody answered her ring she called the super and he used his passkey."

"I take it he notified the police, Mrs. Stewart."

"Yes. And please, don't be so formal. Call me Claire. Your first name is Scott, isn't it? Do you like duck?"

"I beg your pardon?"

"Duck is my favorite dish. I prepare it even better than Maxim's in Paris. I'd like to invite you to dinner some evening this week."

"I'll have to check my appointment book and call you back."

"My number is unlisted." She scribbled it on a card and came over and tucked it into my breast pocket, smiling warmly. "Murray Hill 4-0040. Call soon."

I promised and departed hastily.

Agnes Mahler's bank was the Gotham Trust. I knew it well. The Madison Avenue branch has a most impressive facade. I headed for the desk of Mr. Harry Wharton, third vice-president, a neat compact man with a salesman's smile and a tax collector's eyes. The smile faded as I explained the situation.

"Mrs. Mahler," he said, "was a valued depositor of this institution. A little vague and confused at times, but otherwise no problem. She traveled frequently and had a custodial account. We held her securities, clipped her coupons, collected her dividends, and I advised her on investments and made quarterly reports. Her death shocked us. Of course we stopped all activity in her account until the estate goes through probate. You say one of her checks bounced? Impossible. She was a wealthy woman. Let me check it with Martin Schorr, our assistant cashier."

He dialed three digits on the intercom. "Schorr? Front and center. On the double. And bring the file on Mrs. Agnes Mahler."

A moment later Schorr came trotting through the door, a slight clerical specimen with thick glasses. He was clutching a bulky folder.

"Just tell me," Wharton demanded curtly, "why we refused to honor a check on Mrs. Mahler's account?"

"Insufficient funds, sir."

"Nonsense! Mrs. Mahler keeps much more than eighty thousand dollars in her savings account. We automatically transfer funds to cover her checks."

"There have been heavy withdrawals over the past few weeks."

"By whom?" I asked.

"The depositor, sir." Schorr opened the folder and showed me a bunch of withdrawal slips.

I examined them. But I knew that Agnes Mahler had been out of the country during that time. She could not possibly have conducted these transactions. I had the check she'd given Albert in my pocket. I took it out and compared its signature with those on the withdrawal slips. They were not even remotely similar.

"Someone goofed," I told Wharton. "The signatures on these withdrawal slips are forgeries."

"What? What are you talking about?"

I showed him. He riffled the file for Agnes Mahler's original signature card, then visibly relaxed. "You're mistaken, Counselor. Here is the card Mrs. Mahler signed when she opened the account. The handwriting is identical with the withdrawal slips."

"Then the card is also a forgery, Harry. I have the check Mrs. Mahler gave Albert Osborn. It was written in his presence, so the signature has to be genuine. Observe the capital 'M' in Mahler. A simple letter. Now look at the fancy loops and flourishes on the card and on the withdrawal slips. No similarity at all."

Wharton frowned. "Perhaps Osborn is lying. Perhaps he wrote the check himself."

"Then he would have done a much better imitation. He would have made at least a minimal attempt to copy her signature. But we have other ways to learn which signature is genuine. We can compare it with the handwriting on her will, which was attested by two witnesses. Easier still, go back four or five months and compare it with earlier withdrawal slips."

He nodded and rummaged in the file. His face turned grim. He had to clear his throat twice, then he made a gesture of total resignation. "I'm afraid you're right, Counselor. The handwriting *is* different. Somebody must have pulled the original signature card and substituted a forged one."

"Clever," I said. "Any withdrawals under the new signature would check with your records and be honored. Had to be one of your own people, Harry, fleecing the account. Probably with an outside confederate, a woman who pretended to be Mrs. Mahler. Better tag your employee before he guts the whole damn bank."

Wharton made a face. "Counselor, almost every employee in this institution has access to the signature files. Tellers and cashiers are constantly comparing against those cards."

"I take it you're insured."

"Of course we're insured. But with every fraud and embezzlement our premiums soar." He turned to the assistant cashier. "We'll need a complete audit of Mrs. Mahler's account, from the ground up. Start it rolling at once." After Schorr had left, he appealed to me. "Where do we start? We bond all our people. We check their backgrounds. And still this sort of thing goes on. How can you keep people from stealing?"

"Easy," I said. "Triple all employees' salaries and remove the temptation or the need."

That suggestion did not sit well. He gave me an aggrieved look. "Do me a favor, Jordan. Take your ideas and –"

"Don't say it, Harry. Bankers are supposed to be dignified. You know you'll have to replace all that money in Mrs. Mahler's account. It may ultimately belong to my client."

"Only if you prove him innocent."

He was right. The law is clear. A legatee cannot profit by his own misdeeds. He may not accelerate his bequest by liquidating the testatrix.

But the picture was no longer entirely bleak. Back at my office I thought about it. I knew now that someone else may have had a motive to silence Mrs. Mahler. And I needed to know more about that someone else. The only source of information I could think of was Claire Stewart. I am not especially fond of duck, either roasted, stewed, or fricasseed. But a lawyer often makes sacrifices for the sake of his client. So I reached into my breast pocket for the card bearing her telephone number.

I stared at it, my eyes wide, my pulse quickening – stared at the "M" in Murray Hill with its fancy loops and flourishes. Calligraphy identical with the "M" in Mahler on the substituted signature card in the bank's file. Identical with the handwriting on the recent withdrawal slips.

I did not phone her. Instead I rang Macbeth – Fitz Macbeth, that is – the private eye who practically has a monopoly on investigative work for lawyers. He has a large staff and a number of free-lance operatives on call, all ex-cops who had opted for early retirement.

He listened to me and said, "You want

around-the-clock surveillance of Mrs. Claire Stewart. Starting when?"

"This minute."

"For how long?"

"Until further notice."

"And your description is adequate?"

"The lady is *sui generis*. Nobody around quite like her."

"It's going to cost, Counselor."

"Fitz, have I ever skunked you on a bill?"

He laughed and broke the connection.

I finished the afternoon working on other matters, then took some papers home with me. I ate a solitary TV dinner and was correcting syntax on a pending appeal when the call came – from one of Macbeth's men reporting that Claire Stewart had left her apartment at 9:42 P.M. to rendezvous with a man at a nearby cocktail lounge. Was I interested? I was. He gave me the address and I hurried out and flagged a cab.

I recognized the operative loafing against a light pole. "Still in there," he told me.

I headed for the bar, chin tucked in, hat pulled down. I ordered a Tuborg and encompassed the room through a wall-length mirror. I saw them in a booth, leaning toward each other, speaking intently. They seemed to be arguing. Martin Schorr looked nervous and Claire Stewart was grim. She had her bravura flourishes under control, trying not to attract attention.

This was neither the time nor the place for a confrontation. I ducked out quickly, face averted. "Okay," I told the operative. "Stick with her until the next shift arrives. Can Fitz reach you if necessary?"

He showed me a small box. "Fitz gives me a beep, I call him back from the nearest booth."

Several times in the past both the D.A. and the police have accused me of withholding evidence material to the solution of a felony. The felony here was top drawer. Homicide. So I decided to play this one according to the book. I found Lieutenant Nola at home, watching a televised ballet on NET, one of those thin Dutch cigars smoking itself between his teeth.

He shut off the set and listened while I dumped it in his lap – the bank swindle, the cast involved, the whole works. I said, "You spoke to Mrs. Stewart. You had a chance to size her up."

He rolled his eyes.

"Exactly," I agreed. "And a man like Schorr, a wallflower type, unprepossessing, deprived, he'd be an easy mark for Mrs. Stewart with all those obvious charms. She'd have no difficulty enlisting his cooperation.

What I think happened, one of them panicked when Agnes Mahler blew the whistle and phoned the bank. They took advantage of the fight between Albert and his aunt to divert suspicion to Albert. Mrs. Stewart volunteered that information pretty quick."

He studied the card with her telephone number. "You're certain this handwriting matches those forged signatures?"

"Without question."

"No shenanigans, Counselor?"

"My hand on the Bible, Lieutenant."

"You're saying that Schorr supplied a blank signature card and she filled it out and he substituted it for the original?"

"Yes."

"And where would the Stewart woman get blank checks or a passbook for withdrawals?"

"She and the victim were always visiting back and forth. She could easily have lifted them while Mrs. Mahler was in the kitchen or the bathroom."

"Wouldn't Mrs. Mahler have noticed their absence?"

"Ordinarily, yes. But Mrs. Stewart probably waited until just before Agnes took off on a long cruise."

He pursed his lips. "Damned careless of

the Stewart dame to let you have a copy of her handwriting."

"I never said she had a full deck, Lieutenant. She was probably trying to cultivate me, hoping to wheedle information or exert influence if I got too close."

Nola stood up. "Schorr sounds like the weak partner in this conspiracy. Let's sweat him first. If he cracks we should have no trouble with the lady." He pointed to a telephone book. "Check the man's address."

He managed to commandeer a prowl car. It took us to a five-story walkup on Second Avenue. I anticipated little trouble with Martin Schorr. He possessed neither the Byzantine shrewdness nor the toughness of his accomplice. We found his door partly open – in that neighborhood a fearless act, or a careless one, or perhaps he was expecting someone.

But Schorr didn't even know his door was open. A bullet hole in the left temple had stopped him from worrying about such matters. Or anything else.

Nola bent and touched the corpse. "Still warm," he said harshly. "Dammit, we couldn't have missed the perpetrator by more than minutes." He used the dead man's phone and called it in, then looked at me. "Off the top of my head. The obvious conclusion. A dead accomplice cannot share the loot or implicate his partner. I think we should brace the lady while her adrenalin is still pumping."

"Let me make a call first," I said. "It may save us time." I got through to Macbeth. "Fitz, contact your man and get me a quick rundown on Mrs. Stewart's activities during the past hour. Ring me at this number. It's urgent."

Nola's technical support, with sirens, and Macbeth's response arrived simultaneously. I picked up the handset. Fitz said, "Here it is, Counselor. The lady and her escort left the cocktail lounge about fifteen minutes after you did. They separated immediately. She walked home and he flagged a cab in the opposite direction. She hasn't left her apartment since."

"No other exit?"

"Only the service door, in clear view."

I relayed the information to Nola. "It shoots down your theory, Lieutenant. Schorr was still alive when she left him."

"Then the lady will keep for a while. Where can I get some background on Schorr?" Nola asked.

"From Mr. Harry Wharton, Schorr's boss at the Gotham Trust."

On our way Nola made only one comment,

directed at his driver. "Shut off that damn siren."

Wharton's apartment was far more impressive than Schorr's. He was, after all, in a higher bracket. I introduced Nola and gave Wharton the news about his cashier.

He gaped at us, incredulous. "Schorr an embezzler? Dead? I can't believe it."

"Did the man have any relatives?" Nola asked.

"I don't think so." Wharton shook his head. "Do you know the name of his accomplice?"

"Yes."

"Did she kill him?"

"We have evidence to the contrary."

"How did you manage to identify her?"

"The accomplice blundered and disclosed her identity to Jordan."

"Is the accomplice in custody?"

"Not yet," I interjected. "We had a theory, Harry, and then Schorr's death put a different face on it. We had to scrub our inference that it was Schorr who devised the swindle and set it up. I don't think he had anything at all to do with it. May I use your phone?"

I did not wait for permission. I dialed the Murray Hill number and when I had her voice on the line I said in a tense mimicking whisper, "Claire? Harry. No time to explain. Clear out. Fast."

Sudden alarm strained her voice. "What is it, Harry? What happened?"

I hung up.

The color had run out of Wharton's face. It was now stiff with restraint, tissue-gray, his eyes fixed on mine. I said. "That's all the confirmation I need, Harry. It struck me less than a minute ago. You wanted to know if we had identified Schorr's accomplice and then you asked if *she* killed him. We never told you it was a woman."

He swallowed hugely. "My God, Jordan, that was a natural assumption. It was a woman who withdrew the money."

"Yes. But your calling the accomplice 'she' and 'her' opened my eyes. Then I suddenly remembered your response at the bank – as if you knew nothing about Agnes Mahler's call after her check bounced. Not likely, Harry. Who would she ask for? *Only you*, Harry. You handled her account. You gave her advice. You visited her apartment to discuss investments. And that's where you met Claire Stewart. She's hard to resist. She made a play for you and you tumbled. She's a lady with expensive tastes and the liaison must have required a lot of money. Whose idea was it to plunder the Mahler account? Yours or hers?"

He made a desperate reach for words. "You're mistaken, Jordan, terribly mistaken!"

"I don't think so, Harry. Mrs. Mahler threatened to blow the whistle. It would start an investigation that could sink you. You needed time to cover yourself. And the old lady was expendable. So you paid her a visit. She would certainly open the door for her banker. You saw the urn and you used it. But murder never solves anything, Harry. It only creates new problems. And one of those problems was Martin Schorr.

"He was nosing around. He probably knew you had something going with Claire Stewart – she may have picked you up at the bank several times. I think he knew her name because she too was a depositor at the bank. She must have opened an account as an excuse to see you during the day.

"As soon as Schorr checked her signature he was in the picture. It gave him what he needed, a chance to cut himself in for a piece of the action. And he figured the lady would be easier to handle. A very risky undertaking, after what happened to Mrs. Mahler. So of course Schorr had to be eliminated, and quick. So you moved immediately, right after

Claire phoned and told you what he wanted."

Wharton appealed to the lieutenant. "Not true. Not a word of it," but his voice lacked conviction.

I said coldly, "You shot him, Harry. Did you get rid of the gun? A professional would have dropped it off the Staten Island ferry or one of the bridges. But you're not a professional. So it's probably hidden right here in this apartment. The lieutenant's men know how to search and when they find it, your goose is cooked. They'll collar Mrs. Stewart and she'll sing her lungs out, pinning it on you, trying to clear her skirts."

Nola got to the phone and snapped out an All Points Bulletin on the lady. It sent Harry Wharton into a tailspin of despair. He sank into a chair and lowered his face into his hands.

"All right, Lieutenant," I said. "This one is all yours. Now do me a favor, please. Call the D.A. and start the ball rolling so I can spring my client. I have to earn my fee."

"You've already earned it. But how can Osborn afford your usual whopping fee if he's broke?"

"You forget," I said. "Albert is still Mrs. Mahler's sole legatee. There's a sizeable estate involved, especially after the bank replaces all that embezzled loot."

Nola grinned. "Well, Counselor, he owes you more than a fee. If you ask me, he owes you his skin."

Stanley Ellin

Generation Gap

Stanley Ellin's annual story, written especially for EQMM . . . a contemporary story that will make you ponder and reflect after you have finished reading it. What is the generation gap? Who caused it – the children or the parents? How does it manifest itself – through the truth or through lying? Who can bridge the gap – the young ones or the old ones? And then there is the eternal question: Is anything, from generation to generation, really what it seems to be? . . .

She had been named Elizabeth, but it very soon became Bitsy, and Bitsy it stayed even after she got her growth. Which was a drag, but not so much of a drag that you couldn't live with it. Matter of fact, this was how just about everything in the whole world shaped up: a drag, but not so much of a drag that you couldn't live with it. And when you really started to go down, down, down, there was always The Sound – the delicious blast of it on transistor or stereo – to help pick you up again. Life, let's face it, was at its best when it was strictly audio.

At sixteen, Bitsy just about had her growth. An Aquarius, tall, skinny, and, from the front at least, straight up and down. From the back – well, a few of the boys in school had already let her know that, walking away from them in those jeans, man, she really turned them on. Also, she had that straight blonde hair coming almost down to the handworked leather belt, and those big pale blue eyes – made all the bigger when she laid on the eyeliner and eyelash darkener – and a cute nose, and what with one thing and another she was, as she admitted to herself, definitely on the up side. That is, allowing for some minor skin trouble now and then.

Of course, it still didn't put her in a class with Sis, a ripe twenty, front and back. And, add to the injustice of it, Sis was born with brains enough for two which, as Pa kept pointing out, was a lucky thing because Bitsy herself didn't have brains enough for one. Big joke. But one had to face the facts. There was Sis, out of high school and right into that filing and typing job at the Fort Myers Citizens Bank, and here was Bitsy who could just about make it through roll call in school before the fog set in.

What made Sis bearable at all, really, was that she still had one foot on the right side of the generation gap. There were signs she was already starting to go uptight like Ma and Pa, but she sometimes did remember how it had been for her four years ago and sometimes even acted like a True Friend. Take hitchhiking. Ma and Pa were death on hitchhiking. Somehow they had got it into their pointy little heads that the world was full of evil men just itching to hand lollipops to little girls and then rip them off. But until she had put together enough money to get her own car, Sis had hitchhiked, and while Ma and Pa had never known about it, Bitsy had. And now Bitsy hitchhiked, and Sis knew about it, and True Friend, kept her mouth shut about it.

Well, except for one time.

That was the time Bitsy had hitched all the way back home alone from that Disney World weekend with some girl friends and had carelessly let herself be dropped off at the shopping plaza just when Sis was parking in the plaza one jump away. Sis had ordered her into the car and cut loose then and there. "Was that messy stud with the pickup the one who got you back to town?"

"Mmm," said Bitsy.

"Then you listen to me. Are you listening?"

"Mmm."

"There's plenty of family folks on the road to ride with, and from now on that's who you ride with, stupid. No more studs like that, you hear?"

"Mmm," said Bitsy. She reached out to switch on the radio, but Sis pushed her hand away from it. Bitsy leaned back in her seat and closed her eyes. It wasn't all that hard to get The Sound in your head without even switching on the radio.

"Are you still listening?" Sis said slowly and loudly.

"Mmm."

"Then no more studs, you hear? And another thing. If somebody stops, and you see a six-pack right there on the seat, you stay clear, because it could mean trouble. From now on, family folks only, you hear?"

"The way you talk," Bitsy said, "how can I help hearing?"

Sis often spoke like that to her, a little too slow, a little too loud, the way you'd talk to somebody who was deaf. Or, let's face it, somebody who was so fuzzy in the brain that she had to have things said to her the way they said it in the *Dick and Jane* schoolbooks when she was a kid. Run, Dick, run. Careful, Bitsy, careful.

Except you weren't supposed to show Sis you resented it. If you did Sis resented your resenting it.

"You mind your manners when I talk to you," Sis now told her.

"All right, all right. From now on, only family folks."

Meaning, naturally, uptight old men like Pa. It couldn't possibly mean getting hitches from cars where there was a family team up front. Nothing on the road went by faster than that kind of a car. Maybe the man at the wheel would like to slow down and lend a hand to a sixteen-year-old. Aquarius in tight jeans, but sure as God made little green apples, the lady next to him was not going to buy that package.

Family folks. Like Pa.

She lived up to it too. On trips home from school where she would ask to be dropped off a couple of blocks from the house so Ma wouldn't catch on, and on jumps out of town to kinfolk in Sarasota and Manatee. Truth to tell, although she had no intention of letting Sis in on it, that messy stud in the pickup had scared her a little, what with all the handwork he was trying out on her thigh and meanwhile whooping it down the highway at seventy an hour. And, as if to show that Sis knew what she was talking about, there had been a six-pack on the seat, all of it gone by the time they pulled into Fort Myers. So it really wasn't that much of a drag letting the studs go by and keeping an eye out for something in Pa's class.

She even lived up to it all the way across Florida on the big Thanksgiving trip to Cousin Sheralyn's in South Miami. Big was the word for that trip, because from the way Pa carried on counting out the bus fare, you'd have to believe he was paying for a trip twice around the world. It gave you something to think about all right, how he would carry on if he knew that almost all the bus fares he had been laying out for quite a while were going, not to the bus company, but for the essentials of life. Records, hair stuff, face stuff, clothes, fast food. Put it all together it didn't really add up to all that much, but it was the difference between life and death. Death came when you ran out of your week's allowance two days after you got it and Sis said no, she wouldn't lend you even a raggedy dollar bill because you were just as knotheaded about money as about everything else.

So, Ma's old valise in hand and all that beautiful bus money tucked away in her shoulder bag, Bitsy made it down to Naples as guest of an exterminator-service salesman, a sad case who talked about termite control the whole trip, and then, by way of that straight, wide-open, hundred-mile run along the Tamiami Trail through the Everglades, she was fetched right into the middle of Miami by a bank-president type driving a gilt-edged Cadillac. Not too bad, except that this one kept the radio turned to news broadcasts all the way, even when, after a while, it was the same news broadcasts all over again.

Anyhow, news broadcasts or not, there she was in the middle of Miami, which turned out to be a lot bigger city than Fort Myers, so that she had to ask questions a few times and haul that suitcase a lot of distance before she wound up at the bus depot and phoned Cousin Sheralyn to come pick her up. Cousin Sheralyn was seventeen and drove the family car sometimes. She was also the one who, the Thanksgiving before when she had been Bitsy's guest at Fort Myers, had said that once you did the Thomas Edison house and some hunting for shells on Sanibel Island you just about had Fort Myers, and you really had to see Miami to know where the action was, and that was why this whole trip. Now she turned up at the bus depot in the car, and the first thing she said to Bitsy was, "Did you really hitchhike it all the way, like you said you would?"

"Mmm," said Bitsy. She showed Cousin Sheralyn all those five-dollar bills in the shoulder bag. "Supposed to be bus money. Only now it's fun money."

"Man," said Cousin Sheralyn, her eyes opening wide, "You really do have something going, don't you? I wish I had the nerve."

Then she drove Bitsy to her house, keeping the car radio at full volume so that the two of them would not only hear The Sound but feel it, the way it was meant to be felt, and there was Aunt Willa Mae, and Uncle Frank and the two older boy cousins, a couple of clowns really, all of them waiting to dig into the turkey and trimmings.

"My," said Aunt Willa Mae, "you get taller every time I see you, Bitsy. I bet you're taller than Sis now."

"Mmm," said Bitsy.

"And how's your ma?"

"All right," said Bitsy.

"And your pa?"

"All right," said Bitsy, and that, all formalities attended to nicely, took care of the old folks.

From then on it was one of those holiday

times to remember the rest of your life. Miami was where the action was, no argument about it. Mornings, trying to surfboard off the end of Miami Beach with everybody the right age and all high on sun, salt water, and some grass now and then. Afternoons, a lot of driving around, seeing outside and inside those Gold Coast hotels you'd only see in the movies otherwise, and a lot of souvenir hunting, and along Flagler Street into the record shops, all mixed up with a lot of eating any time you felt like it.

Nighttimes, out to one place after another for the dancing and fooling around and more eating. The fooling around, which Sis had also warned Bitsy about in that Dick and Jane style, turned out to be strictly nothing, since both boy cousins were always nearby and both of them linebacker types. Bitsy agreed with Cousin Sheralyn that it was a drag being supervised like this, but actually she didn't mind it all that much. As far as she could see, it certainly saved her the trouble of making some decisions she'd just as soon not make.

Anyhow, as Aunt Willa Mae said, all good things had to come to an end sometime, so Sunday, right after lunch, Bitsy got her stuff together for Cousin Sheralyn to take her to the bus depot. It turned out that what with all the souvenirs and the new-bought decorated T-shirts and beach hats and the pile of new records, Bitsy found that she needed an extra piece of luggage, whereupon Uncle Frank dug up a good strong carton, and into it went all the extras and around it went a strong piece of cord. So, as if to show what kind of wild weekend it had been, when Bitsy went out to the car where Cousin Sheralyn was waiting to take her to the bus depot she was carrying not only the valise but that carton.

Cousin Sheralyn took a look at the carton. "You got any money left at all?" she asked.

Bitsy opened the shoulder bag and showed her what was left. One dollar and two nickels.

"I thought so," said Cousin Sheralyn. "Well, I'll drop you off Eighth Street downtown. That's the Trail. You can start hitching right there."

"Mmm," said Bitsy.

"But don't you ever let your folks know I didn't put you on that bus. It'll get right back to my folks, and I hate to tell you what would happen to me then."

"A real drag," said Bitsy.

She got off at Eighth Street which didn't look at all like the Tamiami Trail there, just a busy corner full of Latins walking all around and Spanish signs on all the stores, and as soon as Cousin Sheralyn drove off, she arranged the valise and the carton at her feet near the curb, and when a likely-looking car went by, pointed her finger westward. Plenty went by, and for those on the lookout for family-type folks there seemed to be an assortment in almost every car, and none with any idea of stopping.

A couple of one-man cars did pull up and stop, but in both cases this was stud stuff – Latin stud at that – so Bitsy gave them a head-shake, and then, when they persisted in being friendly out of the car window, she just turned her back on them until they took off.

Finally a small truck pulled over, one of those emergency trucks with a hoist in back. The man driving it, strictly family-type except he needed a shave, leaned out and said to Bitsy, "How far?"

"Fort Myers," said Bitsy.

"Nope. Just going back to the shop little past Fort Mile Bend on the Trail. But if it'll help any, hop right in."

So she planted the valise and carton in back of the truck and hopped right in, and that way got as far as a gas station and garage right out in the middle of nowhere, halfway along the Trail. Like every other business along the Trail here, this was on the eastbound side of the road heading back to Miami, so she lugged the valise and the carton across to the westbound side and took up her station there. Trouble was, not much went by, and what did go by looked like it was out to break all speed records. Even the bus she was supposed to have been on went by so fast that it was almost out of sight down the road when she suddenly realized that the sign over its window had said *Fort Myers* and she felt depressed about that. And, of course, the cars that did pull in at the gas station across the road were mostly heading all the wrong direction.

After a while one of the men from the gas station walked across to her and said, "You figure to stand out here like a sore thumb with a red, white, and blue bandage on it, girlie, you are sure going to buy yourself a lot of trouble in about ten minutes when the police patrol goes by. They are real hardnosed about this kind of hitchhike stuff right now. Had a bad time account of it couple of months ago. And not so far down the road from here, neither."

"I have to get a hitch," Bitsy said.

"All the same, girlie, if you don't want cop trouble, you will hang around for a spell in that ladies room over there. I'll let you know when the patrol goes by."

Maybe it was a put-on, but it didn't seem to be. So Bitsy took the valise and carton with her into the ladies room and hung around there looking through the screened window at the swamp country out in back until the man knocked on the door and said, "Okay now, girlie. They just went by."

So it was back across the road with the valise and carton, and, from the way it looked, nothing to do but stand there and watch the cars whoosh by and feel more and more down about it. Then when she was right near bottom, a car slowed down passing her and came to a stop about fifty feet up ahead. She grabbed up the valise and carton, but the car slowly started off again and all she could do was stand there feeling like a fool. The car only went about ten feet more though, and stopped again. It was an old black sedan, looked like something out of the museum, but without a dent in it and with a high shine. A weirdo car all right. And with a wierdo driver too, what with this stop and start business. As if to prove that, he now stuck his jug-eared head out of the window and called back, "You looking for a ride, girl?"

Mister Weirdo himself, because what did he think she was looking for?

She didn't even bother to answer, just

headed down the road as fast as she could with the valise and carton banging her legs, hoping he wouldn't change his mind again before she got there. The one good part of it was that she was still playing by the rules Sis had laid down. The car was sure family-style – it looked like the kind of thing you lay away all week and drive only to church – and when she got up to it she could see that the driver might have been the deacon of the church. A red-neck with gray hair chopped short in a real redneck haircut, but still he was all dressed up in a black suit and white shirt and necktie.

But old Mister Weirdo himself all right. Anybody picked you up on the road was likely to have a friendly way about him. This one, when she came up to him out of breath, looked anything but friendly. Then, when she tried to open the back door to shove her things in, she found it was locked. "Hey," she said, but he made no move to open the door, just looked at her through the open window, taking her in.

"Your folks know you travel around like this?" he asked.

"Mmm," Bitsy said.

"What's that mean?"

"It means they know."

"You sure of it?"

"Yes. Anyhow, what's the difference?"

He appeared to think this over, his lips pulled into a thin line, his eyes squinting at her. "That's the truth," he finally said. "It don't make any difference, does it?" He reached over to unlock both doors, and Bitsy got the valise and carton on the back seat, then got into the front seat with him.

He started the car off. "Where you supposed to be headed for?"

"Fort Myers," Bitsy said. "You going all the way there?"

"No."

All right, but at least she was heading in the right direction. She looked over the dashboard to find the radio dial and found there was no radio dial. No radio, believe it or not. She dug into her shoulder bag and came up with the baby transistor. She put it to her ear, tuning it in to get The Sound, and after a while she did. Mister Weirdo didn't seem to mind. He just kept the car moving along at a speed where anything else going their way easily passed them by.

He seemed to be keeping his eyes straight ahead on the road, but Bitsy could tell that every now and then he was giving her a slantwise look, taking her in from top to bottom. It made her realize that there was no bra under her T-shirt with the *Miami*

Beach written across it and the palm trees painted on it. On the other hand, there was nothing so special under the shirt – as there would be, say, with Sis – to make him pop his cork. So here you had one of those times where what was almost a drag could be kind of a comfort.

Then she caught him looking square at her. He didn't seem flustered by this. Only came on more squinty-eyed and thin-lipped than ever. "Kind of pretty, ain't you?" he said.

Bitsy shifted over in her seat a little, but she was up against the door as it was. She pressed the transistor hard against her ear to cut out that redneck voice, but it wasn't easy.

"I had a daughter about like you," said Mister Weirdo. "Used to travel around the same way, and I never knew about it. So your folks don't really know the way you go hitchhiking, do they?"

"Mmm," said Bitsy.

"What's that mean? You got a mouth, don't you? Why don't you open it up and talk like people?"

Bitsy showed him the transistor. "I'm listening to this," she pointed out. "I can't listen to everybody at the same time."

"Then you listen to me!" He suddenly snatched the transistor right out of her hand

and jammed it down on the seat. The way he did it, he probably wrecked it. She reached for it and he slapped her hand away. "I said you listen to me. I was telling you about my girl. Same age as you. Just as pretty. Same kind of long blondie hair too."

So it wasn't lollipops they came on with when you got to this age. It was talk about their pretty girl just like you. And with blondie hair just like yours, so next thing there would be that big old hand stroking your hair to show you. And working its way right down your back. And that would just be the start of it. No lollipops for grownup girls. Just that slow, roundabout come-on easing things along to big, big trouble.

But even if you could somehow get clear of the car, what do you do about Ma's valise and that carton?

And for sure this was Mister Weirdo's kind of country they were now traveling through. Empty wherever you looked with not even a gas station or hamburger stand showing up any more. Just a lot of swamp greenery and sickly-looking trees. Bitsy pushed so tight up against the door that the handle of it hurt her side.

He was watching her like a hawk now. "You scared?" he asked.

Bitsy shook her head to show she wasn't.

"Yes, you are." He seemed to like the idea. "And that's all right. That's like it should be when you climb in a car with some man you don't even know. That's what you should have in your head before you start climbing in. Afterward is maybe a little too late, ain't it?"

Bitsy started to answer, but it stuck in her throat. She cleared her throat to get it out. "Nothing to be scared about," she said.

"You mean you don't care what a man can do to you? Kind of free and easy with men, is that it?"

"No," Bitsy said. "Look, you can let me out here. It's all right. I can get a hitch from somebody else."

"You sit right where you are. And no tricks, hear?"

"You let me out."

"Like I already told you, girl, it's too late for that. I didn't pull no gun on you and make you get in here, did I? You did it all on your own."

While he was saying this he was slowing down the car, squinting up the road on the other side like he was looking for something there. Then when the car was really slowed down he grabbed her wrist and held it tight so that for the few seconds when she could have just walked out of that door she had no chance to.

With his other hand he turned the wheel hard and pulled the car right across the road and into a clearing among the trees. Dried twigs cracked under the wheels and the car rocked from side to side on the bumpy ground, but it kept crawling further and further away from the road.

"You let me out!" Bitsy said. "I am scared."

"Maybe not enough yet."

There was a freaked-out answer for you. The worst of it was she had heard about crazies like this. They got some of their kicks from what they did to you. But they got even more from watching you be scared because of it. So here she was, acting up just the way he liked. And not able to keep herself from doing it, either.

The road was well out of sight when he stopped the car among some scraggly trees. He reached across her to shove open the door and then pushed her right through it, still holding her wrist and following almost on top of her. He snatched the shoulder bag loose and tossed it on the seat next to the transistor. "Come on," he said. "I want to show you something."

"There's cops out on that road," Bitsy

said. "The gas-station man told me so. They go right up and down all the time. They could be coming right now."

"No," the man said. "They ain't coming now. They only come after it's all over. A couple of months after it's all over. Now look there." He pointed. "Right there."

Bitsy looked. Nothing but a patch of beat-up dead grass. He dragged her toward it, and for all she dug in her heels and tried to hold back it was no use.

"Right here," the man said. He gripped the nape of her neck between his fingers and pushed her head down as if making sure she got a good look. "This is where the cops show up after it's all over. Then you know what they do? They come knock on the door and they say, 'Mister, you remember that little girl of yours that never got back home again couple of months ago? Well, it seems like she was always hitchhiking around, and she finally got picked up by a real bad one. We think we just found what's left of her, so you come along with us and see if it's really her.'"

Those fingers digging into her neck had Bitsy bent almost double now. Her eyes were all filled up so that everything looked watery. "Let go!" she said. "You're hurting me."

He didn't let go. "You ain't hurting," he

said. "You don't know what hurting is. Not till a man does what he wants with you until he's tired of it, and then beats you to death. That's when you'll find out, won't you?"

"Yes," Bitsy sobbed.

Now he took his hand from her neck and let her straighten up and wipe her runny nose with the back of her hand. He turned her by the arm so that she faced him. "Girl," he said, "you understand what I'm trying to get into that dumb babyface head of yours?"

"Yes," Bitsy said, her eyes brimming over. "Look, mister, there's that valise in the car and it's a really good valise. And that other box has a lot of good things in it. I swear it has. You can have both of them if you let me go. And the transistor."

He dropped her arm and stood there facing her like that. All of a sudden he looked beat-up and tired. All washed out. "God Almighty," he said, and turned and started walking back to the car. Bitsy watched him go, not believing it. At the car he motioned to her. "Come on. I'll get you far as Naples."

Bitsy still wasn't moving.

"You better come on," said Mister Weirdo. "You stand around there any longer, you are going to have swamp snakes crawling right over your feet."

This time Bitsy did move.

And he did drive her right to the bus depot in Naples, the old car really putting out all the way. Bitsy sat as far from him as she could tight up against the door again, and after a while she got her mirror out of the shoulder bag and did a job on her face, which was a mess. Then she tried out the transistor and found that even with the banging around it had taken it was still working fine.

Too bad in a way, because when she was let out at Naples she'd have to give it up along with the valise and carton. No sense trying to back out of the deal and stirring up old Mister Weirdo again. The smart thing was to let him go drive away with his loot and then tell Ma and Pa it was stolen from her in the Miami bus depot. They'd believe her all right, because why shouldn't they? Better that than ever let them find out about all the hitchhiking.

But right there at the bus depot in Naples, Mister Weirdo showed he was as freaked-out as ever. He pulled up the car and said to Bitsy, "Tell me the truth, girl. You got money on you for that bus ride?"

"No," said Bitsy.

"I figured not."

And then what did he do but get out of the car with her and haul out the valise and carton and go right along with her to the ticket window and buy her a ticket for Fort Myers. So he hadn't let her go because of him settling for the valise and carton and transistor, and that was just about the weirdest part of it. It was really something to think about. Then Bitsy stood there, ticket in one hand, transistor in the other, valise and carton at her feet, and watched him walk out into the street, that redneck haircut of his finally getting lost among the people there, and that was the last she saw of him.

She waited to make sure he was really gone, then went to the door and peeked out to see if the car was gone too, and it was. So she went back to the ticket window and told the girl there she had changed her mind and wanted to get the money back for her ticket, and, no trouble at all, it was taken care of.

So that was that, and she even had some money to show for it.

Getting up to Fort Myers went the way everything should have gone from the start. Bitsy carried her things out to the street some distance from the depot and made it plain she was looking for a hitch until along came this stripped-down job with kind of a nice-looking stud at the wheel, big beard and a big gold earring, tape deck blasting away so you could hear it right across the Gulf, and he got her to Fort Myers in no time. And except for some pushing and pulling she had to do with that wandering hand of his, with no trouble at all. In fact, he made the run up the coast so fast that she walked into the Fort Myers depot only about an hour after the bus she might have been on checked in.

She phoned the house, hoping it would be Sis, not Ma or Pa, and her luck, it was Sis. Fifteen minutes later Sis showed up at the back end of the depot in her car and helped get Bitsy's stuff into it. By this time Bitsy was really loaded up for Sis. During that fifteen minutes she had wondered if maybe she shouldn't keep it all to herself, but the more she thought of it the more she knew she'd never be able to hold it in. She had too much to settle with Sis.

As soon as they were in the car she said to Sis, "You and your family folks."

"What?" said Sis.

"You know what. You said I should only look to ride with family folks. And that's what I've been doing. And you know what happened on account of it?"

"Suppose you tell me," said Sis, jockeying the car out into the street.

"All right, I will. I got picked up by real family folks on the Trail coming back just now. I mean *real* family folks," Bitsy said, making it slow and loud the way Sis always did. "Like, you know, a shiny old black car and somebody driving it dressed up maybe for a funeral. Real family folks," she said even slower and louder.

"And?" said Sis.

"And first place he could find that was all empty, this nice old man drove off into the swamp there and pulled me out of his nice old car."

"Bitsy!" Sis said. She stepped on the brake, not even noticing they were right in the middle of traffic, cars all going by and honking at them. Then she got her wits halfway together and pulled over to the curb and parked there. "Bitsy, what happened? You tell me straight out what happened, you hear?"

"I *am* telling you. He pulled me out of the car and he showed me where it was going to happen when he was good and ready and he talked wild trying to scare me and he choked me too. Because maybe you don't know about it, but some of those nice old family folks you're so high on are crazies. And this one sure was."

"But what else did he do? Did he –?"

"No," Bitsy said, "he didn't. All of a sudden he just turned off. Just like that. Like he wasn't interested in the whole thing any more. Then he drove me the rest of the way to Naples, and I got another hitch there."

Sis took a deep breath. "You're lying," she said. "You're making up the whole thing."

"I am not lying," Bitsy said very slowly and loudly.

Sis didn't seem convinced. "You mean some man practically kidnapped you? And then when it came time for the big finish he just turned off? Look, Bitsy –"

"But I told you what he was like, didn't I?" Bitsy said. It almost made up for that whole bad scene in the swamp, because for the first time she could ever remember, she was on the telling end, and Sis, like it or not, was on the listening end. "Don't you see? No matter how much he got himself worked up for a big finish, he couldn't do anything about it because he was just too old. Honest to God, Sis, he was at least as old as Pa!"

Florence V. Mayberry

Alone with the Witches

Every story by Florence V. Mayberry stirs the emotions, sometimes in a most disturbing way. Under the surface there is turmoil, torment, and always pain... Here is a hospital story with an unusual situation. Did you know that some drugs make us see witches? Evil witches. Flickering, floating, swooping witches. Witches to be afraid of. But everything we are afraid of isn't real...

They wheeled the woman into my room in the middle of the night. I don't know what time. Except for the day or night, time stood still for me. Nothing marched on except pain, and it went on timelessly, forever and ever. That's peritonitis when one is ready to burst with it – just pain and waiting maybe to die.

The woman was breathing raucously. Otherwise no sound from her. As they lifted her onto the other bed of this semi-private hospital room I caught a glimpse of dark brown hair, long and thick. A pale face. Why wouldn't it be pale? Hospitals are for pale, sick faces.

Two nurses were with her – the fat nurse who was heavy on her feet and made my bed tremble agonizingly when she came near it and who wheezed and sniffed when she was asked for things and the other tall thin one whom I had never seen before, perhaps a ward nurse from down the corridor. Since they were already in the room, I thought it might not make the fat nurse cross to tell her, "I'm hurting. Bad. It won't stop. The pill wore off. Could I have another?"

She turned, her mouth pinched inward as though wanting to bite herself. A sniff, a wheeze. "Miss Jackson, if you would just be sensible!" she snapped. "After all, your doctor did prescribe hypos. Those pills aren't strong enough and you keep asking for another one. A lot of pills or one hypo, what's the difference, really –"

"Morphine makes me see witches," I said. "They gather around my bed and grab at me. Even if they're not real, I see them. Please, just another pill."

"Can't you see we're busy with this poor woman?" the thin one asked.

So I watched them. Watching things

helped to take my mind off my swollen, throbbing belly. I tried to turn to see better what they were doing and the effort made me cry out. "Hush!" It was the thin nurse. "This woman is very sick!"

"Please don't ask the lady to be quiet. My wife doesn't hear anything when she's like this. She's not conscious." It was a deep tired voice.

I looked toward the entrance of the room and saw a large, broad-shouldered man standing in the doorway. It was winter and he had on an overcoat, and carried a dark hat.

"Sir, please wait outside until we're through putting your wife into bed. Then you can come in." As an afterthought the fat nurse asked wheezily, "You won't mind, will you, Miss Jackson?"

"No." Truth was, it helped to have someone in the room. Late at night there were no visitors – no one to help me keep watch to see that death didn't come too close. "Let him stay."

"Good," she said. "Your wife's weak now, Mr. Ober, after all that washing out. She may not come out of it until morning but you can never tell, patients differ. If she does, she's liable to thrash around."

"I know," he said. He looked at me and

said, "Thank you," then stepped back into the darkened corridor.

The nurses raised the guard rails on the woman's bed. The fat one turned to me again. "Listen, Miss Jackson, be sensible, take a hypo tonight, get some sleep – remember, you've got to rest up for that operation. Besides, we're very busy tonight, we can't keep running down here."

I started to shake my head "no," but the movement jarred too much so I whispered, "No. Only the pill."

"But the doctor prescribed –"

"No!"

"God!" said the thin nurse. The fat one snorted displeasure, and the pair left. For a few minutes they talked outside the door with the waiting man. Then he came in and sat quietly in a chair at the foot of his wife's bed. The fat nurse returned with the pill, helped me manage the glass drinking tube, and hurried away.

I spoke to the man. "What happened to your wife?"

"An overdose of sleeping pills."

"Oh." Suicide. My new roommate had reached out for death, and I was struggling to hold it off.

"Will her breathing keep you awake? It's so loud," he said.

"No. I don't sleep. I stay awake."

"Why?"

"Because I'm afraid."

"Oh."

"Sometimes people don't wake up if they go to sleep. Here."

He rose from the chair and came close to my bed, this big dark man. Only the dim night light was left on and this may have made him seem darker than he actually was. Or perhaps it was the shadow of beard growth on his chin and lower cheeks. "They shouldn't have put my wife in with you. I'm sorry. I asked for a private room but they said none was available. They said it wouldn't bother you, that you weren't that sick. But you are, aren't you?"

"It's all right. I don't want to sleep."

"What is it? Your illness. That is, if you want to tell me."

"Peritonitis. Not appendicitis. Something else. They're not sure what."

"That's rough."

What was there to say to that? It was rough.

"But you've made it," he said.

This far.

"Takes hanging on. Apparently you're doing a good job of that."

Am I? Am I really going to make it? I

wanted to ask that for reassurance. But I didn't dare. I was afraid I would start crying, and sobs jerked the pain too much.

He didn't say anything for a while, just stared at the walls, as if he were reading something on it. Finally he nodded toward the other bed. "My wife – she knows about hanging on."

Hanging on? Not a suicide? "Then she took the tablets by mistake? It wasn't –"

"No," he said flatly. "It wasn't suicide. And it wasn't really an overdose either. She intended it to be just enough. To hang on. To me. I make a good bank account for fun and games."

Momentarily I forgot pain, entranced by the choppy bitterness of his words. Fun and games, what did he mean?

I thought the question was only in my mind. But I must have said it aloud because he responded, "Are you sure you want to hear about it? That it won't bother you? Of course you don't have to sympathize or care – we're strangers and you've got your own troubles. Only I need to get it out of me, to talk to somebody. Good lord, imagine, a big drama in the middle of the night when all you want is to get home and have some peace. Are you sure you don't mind listening?"

"I – I think so. I mean, it's all right."

"I didn't know anything was going on. Again. When I left the house this morning – yesterday morning by now – everything seemed fine with us. Kissed her goodbye before I drove to Bakersfield on business. When I told her I wouldn't be back until the next afternoon, she even followed me out to the car for a final kiss. Maybe that's what sent me home early – we haven't always got along so good. Anyway I hurried up the business deal and drove home in the night. Got home early. Too early."

He stopped, as though that was the end, looked over at his wife, and shook his head as though to get the sight out of his eyes.

"She wasn't alone in our bedroom. And it wasn't a girl friend. I left. Pronto. Before I did something I'd be sorry for. An attorney knows better than to be sorry for things like that. The man left in a hurry too. I saw him come out the door and run down the street. I didn't know him, don't want to know him.

"Well, after we left she took the pills. Not to die. To scare me back home. She'd had practise – this wasn't the first time she'd tried that act for the same damn reason.

"She took them and then called the police. Told them what she had done, gave them the license number of my car, said they should check the motels for me. But this time something got fouled up. Maybe she miscounted the pills or the cops were too slow. Whatever, this time she almost made it. All the way."

The strained anger and hurt in his voice echoed in me, made my heart pound against my ribs. The pain sharpened and a small moan escaped me.

"I'm sorry. Forgive me, I shouldn't have burst out this way, I'm sorry. Listen, you ought to try to sleep. I heard what the nurse said, so why not take a hypo? No reason to be afraid of witches when they're not real."

Is everything you're afraid of real? But I must not have said it this time because he didn't answer.

"I see them, even if they're not real."

"With an operation ahead of you, you need rest. Look, I'm sorry I burst out with the whole bit. It's just – well, things get to you in the middle of the night, somehow." He moved to the other bed, stared at his wife. Her breath was still noisy, heavy, plunging. "This time it's taking longer, but by morning she'll be awake." His voice was level, unjoyous. "Ready to have another whack at it. This makes three times she's pulled this drama."

The childhood refrain, "third time's the

charm," rang through my head. He turned sharply toward me. "Think so?" he asked.

"Think so – what?"

"You said, 'third time's the charm.' You mean, this time she may have really done it?"

But now it became too tiring to talk. I shut my eyes, fearing gesture or sound. I longed to lie still – still, motionless in some never-to-be-found ice-cold sea, floating forever in its freezing depths.

I felt, not saw, the man beside me again, felt him look down at me. He stood motionless. Time that wasn't time but only existence stayed on and on and on. My mind drifted.

At last he whispered, "Are you awake?"

I didn't answer, didn't move. I wasn't asleep, but the pain almost was and I didn't want to arouse it. "Can you hear me?" he whispered again.

It was comforting to have him sound anxious. But as he leaned closer, the heat of his body drove away the thought of the ice-cold sea. I grimaced and he moved back, softly, softly. I heard the chair move slightly, heard the faint rub of his clothing against the wood as he sat down.

Thank you – what was his name? – thank you, Mr. Ober, my mind said. It gave me a sense of security to have him there. Even though my eyes were closed, I knew he was watching me intently. Sick people close to death, I had discovered, live by instinct, not by mind. Emotions and thoughts become tangibles, swifter and more precise than words. Such a kind man. So troubled, so anxious.

How long he remained motionless I don't know. He and the room drifted from me as I sought the ice-cold sea.

He was bending close to me again. "Can you hear me?" he asked in a normal voice. Go away, my mind told him, I don't want to move or talk.

"Can you hear me?" he repeated, a little louder.

He couldn't make me talk, I wasn't going to talk. I had listened to his troubles, hadn't I? Now I was tired.

He stepped away, very softly. Then, unhindered, fierce and immediate, caught by the scanning sensitivity that illness brought, his emotion reached me. Anger? Fear? I opened my eyes slightly. Out of the corner of my left eye I saw him lean over his wife and gaze at her steadily, as though he had never seen her before. It tired my eyes to keep watching, so I closed them.

His feet made a swift, soft shuffle on the floor. I opened my eyes again. He stood between me and the woman, his back toward me. He was close to her, his shoulders hunched. He still loves her, I thought; he's kissing her sleeping face. My eyes closed again.

Another shuffle, this time quicker, and again I looked. He was raising a pillow from his wife's face. Her heavy breathing – had it vanished? Been forced back into her lungs? He turned, tiptoed to the dressing cabinet, placed the pillow on it where the nurse had left it. It was my pillow, the one they sometimes put under my knees to relieve pressure.

He tiptoed back to his wife, tilted his head as though listening. Her breathing, where was its sound?

The cord of my call button was pinned to the sheet beside me. I pressed the button, praying, Come quickly, nurse, she may still be alive. This nice man is a murderer!

Rubber-padded footsteps approached heavily. The fat nurse poked her head in at the door. "Yes, sir?" she said breathily to the man who had moved quickly to his chair at the sound of the footsteps. "Is your wife waking up?"

"No. She's resting quietly."

"Nurse, I called you. Please come here!"

"Miss Jackson, I warned you that pill wouldn't work. If you would only –"

"Not that. Please! Come close."

"You want the bedpan?"

"No! Oh, please –"

"Then it will have to wait. There's an emergency down the hall and I need to stay with the patient until the doctor gets here. I'll be back as soon as –"

"He smothered her with my pillow! The woman in the other bed. Look at her, please, she may be dying!"

"Miss Jackson! What a terrible thing to say! Now you've got witches from the pill, you might better have had that hypo."

"No! Not witches, it was real! He put the pillow over her face. Look at her, please!"

"Just ignore this, Mr. Ober," the nurse said to the man who had started up from his chair. "Don't mind it. She has this bad reaction to medication – keeps seeing things that aren't there."

"What a shame," he said, in an empty voice.

The nurse went to the other bed and looked down. "Oh, she's nice and quiet now. That's good. That heavy breathing can be a strain on the heart. Now if this is all it was, I have to go. We've got a bad hemorrhage down the hall." She hurried out and the door softly closed.

I stiffened as the man arose and came to my bed. He said, "You had a bad dream."

If he put the pillow on my face, what could I do? Call the nurse again? Too soon, she would ignore it. Struggle? I couldn't even turn in bed. Scream? My voice was no more than a whisper.

"I tried to talk to you but you were asleep. Then I went to see how my wife was, to straighten her cover. You saw me do that. A bad dream. Or like the nurse said, your witches again."

Did I dare argue? The pillow would be heavy and hot, and I couldn't bear more heat. Perhaps I would struggle, pain or no pain, and the pain would kill me. Pain or the pillow, or both.

I began to cry. It hurt to cry. "She's so quiet. Before she was noisy. Now I can't hear her breathe."

He stretched out his hand and a scream tried to get past my throat. But his hand only touched my forehead, very gently, stroking it. "Poor little girl. She shouldn't be here, you shouldn't be bothered. Shut your eyes and go back to sleep."

I shut my eyes and desperately pressed the call button.

An eternity seemed to pass before the fat nurse appeared. With her shape, like pillows stacked together, she should have been cuddly, comforting. She wasn't. She was frowning and her underlip thrust forward pugnaciously. "Yes? What now?"

"I don't believe she's breathing!" Sobs tore at my belly, releasing fiery pain. "Examine her, please, please, *please!*"

"Hush! You keep this up, you'll be in surgery tonight! Now, young lady, no more arguing, you've got to have that hypo. You can't be allowed to disturb the other patients."

"Please, it's our fault," Mr. Ober put in. "She can't rest with someone else in the room."

"Well, after all this is *not* a private room, it's a semi-private. She has to expect others in the room."

"She's too sick to expect anything. They should have told me she was this sick and I would have insisted on some different arrangement. My wife gets noisy as she comes to."

"It's mostly nerves, she's such a nervous thing," the nurse said, as though I couldn't hear. "Won't eat, won't turn in bed, won't try to help herself. Just a bundle of nerves. And the doctor insists that she build up her strength for surgery. Miss Jackson, we *must* have that hypo. After all, the doctor knows better than you."

"No!"

"I can't keep running in here. There's only two of us in this section tonight – some are off sick at the last minute. Honest, Mr. Ober, nobody thinks nurses get sick, but we get sick too."

She flounced to the other bed. "She's resting, that's all. Like you're supposed to do."

I began to cry again. "He did! With the pillow! I saw him!"

"Mr. Ober, please go outside for a bit. She's – well, I'm going to call her doctor. Miss Jackson, so you'll be satisfied, I'll check with your doctor about your medication."

She followed Mr. Ober into the corridor. Whispers are sibilant, they carry, and I heard her say, "She'll have to have that hypo, she's next door to hysteria. Then after she's asleep you can go back in. That man down the hall can't be left, and it will be good to have someone watch the pair of them." She padded away.

I tried to raise up to see the woman better, then fell back.

The nurse returned, a hypodermic needle in her hand. Coy, trying to smile. "Now we can't have you wearing yourself out, can we? A little rest and we'll feel better." Up went the covers. Jab went a needle. Though I knew the witches were watching and waiting, I was almost glad. Soon there would be no pain.

Outside the room the nurse whispered again. "She'll sleep after a bit. Those witches are hallucinations – morphine often does that. But she'll soon sleep and won't know you're here."

"She said she doesn't sleep, that she's afraid to sleep."

"Oh, goodness," the nurse said, "if you only worked here, you'd hear a lot of that. They complain they don't sleep, then you catch them snoring. The sick aren't normal, they don't reason right – you have to remember that. Like maybe your–" She stopped.

"Like maybe my wife."

"Now, Mr. Ober, just wait a bit, take a peek in to see when she dozes off, then go in."

She left. He waited. So did I. My eyes were heavy, but not from sleep. I felt I could never sleep again. Little by little the drug detached my mind from my body, and pain began to slip into the shadows to alert the witches. Finally pain became a memory that I was forgetting more and more.

Then the memory left and the first witch flickered over the wall at the foot of my bed. She faced me, leering wickedly. I tried to swallow but my mouth was dry and heavy.

Another witch joined her and together they floated back and forth between the wall and my bed, each time swooping nearer. It was a relief to see the man beside my bed. "Make them go away," I begged. "Don't let them touch me!"

"Who?"

"The witches. Against the wall. Can't you see them?"

"No. You're imagining them. Like you imagined you saw me put the pillow on my wife's face. It was a bad dream."

One of the witches glided into him and the face above me twisted, leered, fanged at me. Its mouth writhed into sound, "It was a bad dream, it was a bad dream..." – over and over.

Then I heard it. A caught, snaggy sound. Like a swallowed snore being forced out again. The witch whirled up to the ceiling and left the man behind. He walked swiftly to the other bed, bent close to his wife. "Oh, God!" he whispered. Whispers were so clear.

I grasped the call button, pressed it, and

began to cry wildly, "Help! Help, somebody! He'll do it again!"

Footsteps ran in the hall. Then the man and the nurse and the witches jumbled themselves together and advanced on me. "As if one emergency wasn't enough!" Furious. Nurse or witch? "Never saw it fail, they come in bunches. Well, that poor man down the hall won't need his bed any longer. Mr. Ober, I think we ought to move your wife down there as soon as we can arrange it. It's a private, costs more, but with this one into hysterics –"

"Yes, please, as soon as possible. The cost doesn't matter. It's a shame we've upset this lady."

"Already upset," sniffed the nurse. "So, Mr. Ober, if you will just go down to the office and fix up the transfer. Tell them to call us, we'll explain."

He nodded and left. The nurse turned on me determinedly. "See here, young lady, you just settle down. You shouldn't be having pain now, you'll run up a temperature."

"You'll leave him alone with her, he'll kill her! Then he may kill me too! Because I saw him try to smother her!" The little lost voice hung above me, then slid down my throat, choked me as the witches laughed from the ceiling. *Hush hush HUSH HUSH!* Nurse or witch?

It must have been the witch, because the nurse was gone. Leaving me alone, helpless, with a snoring woman who didn't know she was going to be killed. "Mrs. Ober, wake up! Wake up! Your husband is going to kill you!"

The two nurses and an orderly rushed in. "Get her out of here quick before her husband gets back and hears this! That Jackson goes crazy, absolutely nuts from morphine. I wish to God I dared give her another shot –"

"Better not or she'll turn into a witch herself," the second nurse said. "Some night, this."

"Get moving, gals," the orderly said. "I'm crowded tonight. I'm due to wheel another one up to surgery right away. Hey, this dame's breathing funny, give a look, willya?"

"Take a handful of sleeping pills, you'd breathe funny too. She's lucky she's breathing at all. I checked her a while ago. Jackson gave me the willies, screaming the husband put a pillow on her face, but she was okay, just breathing quieter. So now she's loud again. What do you think, the doctor should be phoned about her?"

"This dump," said the other nurse. "No

house physician. No, don't call the poor guy, he probably just got to sleep again. Like you said, she's breathing."

"God, will I be glad when morning comes!"

They let down the protective bars on the sides of the woman's bed, wheeled her away, turned out the light, and closed the door.

In the dark I couldn't see the witches but I could feel them slithering around me. Did death wait beside them, carried by them like a contagion? And if death came for me now, would the witches follow to torment me forever and ever? I burned all over and raised my hand to wipe the sweat from my face. But there was no sweat, only burning.

The door opened a crack that slowly widened. The man's bulk stood dark against the dim light of the corridor. I held my breath, let it ease out slowly. If he doesn't hear me breathe, he may think I died and go away, and there would be no need to smother me –

He tiptoed to the other bed, saw it was empty, then came to my bed. "I'm sorry we upset you."

I didn't answer.

"It was a nightmare, you know. About the pillow, I mean."

He was insisting too much. Besides, I

knew when it happened. Before the hypo, before the witches. It was no nightmare. It was real. But now it was different, for the lighted doorway revealed the gathering forms of the witches. One left the group, swept against my face, sucked at my breath. I panted, gasped to get it back. The sleeping pain in my belly stirred, warning that it was merely patient, that it would never leave me.

"Poor little girl," he said. He bent down, down, down. How terrible to be killed so gently! His lips barely touched my forehead. "Good night. Thank you for letting me talk to you."

At the door he stopped and looked back. "Don't worry. Third time won't be the charm."

He left, and I was alone with the witches.

"Well, Miss Jackson, we gave the night nurse a bad time last night, didn't we?" It was the nurse's aide, a pleasant girl who worked the morning shift.

I looked at the clock on my bedside stand. Seven. The window was light, but I hadn't noticed. Ever since the pain had returned I had been lying in a gray haze, acquiescent to it.

"Better wash our face, hadn't we? The nurse didn't want to disturb you, you were resting so nice. Now maybe today we'll be good and eat some breakfast."

"How is she?" I asked. "Did she – wake up?"

"Huh?"

"The woman, the one in here last night. Mrs. Ober. The one who took sleeping tablets."

"Oh, that one. Well..." She cocked her head on one side, listening. Then I heard it. A distant, jumbled yell, words tumbling over each other in meaningless sound.

"Her again," the girl said. "Listen, do you suppose you can wipe off your face and hands yourself? She's been trying to throw herself over the bars, they may need help." She dropped the washcloth in the bowl and turned to the door. "You know, the woman you're asking about. Sometimes they come out wild after an overdose."

She left, and I tried to reach the washcloth, then gave up and stared at the monstrous swollen belly that had raised the bedcover from the skeleton legs.

The yells kept coming, now high, now low, shooting out in tangents. At last muted. Then gone. Were they smothering her?

Later, I don't know how much later, I saw Mr. Ober walk past my room toward the elevators. If he had been a small man, perhaps he wouldn't have looked so sad. But the slump of his walk, his chin black with beard growth dropped toward his thick chest, the drag of his feet below his big body, all were so out of keeping with the virile size of him. Sad, sad.

Even after his footsteps were swallowed up by the elevator, his sad hopelessness stayed with me. Sick people close to death live by instinct, and emotions and tangibles. I began to sob for him, softly at first, then in great jerking sobs, louder and louder. The room filled with fog. Figures struggled through it toward me, nurses, finally my doctor.

That was the day they operated. They hurried it up. I was in no condition to wait.

It was a long time after the operation. I was well again – no more skinny legs and distended belly. Back on my job. Quite a long time afterward, and I kept trying to remember where I had seen that name before. The name I read in our county newspaper. It belonged in another small town – all the towns in my sprawling southern California county were small – it wasn't the name of anyone in my own community. Even so, the name kept bothering me, struggling to make some connection. Anesthetics do queer things to one's memory – names go away.

Then I did remember. I hadn't seen the name. I had heard it. Ober. Maria Ober, 37, died yesterday approximately at midnight. Heart attack. Awakened her husband complaining of a smothering sensation and was dead on arrival of the doctor. A long history of illness. Amateur artist, former dancer, born in South America. Leaves her husband, Robert Ober, prominent attorney, no children, one brother residing in Argentina.

Third time won't be the charm.

But he didn't say anything about the fourth.

Still, that wouldn't be much to offer a District Attorney, would it? About another attorney?

Jack Ritchie

Nobody Tells Me Anything

There is an open-air café in Paris where if you sit at a table long enough, it is said, everyone you know will pass by. The legend (surely that's all it is) popped into our mind as we began to prepare this story for the press. We couldn't help thinking that if we sit long enough at our editorial desk, a manuscript from every mystery writer we know will come our way. With this offbeat preamble we now announce how happy we are to bring you the first story by Jack Ritchie to appear in EQMM – and what a delightful story! Ingenious, fast-reading, and with that special brand of Ritchie's humor...

He was my first client.

"Mr. Turnbuckle," he said, "I'll pay you fifty dollars for each day's report. How does that strike you?"

It struck me as being a bit frugal, but possibly he was prepared to be generous with expenses. I voiced the thought. "Fifty dollars and expenses?"

"I don't forsee any expenses. Just fifty dollars for each day's report. Thirty reports."

I smiled tolerantly. "Fifty dollars a day for confidential investigation might have been a munificent sum twenty or thirty years ago, but by today's standards –"

He held up a hand. "It will not be necessary for you even to leave this office. Just sit down at your typewriter, insert the stationery of your agency, and type the reports, one after another until you are finished. Thirty reports to cover thirty days."

I glanced down at my notes, which consisted of just two words: Paula Smith. "You mean you *don't* want me to find this Paula Smith?"

"Exactly. I want you to do no searching at all. However, fill out your reports as though you had been exceedingly busy. Use your imagination. Trace her across the country – on paper – and finally lose her in, say, San Francisco or Seattle. Make it appear that you are sending your reports back here, where a secretary transcribes them, and forwards them to me."

I considered that. "Wouldn't it be cheaper if you had a few letterheads printed and then filled in the reports yourself?"

"I suppose so. But it would be quite a bother, and besides, I simply don't know the forms used, the methods of search, and the jargon or whatsoever used by private detective agencies, and I want these reports to appear as authentic as possible. I will also need thirty envelopes with your agency imprint."

I nodded to myself. He's going to mail the reports to himself – one at a time – and when they arrive, he intends to show them to one or more other people.

My client was a tall distinguished man in his fifties, graying at the temples, exceedingly well-dressed, and he had refused to tell me his name.

I consulted my sheet of paper again. "Is Paula Smith her real name?"

"Just fill out the reports."

"To whom shall I address the reports?"

"Leave that part blank. I'll fill it in later myself."

I sighed. "Just to recapitulate, we have a missing person, one Paula Smith. You do *not* want me to find her. But she *is* missing, isn't she? Have you gone to the police perhaps?"

He regarded me for a few seconds. "Paula Smith is quite well and, I presume, happy. You need to know no more than that. How long will it take you to compile those reports?"

"Probably a week. I'll have to do some research at the library – things like the names of streets, hotels, restaurants, and the like in various cities. Where was Paula Smith last seen?"

"Why do you need to know that?"

"If she were last seen in the Sahara, I can hardly begin my report by taking up the trail at the North Pole."

He nodded reluctantly. "Begin your report with the statement that you located the taxi which took her and her luggage from 'your residence' to the airport or the bus station. You do not specifically need to know my address."

"What was the date and time she was last seen, and by whom?"

"You do not need to know by whom. But she was last seen Sunday at approximately ten o'clock in the evening when she went up to her rooms. Do you suppose I could have the first report by noon today? I'd like to get on this as soon as possible before somebody else –" He stopped and reached for his wallet. It was a fine piece of leather with the initials A.B. in one corner. He handed me two twenties and a ten.

I took the bills. "How did you happen to select my agency?"

"I walked through the yellow pages of the phone book and there you were." He went to the door. "If you have any idea of following me, forget it. I intend to take all due precautions."

When he was gone, I proceeded to think.

What did I have here?

I was being asked to fill out a series of false reports. Why? Obviously to fool someone – to make some person or persons think that this Paula Smith was indeed being searched for, though my client did not have the slightest desire in the world that she be found.

And what about the name Paula Smith itself?

Was the name fictitious? Or did such a person really exist?

I reached for the telephone book and turned to the Smiths. There were legions of them, of course. Several Peter Smiths, but no Paulas or even P. Smiths.

And what about my caller, A.B.?

For one thing, he had said that he had walked through the yellow pages until he found my name and address.

But that was hardly possible since the name of my agency was not yet listed in the book. I had just opened my office three weeks ago. My name would appear in the next issue of the phone book which was not due for distribution for another two months.

Then why and how had he chosen me?

If not by means of the telephone book, had he simply wandered the corridors of downtown buildings until he saw the lettering on my door? Hardly likely. I am on the eighth floor of a twenty-six-story building and there are at least a hundred tall buildings in this city.

Or was it possible that he actually worked in this very building and that during the last three weeks while waiting for the elevator to take him up to his floor he had noticed my agency's name on the directory on the wall? And had it been filed in his memory bank until, when he needed the services of a private detective, it had suddenly leaped to his mind?

I rubbed my neck. Should I restrain my curiosity, mind my own business, and collect the $1500 as per order? Is that what an experienced private detective would do?

My phone rang. It was Ralph. He is a detective sergeant on the police force and I was his partner until three weeks ago.

"How are you doing, Henry?" he asked.

"I just got my first case."

"Congratulations. My wife and I were a little worried. I mean it's been almost a month since you opened your office."

I cleared my throat. "I just realized that most people consult the yellow pages of the phone book when they want to hire a private detective and I won't be in the book for another two months when the new edition comes out."

"You picked the wrong time of the year to open for business. Why not advertise in the newspapers?"

"I'm not sure that's professionally ethical."

"Henry, I wouldn't worry about ethical as far as the private detective scene is concerned. What's your first case about?"

"A missing person. Paula Smith."

"Smith? Well, I suppose the Smiths get lost now and then too. My wife's wondering if she should bring over some chicken soup or something?"

"No, Ralph. I'm doing just fine."

After he hung up, I went downstairs to the lobby and studied the directory next to the bank of elevators.

I found twelve companies and individuals listed under B. Albert Bancroft, Investments, seemed to be what I was looking for.

I went to the nearby public phone and

turned the white pages of the book to the Bancrofts. I found only one Albert Bancroft listed.

I glanced at my watch. It was nearly ten in the morning. Where was Bancroft at this moment? Probably upstairs in his office poring over municipal bonds or something equally exciting.

I checked his address and phone number and then dialed.

The phone was picked up by a man who said, "Bancroft residence."

"Could I speak to Paula?"

There was a pause. "Paula?"

"Yes. Paula Smith."

Another pause. "I'm sorry, sir, but she is no longer in our employ."

Ah, so there really *was* a Paula Smith. And whom was I talking to? He had used the words "Bancroft residence," and had called me "sir." Was he the butler? After all, people who listed their trade as Investments and lived in Bancroft's neighborhood probably could afford to hire butlers. "Is this Jarvis?" I asked.

"No, sir. This is Wisniewski."

"Wisniewski?" I laughed lightly. "Jarvis. Wisniewski. I always seem to get those two names mixed. But you *are* the Bancroft butler, aren't you?"

"Yes, sir."

"Of course," I said. "Paula wrote to me about you."

"Miss Smith wrote to you about *me?*" He seemed cautious. "What did she say?"

"I don't remember the exact words, but they were nothing but good."

"Who is this speaking, sir?"

"John Smith. Paula's cousin, twice removed."

"I understood that she had no living relatives."

I chuckled. "I don't blame Paula for not mentioning me. But I'm on parole now. Did she leave a forwarding address?"

"No, sir."

"You mean she just disappeared into thin air?"

"Not exactly into thin air, sir. She just packed up during the night and left. I understand there was a note, sir, but it did not mention where she was going."

What had Paula's job been at the Bancroft's? Cook? I chuckled again and quoted H. H. Munro, better known as "Saki": "She was a good cook, as cooks go. And as good cooks go, she went?"

"Sir?" Wisniewski said.

I had evidently missed the mark. "The *last*

place Paula worked, she was a cook," I said. "I just assumed –?"

"She was the housekeeper here, sir."

Housekeeper? What did housekeepers do? Oh, yes. They supervised the other servants, kept the household accounts, and generally feuded with the butler.

When I hung up, I pondered a few moments, then decided that further investigation at the scene was in order.

I left the phone booth for the multi-level garage where I park my car and drove to 217 Lake Crest Drive.

The entrance to 217 Lake Crest Drive was flanked by fifteen-foot stone pillars. The gates were open, but I had the feeling that a door-to-door salesman would hesitate before considering that an invitation to enter.

I turned into the driveway and followed it through the shade of elms and other greenery until I reached a large Tudor-style structure.

I parked, ascended the wide stairs, and used the knocker. While I waited, I watched an ancient gardener trimming a hedge.

To circumvent the possibility that Wisniewski might recognize my voice, I had intended to speak in a Scots burr, which I perfected while playing the part of Macbeth in my senior year in high school, but a uniformed maid answered the door instead. "Yes, sir?"

Where was Wisniewski? Probably in the pantry polishing the silver or in the cellar turning wine bottles.

"Could I speak to Mr. Bancroft?"

"He is not at home, sir."

"Mrs. Bancroft?"

"I'm afraid not, sir. She died three years ago."

That certainly eliminated her. "Are there any other Bancrofts on the premises?"

"There is Miss Bancroft, sir. Mr. Bancroft's daughter."

"She will do nicely."

"Who shall I say is calling, sir?"

"John P. Jones, Attorney."

She left me there, but returned a minute later and led me to one of the drawing rooms.

Miss Bancroft appeared to be in her early twenties, wore shell-rimmed glasses, and had possibly been reading the open book on the cocktail table.

"I'm Marianne Bancroft," she said. "What can I do for you?"

"I understand that you have in your employ one Miss Paula Smith? Could I speak to her?"

"Paula?" Marianne Bancroft shook her head. "Paula is gone. She left sometime before Monday morning when we were all asleep. Bag and baggage. There was a note, but it didn't say where she was going."

"Did it say *why* she left?"

"She said she was just fed up here and had decided to move on. Why do you want to find her?"

"Her uncle Theophilus Smith died and left her some money."

"Was it a lot?"

"Not really. About a thousand. I know very little about Paula Smith besides her name. How old was she?"

"About forty. But she looked younger when she tried."

"How long was she the housekeeper here?"

"Less than a year."

I noticed a framed photograph of three people on the corner shelf. One of them was my client, Albert Bancroft, another Marianne, and the third probably Bancroft's son, a younger, thinner, and taller version of his father.

"Did anyone see Paula leave?" I asked.

"If they did, no one's said so."

I assumed a thoughtful pose. "You don't suppose I could have a look at her room just on the off chance that there might be some indication of where she was going? Perhaps some scrap of paper or some underlined portion of a bus schedule?"

She led me up to the third floor. "You look familiar. I could swear that I've seen you somewhere before." She opened the door to Paula Smith's suite. "Sitting room, bedroom, bathroom."

I opened the sliding doors to a large closet. It was completely bare except for a few wire hangers, but the scent of perfume and powder still lingered. "I always think of housekeepers as wearing uniforms. With maybe a dress or two for going out?"

"Housekeepers don't wear uniforms any more. At least I can't think of any who do. Paula probably had that closet full of clothes. I know she was always sending things to the cleaners or getting them back. Are you going to scour the ends of the earth until you find her?"

"Not for one thousand dollars. We'll just put it in escrow and hope that someday she'll get in touch with somebody who'll tell her about us. You don't happen to have a photograph of her?"

"No."

"What did she look like?"

Marianne shrugged. "Quite tall and – well-developed. Blonde."

"There isn't any shortage or anything of that nature in her household accounts?"

"Nobody's checked yet, but I doubt it. I'm willing to bet that her books are in perfect order. She was after bigger –" She stopped. "Are you sure you're not some kind of detective?"

I smiled. "Well, there *is* quite a bit of detecting involved in tracing heirs." I moved to a door on the farther wall of the bedroom and opened what appeared to be another closet or storage area. A large steamer trunk stood upright but open. It appeared to be almost fully packed with dresses, skirts, and coats.

"Paula's?" I asked.

Marianne moved closer. "It appears to be. I recognize some of the clothes."

"Why would she leave this behind?"

"I don't know. Maybe she intended to send someone back for it."

"But wouldn't she at least *close* the trunk and probably lock it before she left?"

"Perhaps she just decided that it was all too much to take along with her."

"It all looks like fairly good quality. Would she abandon it?"

"Why not?" Marianne said a bit testily. "She could always buy more. She didn't leave here exactly empty –" She stopped and smiled sweetly. "Anything else?"

"Did Paula own an automobile?"

"No."

"Did she have any other luggage besides this trunk?"

"I seem to remember two suitcases when she came here."

"This note she left? Do you mind if I see it?"

"It doesn't exist any more. I tossed it into the fireplace."

"Why?"

"Because I felt like it."

When I returned to my office, I phoned police headquarters and left a message for Ralph to call me when he next checked in.

Then I sat down at my typewriter and began composing my first report for Bancroft.

At ten after eleven Ralph phoned.

"Ralph," I said, "I'd like you to find out if Paula Smith left a forwarding address at the post office and also if she had or has any savings or checking accounts in her own name. I'd do it myself, but you're on active duty and that opens doors and saves time."

Ralph clicked his tongue. "Shame on you, Henry, using a public servant for private business. The post office will be easy, but the bank accounts won't – do you know how many banks there are in this town?"

"Try the branch banks in the Fiebrantz shopping center. It's only half a mile from the Bancroft place."

"And what is the Bancroft place?"

"That's where Paula Smith worked until the night she disappeared."

At noon, when Bancroft stepped into my office, I had two reports ready for him. "So far I trace her from your residence to a pizza parlor in Billings, Montana."

He read and nodded. "These look fine."

I offered him two envelopes. He put the second report into one of them, but not the first, from which I deduced that he intended to show the first report to someone immediately and did not want to wait out the time lag of mailing the report to himself.

He produced his wallet and handed me another $50 for the second report. "I'll drop in every day to pick up whatever reports you've finished."

After he left, I paused to wonder again why he preferred to remain anonymous. Was he just embarrassed over the charade, or was he afraid that I might possibly attempt to blackmail him later. After all, he obviously had something to conceal and if I knew his identity I might find out what it was all about and attempt to profit from it.

Ralph phoned me in the afternoon. "The post office says that Paula Smith left no forwarding address. And according to the First National Branch at Fiebrantz, Paula Smith still has a checking account there. Balance $112.16. The bank's records show that she deposited her paycheck into the account each month and was usually overdrawn by the time the month was over."

"Why would she leave $112.16 behind?"

"That isn't necessarily a final balance, Henry. There might be some checks outstanding. She could have closed the account for all practical purposes."

"Ralph, when Paula left the Bancrofts' place she probably took along a couple of suitcases. She didn't own an automobile, so she must have taken a taxi."

"I'll check on it. But maybe someone in the Bancroft house drove her to the airport or bus station or whatever."

"If anybody did, he certainly hasn't volunteered the information."

In the afternoon I dropped in at the main library for research that carried Paula from Billings to the Custer Battlefield National Monument and then on to the Cheyenne Frontier Days Rodeo.

That evening, at home in my apartment, I created and consumed my supper, and then sat down to TV, turning, as usual, to the educational channel. I was quietly engrossed in the history of barrel making when my door buzzer sounded.

I identified my caller immediately as Albert Bancroft's son. He looked even taller and thinner than his photograph.

He introduced himself. "My name is Jerome Bancroft. Are you the Turnbuckle of the Turnbuckle Detective Agency?"

I nodded.

He cleared his throat. "I understand that my father is employing your agency to search for Paula Smith? My father showed me your first report this evening and I memorized your letterhead." He stepped into the room. "I knew you wouldn't be in your office at this time of the night, of course, so I looked in the white pages of the telephone book. You are the only Turnbuckle listed."

I beamed proudly. "The Turnbuckle line is long but narrow. What can I do for you?"

He seemed uncomfortable. "Do you think your agency will find Paula?"

I shrugged. "One can only do one's best."

He took the chair I offered. "I don't know what father is paying you to search for Paula, but I'm willing to double it – if you do *not* find her."

I raised an eyebrow. Here was someone else who didn't want Paula Smith found and was willing to pay handsomely for it. "Why don't you want her found?"

"It's a personal reason. I really don't think it's necessary that you know."

I went to my TV set, which at the moment featured a cooper spoke-shaving some barrel staves, and turned it off. "I have the strangest suspicion about this case. Is Paula Smith still alive?"

He seemed surprised at the question. "Alive? Of course she's alive. I just don't want her to be found and persuaded to return."

"Do you know where she is now?"

"No."

"Why did she leave in the first place?"

Jerome Bancroft took half a minute to wrestle with a decision and then sighed. "I guess I might just as well give you the whole story. I *paid* Paula to leave. Twenty thousand dollars, to be exact. I felt that Paula had an undue influence on my father and that it was just a question of time before he asked her to marry him."

"You didn't think that Paula Smith was a suitable stepmother?"

"Frankly, no. As a matter of fact, she was considerably free with the amount of personal attention she paid to *me* too."

"You were attracted to her?"

"Actually she frightened me half to death."

"But still you were afraid that she might seduce you?"

"No. Frightened or not, I do have a mind of my own. I would have been able to resist her, regardless of temptation or perfume, both of which were considerable. But I was worried for Dad's sake. I don't know how strong he is in matters of this nature."

"Did the fact that Paula Smith, as your father's wife, would be in a position to claim a considerable share of your father's wealth disturb you?"

"Not particularly. Both Marianne, that's my sister, and I have quite enough money in our own right. Personally we both feel that Dad ought to remarry, but we can think of a number of more suitable candidates."

"So you offered Paula Smith twenty thousand dollars to leave the household?"

He frowned thoughtfully. "Now that I think it over, I'm not quite positive whether I offered or she *suggested* that I give her the money and she would leave. Anyway, I handed her twenty thousand in cash on

Sunday afternoon. She promised that she would leave on Monday while Dad and I were at the office. She said she'd leave a note saying that she was just fed up with the job and had decided to get out. The note was so that Dad wouldn't think she'd been kidnapped or something and call the police."

"And she left the note?"

"Yes. On her bedroom dresser."

"But instead of leaving Monday she left sometime between ten P.M. Sunday, when she was last seen going up to her rooms, and seven A.M. Monday, when she was scheduled to report for duty, so to speak?"

"Yes. I don't know why though. Maybe she thought I'd think things over and demand the twenty thousand back. So she decided to skip while the skipping was good."

I debated whether to tell him that his father apparently had as little desire as he to have Paula Smith return, then I decided that this case needed a little more investigation first.

Jerome Bancroft brought out his checkbook. "How much would you like as a retainer?"

I pondered. What would your average private detective do? Take money for not doing a job for which he was already being paid for not doing? I'd have to think it over. "A retainer will not be necessary," I said. "I prefer to bill at the completion – or in this case, the noncompletion – of my job."

When he was gone, I turned on the TV set just in time to catch Winnebago Indians harvesting wild rice.

The next morning I completed several more reports tracing Paula Smith to Salt Lake City, where by finding a ticket stub in a room she had just vacated at the Excelsior Motel, I deduced that she had the night previous attended a concert of the Mormon Tabernacle Choir.

In the afternoon Ralph phoned.

"No taxi picked up a fare anywhere near the Bancroft residence either on Sunday or Monday," he said. "Maybe she phoned a relative or a friend to pick her up?"

"She told the butler she had no living relatives. As for friends outside of the household, I don't know. Nobody's mentioned any."

"If someone from the house drove her away, why is he so shy about mentioning it?"

"Maybe she wasn't alive when he drove her away."

Late in the afternoon a silhouette appeared at the opaque glass of my door and the knob turned.

Marianne Bancroft entered my office.

Her eyes widened. "*You? You* are the Turnbuckle Detective Agency?"

I thought for a flashing moment of telling her that I just happened to be visiting, but there I was coatless and before a typewriter.

So I admitted the fact. "Yes, I am Henry Turnbuckle. I'm sorry if I misrepresented myself yesterday, but it was necessary in my pursuit of information."

She regarded me with narrow-eyed suspicion, but nevertheless got to the point. "I understand that my father hired you to find Paula Smith."

I dodged the exact point delicately. "I am in your father's employ, yes."

"All right. I don't know what he's paying you to find her, but I'll double it if you *don't* find her."

I had heard those words before, of course, and I repeated my part of the dialogue. "Why don't you want her found?"

"I really don't think it is necessary you know."

I closed my eyes for a few reflective moments and then opened them. "The pieces are beginning to fall into place. You do not want me to find Paula Smith for the simple reason that you *paid* her to leave. Possibly twenty thousand dollars?"

Naturally she was astounded. "How did you know that?"

I tapped my forehead with a finger. "Sheer deductive reasoning based solidly on coincidence. And the reason you paid her to leave and do not want to have her found and returned is that you feel she was on the verge of entrapping either your father or your brother into matrimony."

She was, for the moment, speechless.

I smiled understandingly. "My dear Miss Bancroft, neither your father *nor* your brother has the slightest desire ever to see Paula again. As a matter of fact, your brother also offered me double what his father was paying me if I also did *not* find Paula."

She was confused. "Why did father hire you in the first place, if he doesn't want Paula back?"

"I believe he was under the impression that your brother was infatuated with Paula. She seems to have been clever at creating conflicting impressions. It wouldn't surprise me at all if your father *also* was conned into paying her to leave. And it occurred to him that when Jerome discovered that Paula was gone, he might be heartbroken enough to decide to employ a private detective to find her. And he might have, at that. So to forestall that possibility, your father hired me not to look for her, but to prepare a number of reports to make it appear as though I was conducting an extensive search. He would show them to Jerome to indicate that everything was already being done to find her."

Marianne sighed. "I guess the three of us will just have to get together and compare notes." She regarded me for a few moments and then frowned. "Now I remember where I saw you before. When the Culbersons had that break-in and jewel robbery at their place a couple of years ago, I dropped in because I wanted to hear all about it from Jenny Culberson. The place was overrun with police and detectives." She nodded reflectively. "And you were there questioning one of the maids. You and another man, both in plainclothes. He was kind of chubby, with straw-colored hair."

"That was Ralph, my partner."

She stared at me accusingly. "You're not a private detective, you're a public detective."

"Well, yes and no. At the moment I'm on educational leave from the department. I'm doing my Master's on quasi-police organizations – like the Merchant Police, security guards, private detective agencies, and things like that. As part of my research, I'm putting in a spell as a private detective. My license cost me fifteen dollars, but I expect it's worth it."

She was still dubious. "You mean the police department put you on leave for something like that?"

I nodded. "Frankly, I *did* feel a little guilty about being absent from the force for one whole year and possibly letting them down in some way, but Captain Wilkerson was very understanding. He not only approved my application, but actually urged me to take the year off. As a matter of fact, he generously suggested that I make it two or three years."

She smiled faintly. "I know one thing for certain, Henry Turnbuckle, you'll never become a *rich* private detective."

I shrugged. "Well, I certainly have never expected to."

"I mean now that you've cleared the air, it isn't necessary any more for either me or my brother to double the money Dad is paying you, is it? And as for Dad, I don't know what he's given you so far, but he really has no reason now to pay you any more, does he?"

Good heavens! She was right. In my moment of candor I had shot down my own financial balloon. I frowned. What would an experienced private detective do in a situation like this? Threaten to find Paula Smith on his own and bring her back unless the family paid? I rejected that after a few moments' consideration. No, that would be blackmail.

Marianne seemed about to pat me on the shoulder. "I'll tell you what, Henry, I'll take you home and the family will come through with some kind of settlement that won't leave you exactly empty-handed."

We used her car for the transportation to the Bancroft mansion and I'm afraid I was a bit moody during the ride. When we arrived, two other automobiles were parked in front of the house.

"Dad and Jerome are home," Marianne said. She led me to a drawing room where we found Bancroft Sr. and Jerome.

A large man, well over six feet tall, balding, and wearing a butler's uniform stood at the liquor cabinet making drinks. I deduced that this was Wisniewski.

Both of the Bancrofts blanched when they saw me.

"It's all right, Dad," Marianne said. "I'll explain everything." She did, and during the course of the explanation and clarification, I learned that Bancroft Sr. had also paid Paula Smith $20,000 to leave.

I had been thinking heavily while they talked and suddenly I saw the light at the end of the tunnel. "Ah, hah!" I said, gaining their attention.

I smiled tightly. "Paula Smith privately assured each one of you that she would leave secretly on Monday while all of you were gone from the house for one reason or another, presumably to 'prevent' some member of the family from pleading with her to remain. And yet she left suddenly the night before. Why?"

None of them had the answer.

I continued: "It is my belief that Paula Smith was murdered here some time after ten P.M. on Sunday – when she was last seen alive – and before seven A.M. on Monday, when she normally assumed her duties for the day, and that her body was removed from the premises by her murderer."

They blinked, of course, and Marianne said, "Are you intimating that she changed her mind about going and that one of us killed her to get her out of the way?"

"No. I think she planned to go. She had milked all three of you for about as much as she could expect and she probably thought that you were on the verge of comparing notes and learning that none of you actually wanted her to remain. You might even decide to go to the police. After all, the entire scheme was a form of extortion. No, she had decided to leave, but before she could go voluntarily, she was murdered. You ask why? And by whom?"

None of them did, but I felt that the questions were implied.

"The Why is obvious," I said confidently. "For the sixty thousand dollars in cash which she had accumulated."

Albert Bancroft seemed shocked. "I know that *I* certainly would not kill *anyone* for *any* amount of money."

Jerome agreed. "Neither would I. Besides, I couldn't strangle anybody. My wrists are too weak."

I thought that over and regarded Jerome piercingly. "What makes you think she was strangled?"

He shrugged. "Nobody seems to have heard a shot and if a knife or a bludgeon were used, there would be blood sprayed about, I imagine, but nobody's mentioned any. So I opt for strangulation."

He seemed to have a keen mind. I continued: "The fact remains that Paula was murdered and that her murderer knew that she planned to leave on Monday and used that fact as a coverup for the murder. And after killing her he carried her body downstairs and put it into an automobile or a station wagon and then returned to her room, finished packing her suitcases, and then took them away with him."

"Why didn't he take the trunk too?" Marianne asked.

"Either he didn't know it was in that closet or, if he did, he probably felt that it was too great a risk attempting to carry a fully loaded trunk down three flights of stairs in the dead of night without making enough noise to waken someone. Or possibly he thought that each of you would just assume that Paula had decided at the last moment to abandon the trunk of clothes. After all, she had plenty of money to buy more."

Marianne nodded. "And you think that a man has to be the murderer because of the heaving and hauling involved with the body? After all, Paula was rather a full-bodied woman."

"Exactly. And who in this household, besides your father and your brother, is capable of carrying a hefty body down three flights of stairs?"

"Who?" Marianne asked.

I smiled. "Shall we consider the gardener for a moment?"

"Hector?" Marianne shook her head.

"He's sixty-five and I doubt if he weighs over one hundred and twenty pounds."

I agreed. "You are quite right, Marianne. The murderer couldn't have been Hector."

Wisniewski had been doing make-work at the liquor cabinet so that he could remain in the room.

Now I turned to him and pointed triumphantly. "You, Wisniewski, *you* are the murderer of Paula Smith!"

He regarded me coldly. "Utterly ridiculous, sir. How could I possibly have known that Miss Smith had sixty thousand dollars in her possession?"

I chuckled meaningfully. "Miss Smith was a woman who, shall we say, came on strong. She lived in this house for almost a year, all the while apparently getting noplace at all with any member of the opposite sex, and frankly, in her case, I think that would have been both unendurable and unbelievable. She had to find some man who would prove more compliant and more willing –"

Wisniewski's crown reddened. "Preposterous, sir. She was definitely not my type."

Albert Bancroft was still aghast. "You mean that in this case it was the *butler* who did it?"

"Yes," I said firmly. "The butler." I

scowled at Wisniewski. "And so there you were with a body on your hands. What did you do with it? Hide it on the grounds? No. A bit too risky. You might be seen or the body found at some future date. No, you had to take the body somewhere else to dispose of it. A lake? A river? But bodies have a nasty habit of floating to the surface eventually. Or did you bury Paula? Do you own some property around here? Perhaps a cabin on a lake? Certainly an ideal remote burial place."

There was silence.

The Bancrofts and Wisniewski had assumed a stance of deep thought.

After a while Marianne spoke. "Meadows is the murderer."

"Meadows?" I said. "Who is Meadows?"

"The chauffeur."

"Chauffeur?" I said. "What chauffeur?"

"He has quarters over the garage," Albert Bancroft said.

I frowned. "Nobody told me you had a chauffeur."

"Come to think of it," Jerome Bancroft said, "Paula and Meadows were a sort of package deal from that employment agency, weren't they, Marianne?"

I was getting a bit warm. "No one said a damn word about Meadows and Paula coming here at the same time from the same employment agency."

Wisniewski rubbed his chin. "Now that I reflect on it, there were a number of times when I saw the two of them together in what one might call close circumstances."

"Now look here," I said, my voice rising a bit. "How can anybody expect me to solve anything if I'm kept in the dark? No one even hinted that Paula and Meadows were the *least* interested in each other."

"Meadows is about twenty-five," Marianne said. "And Paula was at least forty and it was beginning to show. She must have told him about the sixty thousand dollars and they even planned on going away together. But he was getting tired of her and figured that this was the time to split, and with the money."

I glared out of the nearest window. "Suppositions, suppositions."

Wisniewski brightened. "I believe that Meadows once mentioned that his uncle had a hunting cabin on an acre of land up north. An ideal place to bury Paula. It's probably miles from neighbors."

I turned back to them. "Now there's another example. No one had the decency to tell me that Meadows had an uncle or that this mysterious uncle had a hunting cabin."

"The money," Marianne said. "If the police find the money on or near Meadows, that ought to incriminate him."

"Ha," I snorted. "But suppose they don't find the money on or near Meadows? Then what?"

"In that case they'll tell Meadows they're going to go over his uncle's land with a fine-tooth comb. That ought to crack him wide-open."

"Nonsense," I said. "Nobody cracks wide-open just because someone threatens to search the land around his uncle's hunting cabin."

Wisniewski phoned the police and told them what we knew and what we suspected.

When they arrived, they talked to Meadows and in the course of questioning mentioned that they were going to have a look at the land surrounding his uncle's hunting cabin.

Meadows cracked wide-open.

My phone rang.

It was Ralph. "Well, everything's wrapped up. Meadows led us to the spot where he buried Paula's body and her two suitcases. The money was hidden under the floorboards of his uncle's cabin."

My fingers paradiddled on my desk top.

"I knew positively that the murderer had to be a man because to carry a deadweight body down three flights of stairs –"

"Actually he killed her in the garage," Ralph said. "He waited until she wrote the letter she was going to leave and then he lured her down there. Hit her over the head. We found bloodstains on the cement floor."

"Hm," I said thoughtfully. "Undoubtedly he used a tire iron."

"Henry," Ralph said. "You don't find tire irons around private garages any more. The murder weapon was a geologist's hammer."

"What the devil was a geologist's hammer doing in a garage?"

"Meadows and Paula Smith were a team. They pulled the same stunt at other places. When the money ran out, they'd get another job and work the routine again. But Meadows got tired of Paula. She was a lot older than him. So Meadows decided that while it was a nice racket, he'd just as soon work with somebody younger. Like Fifi."

"Fifi?" I said. "Who's Fifi?"

"The Bancrofts' upstairs maid."

"Nobody told me that the Bancrofts had an upstairs maid named Fifi."

"She wasn't in on the murder, but Meadows told her about the racket and she was ready to take Paula's place. She's gaga about Meadows."

"Ralph," I said a trifle reproachingly, "nobody told me that Fifi was gaga about Meadows. If people persist in withholding information, it only makes things that much more difficult for me."

Soon after Ralph hung up, a familiar silhouette appeared against the glass of my door.

Marianne entered and smiled. "Hi. What time is it?"

I consulted my watch. "Two minutes to eleven."

My phone rang.

It was a woman's voice. "I suspect that my husband is having an affair and I'd like to have him followed."

I wondered idly how the caller had got my phone number. "Certainly, Madam. I'll put one of my best operatives on the job. Your name, please?"

"Darlington. Mrs. Darlington. Could I see you this afternoon?"

"Just one moment, please, I'll have to check my appointment book." I waited twenty seconds and then said, "Ah, yes. Would two o'clock be convenient? I have an opening then."

"Fine. I'll be there."

I put down the phone and smiled. "Well, Marianne, I've got another case. A Mrs. Darlington and possible infidelity."

Marianne nodded. "Winifred should have suspected long ago."

"Winifred?" I said. "Who's Winifred?"

"Winifred Darlington. I gave her your phone number and said to call at eleven. I'm just dying to find out who Edward's been going out with."

"Edward?" I said. "Who's –" I stopped. "Never mind. I can *guess* who Edward is and I have to guess because nobody ever tells me anything." I stalked to my filing cabinet and opened the bottom drawer. I pulled out the bottle and drank two stiff fingers of sherry.

Isaac Asimov

A Case of Income Tax Fraud

Pull up a chair, unfold your napkin, and join the Black Widowers at one of their monthly dinner meetings, complete with preprandial argument (this time between artist Mario Gonzalo and writer Emmanuel Rubin) and postprandial puzzle, this time a brilliant baffler that once again is unraveled by old reliable Henry the waiter (long may he wait!). As to the problem brought by the guest of the evening, it is the kind of problem that might have been conceived by a scientist and a fiction writer collaborating – or, more precisely, by a mathematician and a detective-story writer working together...

Mario Gonzalo, the artist-member of the Black Widowers, seemed oddly disheveled as he said vehemently, "I *cannot* teach what I do because I don't *know* what I do, but that doesn't mean I can't *do* it."

And Emmanuel Rubin, his straggly beard seeming to shoot sparks out of each gray bristle, raised his eyes, magnified through their thick lenses, and said, "If you don't know what you're doing, you're a paint-dauber and not an artist."

"You're a madman, Mannie. If knowing were everything, Michelangelo could teach you to be Michelangelo, but the fact is that Michelangelo couldn't teach anyone to be Michelangelo. For that matter, no one could have taught Michelangelo to be Michelangelo either. He was *born* Michelangelo."

"You miss the entire point. Teaching doesn't necessarily imply the making of an equal. Michelangelo could give the kind of instruction from which others might profit. If he couldn't create equals, he could create more skillful marble-tappers. You bet he knew what he was doing even if he could only pound a limited amount into the heads of mere mortals."

"Ah," said Gonzalo gleefully. "Mere mortals! And what made them mere mortals? The lack of genius. And what were the components of that genius? Did Michelangelo himself know?"

Thomas Trumbull, the code expert, staring over his Scotch and soda and apparently irritated at being excluded from a conversation which the loud voices of Gonzalo and Rubin had made into a private dialogue, scowled and said, "Since Michelangelo is dead and can't be consulted on the subject, why don't you drop this foolish argument?"

"No," said Gonzalo passionately. "I appeal from the sublime to the ridiculous and ask Manny. You're a writer, Manny – after a fashion. Can you teach what you do?"

"I not only can," said Rubin, "I have. I've written articles for *The Writer* and I've lectured at writers' conferences."

"And you've told them about query letters, and the necessity of rewriting, I suppose. Do you tell them how you know where you start your story, just which incident you put after which, how you break up your dialogue, how you make the denouement inevitable without telegraphing it?"

"I can do that."

"Then do it right now. Explain it to me!"

Roger Halstead, a teacher of mathematics, flushing to the roots of his receding hairline, said in his soft voice, "Don't do it, Manny. We'll be sitting here all night and none of us is interested. Not even Mario."

"I won't – but I can."

"You *can't,*" said Gonzalo, "because you can't describe the intuition involved. Enough intuition is talent, and a hell of a lot of it is genius, and intuition can't be taught."

Geoffrey Avalon, the patent attorney, said in his solemn baritone, "You stand with the Greeks, Mario. They were quite certain that any outstanding ability was the result of divine inspiration, the working of a god who possessed the person. The word 'enthusiasm,' expressing this process, means 'the god within' in Greek. Naturally, one can't explain the workings of a god to a mere mortal and that, I take it, is your position, Mario."

"Bull!" said Rubin. "Bull to you, Jeff, and to Mario. There is nothing at all mysterious about intuition."

"If you understand it," said Mario, "explain it."

"I will," said Rubin. "All a man knows is what he observes and learns. There is nothing innate except a few biological instincts – certainly nothing cultural. It may be that with experience – with *experience,* Mario – a person learns to interpret what he observes, or to draw inferences, or to do something based on deduction or induction from those observations and past experiences. He does it so rapidly that he generally doesn't bother to isolate the steps in the procedure or even to be aware they exist, so he calls it intuition. – Yes, Henry?"

Henry, the perennial waiter at the Black Widowers' monthly dinner meetings, his bland and uncreased sixtyish face displaying no emotion, said gently, "Dinner is served, Mr. Rubin. If you will sit down, I am sure the rest will follow."

Rubin said, "I suppose I *am* the natural leader."

"No," said James Drake, the organic chemist, stubbing out his cigarette, "as host tonight, I'm the leader. However, the rest of us are naturally afraid you'll eat everything in sight if we don't all sit down to protect our rights."

"That depends," said Rubin, "on what we are having tonight. Henry?"

Henry said, "The chef is in an Old English mood, so it will be rib roast and Yorkshire pudding, preceded by a seafood quiche."

"*That's* not Old English," said Rubin.

"The chef is rarely consistent," said Henry, "and I'm afraid his judgment of what will constitute a success for dinner is largely intuitive."

"And largely right too," said Gonzalo, approving. "Whatever you say intuition is,

Manny, some people have more of it than others, and why is that?"

"Some people have more talent than –"

"*Aha!*" said Gonzalo.

Rubin looked haughty and said with stiff politeness, "*If* I am to be allowed to finish my sentence, I will go on to explain that talent is the capacity for fast thought plus, perhaps, muscular deftness, and undoubtedly depends on the physiology of the brain and on nothing more mysterious than that."

"That's mysterious enough," said Drake.

"Mysterious now, but not necessarily forever," said Rubin, "and when we learn enough about the brain, talent and genius will be as non-mysterious as eye color."

"That's just your intuitive guess," shot back Gonzalo.

Rubin's reply was lost in quiche and the dinner conversation grew more general.

Throughout the argument the guest of the evening had maintained a steady and clearly amused silence. Quietly he listened and as quietly he sipped his martini.

His name was Simon Alexander. His black hair and black mustache, each thick and luxuriant enough to give him a Satanic appearance, or, failing that, a Levantine one, were his most prominent features. The small and persistent smile on his face seemed to accentuate the Satanism.

When the coffee was served, however, and Drake tapped his spoon against the water glass, Alexander, as though in anticipation, grew serious.

Drake said, "Gentlemen, it is time to grill our esteemed guest, and Manny, since you've been clattering away more insupportably even than usual, suppose you supervise the grilling."

Rubin said, "I'm sorry you find mental stimulation insupportable, Jim, but I'm not surprised." He took a quick sip of his coffee, signaled Henry for a bit of a freshener, then said, "Well, Mr. Alexander, or, if you prefer, Simon, how do you justify your existence?"

Alexander's smile returned. "By seeing to it that the American people pay their legal income taxes in full and on time."

There was a stir about the table and even Henry was betrayed into pausing in the precise performance of his duties long enough to cast a penetrating glance at the guest.

Trumbull said, with a distinct suggestion of outrage, "Are you in the employ of the Internal Revenue Service?"

"I am," said Alexander. "I'm in the division of fraud."

"Good God," said Trumbull, "and you offer that as justification for your existence? Horse-whipping with barbed wire is what it justifies." He cast a lowering glance at Drake.

Drake said, "Give him a chance, Tom. It takes all kinds to make a world and, aside from his profession, Simon is one of Nature's noblemen."

Alexander waved his hand. "It's all right, Jim. Tax collectors have always been the favorite villains of humanity from the moment they first appeared in ancient Sumeria five thousand years ago and invented writing in order to keep score. Besides, I think Mr. Trumbull was merely expressing himself colorfully and didn't really mean it."

"The hell I didn't," muttered Trumbull.

Rubin, who had held his peace in a markedly aggrieved manner, now raised his voice. "Since I'm grilling today, may I continue? Do you mind keeping quiet, Tom?"

Trumbull said, "Circumstances moved me."

Rubin waited for silence, then said, "Mr. Alexander – I withdraw the Simon, since through the common law of humanity you can have no friends here, or possibly anywhere – how can your role in tax collection be taken as justifying your existence?"

Alexander said, "I think it is not difficult to see that the I.R.S. represents the single essential arm of the government. Presidents can die and be replaced at once. Congress can bumble, the Supreme Court can drag, and we can lose ground diplomatically, economically, even militarily, yet perhaps make it all up afterward.

"However, let the tax structure of the nation falter and the government can no longer function. That would mean a spreading paralysis far wider, longer, and deeper than anything that can possibly occur short of a thermonuclear war."

Rubin said, "But the tax structure is not likely to falter, is it?"

"Not in the sense that the physical machinery is likely to break apart or that the computers will stop working. No, the weak link is the taxpayer himself. The American budget now approaches one-third of a trillion dollars annually and the largest part of this is collected out of the unwilling wallets of Americans everywhere."

"Sorry, Manny," said Trumbull angrily, "but I've got to interrupt. What the hell has 'unwilling' got to do with it? You enforce your own interpretation of the rules, act as prosecuting attorney and judge, hound us relentlessly, treat us as guilty till we prove ourselves innocent, and are perfectly ready to jail us if you can. What do you care if we're unwilling?"

"In the first place," said Alexander, "our judgments can be appealed to the courts. We are not the last word. Secondly, it would be much more harmful if we were not relentless. Despite everything we do, we cannot audit everyone, we cannot check into everything. If we tried, the cost would far outweigh what additional money we could collect. No, we are forced to depend on the average American filling out a reasonably honest return and we can count on this only so long as that average American is convinced of the essential honesty of the system. Within the bounds of the law – and the law is not completely equitable, but that's not our fault – we must show neither favor nor mercy or the structure will break down.

"Thus, although Al Capone could commit theft on a grand scale and could even murder with impunity, he could be caught and punished on income-tax evasion. There is nothing ironical in this. Income-tax evasion is the greater crime. Similarly, nothing that Nixon and Agnew did prior to their forced resignations was as mischievous as their tampering with the I.R.S. and their making out of dubious income-tax returns. That they were willing to shake the faith of the American people in the honesty of the tax structure was of all their misdeeds the most unforgivable."

Rubin said, "You're serious about this now? You're not pulling our legs?"

"Dead-serious."

"Good God, Jim," Rubin said, "we ought to ask for your resignation. You've brought in a guy who's going to make it difficult for me to indulge in a little bit of honest expense-padding next time round."

Avalon cleared his throat. "I don't consciously pad, but I must admit that the I.R.S. and I might not agree on just what constitutes a deductible expense."

"Then you deduct it till we tell you otherwise," said Alexander agreeably. "That's the tax-man's version of keeping you innocent till proved guilty – but none of this is what I came here prepared to talk about."

"Oh," said Rubin, "what are you prepared for?"

"Jim told me," said Alexander, "that the Black Widowers like to hear some tale that involves a bit of a puzzle and I happen to have one."

"Jim was wrong to tell you that," said

Avalon austerely. "We meet for the purpose of participating in stimulating conversation and a puzzle is not necessary. However –"

Alexander smiled. "In that connection, I was amused by the preprandial quarrel over the nature of intuition, since it is with a matter of intuition that my story is concerned."

"Telepathy!" said Gonzalo at once.

"No, I think not," said Alexander. "Actually, the whole conversation illustrated Mr. Rubin's thesis. I agree with him that intuition is undetected observation and deduction, and I would like to point out that what is often considered telepathy is the same. Thus, when Jim introduced me, he said – and I think these are his exact words – "This is Simon Alexander, an investigator of sorts and a very good one. I think he can sense criminality by some kind of inner magic.' Isn't that what you said, Jim?"

"I think so," said Drake.

"I notice you said 'an investigator of sorts,'" growled Trumbull. "Jim didn't say you were from the I.R.S."

Alexander said, "I am trying to make the point that the introduction took place when the drinks were being passed around – as the brandy is now, I see. – Henry, do we have any Curacao?"

"I believe so, sir."

"I'll have some then. With everyone concentrating on alcohol, I don't think anyone heard the introduction. Does anyone recall having heard it?"

There were no bites on that one, and Alexander smoothed his mustache with one forefinger and accepted the small glass with its orange-colored content from Henry.

"But if Rubin and Gonzalo did not *consciously* hear it," he said, "they nevertheless heard it, I'm convinced, and that bit about sensing criminality by some kind of inner magic is what sparked the argument on intuition. Of course, I *don't* use some kind of inner magic. I use reason and I am always quite conscious of the details of the reasoning. Except one –" He looked thoughtful.

Drake lit a cigarette from the dying stub of his old one and said, "Tell us, Simon."

"I intend to," said Alexander, "but it has a certain personal confidentiality about it. I have been given to understand that everything that goes on here is confidential."

"Everything," said Trumbull pointedly, "and that includes everything *we* say. We take it for granted that nothing *you* hear can be used against us as far as our taxes are concerned."

"Agreed," said Alexander, "but please be careful what you say, as I would rather not be asked to place too great a load on my integrity."

He sipped his Curacao, looked pensive, and, for some reason, particularly Satanic.

"You know, of course," he said, "that computers are now the life-blood of the I.R.S. We couldn't operate without them. Because they never hesitate, never tire, never grow bored, they are our great strength. Because they never think, they are our great weakness.

"To exploit a computer, however, and take advantage of its weakness, one must know every detail of a computer's working, and this eliminates almost all the human race. And it puts us off our guard.

"Some years ago the I.R.S. was royally diddled by someone who knew his computers, by a mathematician who was tired of the type of remuneration that mathematicians receive."

Halsted, who taught mathematics at a junior high school, sighed and said, "I know the type."

"The specific details of his operation don't concern you, but he managed to get a job that would involve the servicing of certain of our computers. For the purpose, he built himself a new statistical background, a new name, a new appearance, all the way down to a new social security number. How he managed that I won't tell you since, confidentiality or not, there is no point in spreading knowledge of the techniques of successful knavery."

"I agree," said Avalon, nodding.

"Nor," said Alexander, "will I tell you exactly how he managed to reprogram one key computer – for, the truth is, I don't understand it myself. I am no scientist or mathematician. Still, it was done. For a period of five years our mathematician – let us call him Jarvis – received large tax refunds while paying no taxes. He received more money in that interval than he could have earned in a lifetime of honest endeavor.

"He might still be receiving the money but for the accidental uncovering of an inconsistency in the program. The detection was the result of a most unusual coincidence, and I assure you the I.R.S. could not have been more dismayed, or embarrassed, at the event. Naturally, two things were at once essential. The money leak must be stopped and the computer programs so modified as to make the Jarvis type of fraud impossible in the future. That was carried through at once in the greatest secrecy. The secrecy was needed not so much to keep the individual officials from looking ridiculous, though that was a factor, but to keep the Service itself from losing the confidence of the American people."

"They shall never learn the truth from any of us," said Gonzalo, with suspiciously intense gravity.

"The second thing," Alexander went on, "was to catch Jarvis, make him return what money was left, and clap him in jail for as long as the law would allow. It was the Al Capone reasoning, you see. Jarvis might get away with murder without shaking the foundation of American civilization, but he could not be allowed to get away with income-tax fraud. – And that was where I came in. I was put in charge of the case.

"My reputation in the Service is, perhaps, an exaggerated one. More than one person there suspects, as Jim told you, that I solve my cases with some inner magic, with some mysterious intuitive faculty that defies analysis. It has been said among us, for instance, that I can look at a tax return that seems somehow absolutely clean and yet tell that somehow money was clinging to the taxpayer's fingers. Or that I could interview a person and know for certain that there was a thief hidden inside the saint.

"Actually, there is no magic in it at all. I

have a certain cleverness at observation and reasoning and a great deal of experience. My memory is excellent and I have encountered all varieties of behavior patterns – and all the ways of laundering returns too. What seems like magic or intuition boils down to noting small things that others don't and attaching the proper importance to them.

"It works the other way around too. I can often detect the saint inside the thief. I am quite certain, for instance, that you, Mr. Trumbull, are not short on your returns by even as much as fifty dollars. I suspect that you are ashamed of your relative honesty, and take it out by vilifying the office you do not defraud. And that's not a guess. I've met others like you."

It was hard for Trumbull to flush through his tan, but his expression made the flush unnecessary.

Avalon said, "I'm afraid your reputation is ruined, Tom. – Please go on, Mr. Alexander."

"To put it in figures, in nearly a quarter of a century at my job, I have almost never pointed a finger in the direction of either guilt or innocence and been proved entirely wrong."

"A quarter of a century?" said Avalon. "How old are you, Mr. Alexander?"

"Fifty-two."

"You don't look it," and Avalon's finger went unconsciously to his own mustache.

Alexander said, "There's gray in my hair, too, but I touch it up a little. Not so much out of vanity, you understand, as because the darkness seems to give me a forbidding appearance that is useful to me in my line of work. However –

"Jarvis was not an easy quarry. He could tell, somehow, that the game was up, and when the next refund came to him – this time under the eyes of the Service – it remained uncashed. It's not impossible he had an ally within the Service, but never mind that. Tracing him wasn't easy. He had quit his job long before and all records we had concerning him were false, down to his social security number, which, we suddenly discovered, was attached to no human being.

"I was forced to follow the most evanescent clues and to build up the picture of the human being who had done the deed. We left absolutely nothing unturned that might lead us to the identity of the thief and we finally had several possibilities, all dim and uncertain. Different operatives were assigned to each lead. The task was somehow to locate enough evidence to warrant a concentration of forces, a full-scale investigation of one particular man – and an arrest, if possible.

"My own target was a rather mousy man of average weight and height and of undistinguished appearance. That, in itself, was a good sign, because the fraud had to be carried out by someone who could be unnoticeable at crucial moments. He had a vague background that could not easily be traced without tipping our hand too soon – again an encouraging circumstance. At crucial periods he seemed to be particularly untraceable.

"Unfortunately, all this was negative and such things could never be made to stick. We needed some *positive* linkings. We had to locate him at the site of action each time, prove computer expertise, and so on. For that kind of evidence I haunted him like the ghost of a vulture. In fact, I managed to collect a circle of acquaintances in common with him, and I managed to be present at social gatherings along with him.

"Then, at one gathering in early November – he quiet and watchful, nursing a single drink for an hour, and I almost as quiet, certainly as watchful, and equally abstemious – the host spoke of Halloween. He had a seven-year-old daughter who had gone out trick-or-treating, along with several older friends, and who had come back in ecstasy.

"That rang true to me for I remembered very well my own daughter's first experience of the sort and I said, 'Yes, I have always thought that, were it not for the enormous commercial overweighting of the Yuletide, a child's spontaneous reaction would be to treat Halloween with the full excitement of Christmas.'

"And, surprisingly, my quarry spoke up. As though overwhelmed by an emotion that forced his naturally quiet personality into the limelight, he said, with a warm smile that lightened and almost transfigured his face, 'You are quite right. In a way, Halloween may be considered precisely equal to Christmas.' Those were his exact words, gentlemen, for I noted them at the time with particular care."

Rubin asked, "Why?"

"Because, as a result of that comment, I instantly and completely eliminated him as a suspect. So certain was I, that I remember having the distinct impulse to clap him on the shoulder and invite him out for a drink to celebrate his innocence. I couldn't though, for I suppose his own unexpected warmth had embarrassed him. As soon as he made the remark, he looked frightened and melted away. My own attention was distracted for a moment, and when I turned to find him, he was gone."

Alexander paused and finished the last of his Curacao. He said, "At the time, my sudden conviction of innocence might have seemed pure intuition – even to myself – but it wasn't. I cling to Rubin's hypothesis that intuition is undetected reasoning. Here is the reasoning as I figured it out later.

"Working laboriously from the tiniest beginnings, we had drawn a picture of our criminal, this Jarvis. He was a mathematician and had no family. The chances were that he was not only unmarried and childless, but that he had no siblings and that his parents may have died while he was young. He was cold, utterly cold – and I don't mean that he was ruthless and sadistic – merely that he lacked any desire or occasion for love and affection. Let me put it in a way that has great significance for me. He was not what I call 'a family man.'"

Halsted pleated the tablecloth absently and said, "You, I take it, *are* a family man."

"Completely. My parents, two brothers, and a sister are all close. I married a childhood sweetheart, have three children, and a grandson newly born, plus nieces and nephews. I know the emotions of a family man and no one, *no one*, could have spoken with such genuine warmth of children's holidays unless he had experienced the kind of love and affection that accompany those days. My quarry spoke that way; Jarvis could not have; conclusion, my quarry was not Jarvis and was innocent. What seemed like intuition was, after all, a process of reasoning.

"Intuition or reason, I reported my belief in his innocence to my superiors and the tracking down of the remaining possibilities grew correspondingly more intense. Five months later we caught the criminal and he is now in prison and likely to remain there a long time. Some of the money has been recovered; not all, of course."

He paused and Avalon broke the short silence that followed, saying, "I am delighted to have a happy ending for the department, but you spoke of a puzzle and I see none."

Simon Alexander sighed. "The happy ending is a qualified one. Having dismissed my suspect, we nevertheless found the other suspects fading as well. One after another they proved to be incompatible with the conditions of the fraud. One day, out of nothing but desperation, I returned to my own dismissed suspect and something unexpected arose that cast a new light on the affair. Astounded, I followed it up and had him – my own suspect whose innocence I had previously maintained and, virtually, guaranteed. He was the criminal after all.

"What puzzles me and, even now, keeps me awake occasionally, is the incongruity of it. He did indeed turn out to be what we had suspected all along – a man without family, love, or affection. Yet his remark about Christmas and Halloween, and the tone in which it was uttered, indicated precisely the reverse. How is this contradiction possible and how could he have used it to throw me off the scent?"

There was a silence around the table as Alexander waited for an answer.

Avalon finally spoke, staring at his empty brandy glass. "Mr. Alexander, despite easy theorizing, the fact remains that human beings are complicated and inconsistent creatures. There are undoubtedly contradictory aspects in the character of your suspect or of any man. You'll have to chalk it up to a bad break."

"I'd like to," said Alexander, "and I've tried to do so, but it is my experience that in fundamentals human beings are *not* inconsistent. A man who always puts on his left shoe first, may switch party allegiance and swap wives, but he will always put on his left shoe first."

"Nothing will stop him from putting on his right shoe first, however uncomfortable that might be," said Halsted, "if it is necessary to do so to fool someone. He stepped purposely out of character to mislead you."

Alexander didn't answer at once. Then he said, "I doubt that. Even if he knew I was at his heels, and that's conceivable, he couldn't possibly have known me so well as to be sure that one short, apparently irrelevant sentence, would deflect me."

Rubin said, "The remark might have been misanthropically in character, and you interpreted it wrongly because of your own happy associations with the holidays. What the suspect might have meant was that Christmas was just as full of superstitions as Halloween."

Alexander said, "An interesting thought, but the expression on his face and the tone of his voice belied that. The expression was happy and very delighted. I am *still* sure he meant it as a loving remark."

Gonzalo said, "He could be a *Peanuts* fan and was thinking of Linus' 'Great Pumpkin,' which is a kind of satire on Santa

Claus. That would set up a strong association between Halloween and Christmas."

There was a general hoot from the audience, but Alexander held up his hand. "Actually, that's the first suggestion I hadn't thought of myself. It doesn't sound in the least likely to me, but I will check whether or not he was a *Peanuts* fan."

Trumbull said, "We don't have enough to go on. I don't think anything can be deduced from what he said to set your mind at ease. Sorry."

Drake said, "I agree, but we haven't heard from Henry yet."

"Henry?" said Alexander in surprise, swiveling in his seat.

Henry cleared his throat. "I admit, gentlemen, that a thought entered my mind the moment Mr. Alexander gave us the suspect's remark."

"Oh?" said Alexander, "and just what thought was that?"

"The suspect, sir, did not say, as you or I might have said, that Halloween was just like Christmas or just as good as Christmas, or even equivalent to Christmas. If you quoted him correctly he said Halloween was 'precisely equal' to Christmas. Surely that sounds like a mathematician speaking and would be in character."

Alexander snorted. "Feeble. A non-mathematician might have happened to put it that way if he were an extremely meticulous person."

Henry said softly, "Perhaps. Yet we might find more in the statement if we treat it mathematically than anyone has yet pointed out. After all, if your suspect were indeed the guilty man, he would be not only a mathematician, he would also be a computer specialist."

Alexander looked annoyed. "What has that to do with it?"

Henry said, "Mr. Alexander, listening to the gentlemen of the Black Widowers month after month is an education in itself and there have been times when I have pursued my reading in the directions they have opened up for me. Mr. Halsted, for instance, once discussed the rationale behind positional notation, the manner in which our Arabic numerals are constructed, and I went on to read further about the matter. If you'd care to have me explain it, I'm sure Mr. Halsted will be glad to correct me if I make a mistake."

Halsted said, "I'll be glad to, Henry, but I don't see what you're driving at."

"You will in a moment, sir. Our ordinary numbers are written to the base ten. The first column at the right are the ones. The next to the left are the tens, the next are the hundreds, or ten times ten, the next are the thousands or ten times ten times ten, and so on. Thus, the number, 1231, is *one* times a thousand plus *two* times a hundred plus *three* times ten plus *one,* and that comes to 1231."

"Right so far," said Halsted.

"But there's no need to consider ten the only possible base for a number system," said Henry. "You could use nine, for instance. The right-hand column in a nine-based system would be ones, the next to the left would be nines, the next would be eighty-ones or nine times nine, the next would be – uh – seven hundred twenty-nines or nine times nine times nine, and so on. The number 1231 would, in the nine-based system, be *one* times seven hundred twenty-nine plus *two* times eighty-one plus *three* times nine plus *one.* That would be, if you would allow me a moment to work it out, the equivalent of 919 in our ordinary ten-based system."

He scribbled hastily on a menu and held it up. "You could write the result this way: 1231 (nine-based) = 919 (ten-based)."

Halsted, Drake, and Rubin nodded. Avalon and Trumbull looked thoughtful, and Alexander shook his head impatiently.

Gonzalo said, "But why would anyone use a nine-based system and multiply nines?"

Halsted said, "The other number-bases look complicated, Mario, only because our number system is designed to fit ten as a base. Mathematically, all are equally rational, though some are more convenient than others. For instance, in computers, it is particularly useful at times to use – uh, oh –"

He looked at Henry with a grin and said, "I get it, Henry, but you keep on and finish."

"Thank you, sir," said Henry. "As Mr. Halsted was about to say, the eight-based system is, I understand, useful to computers. The number thirty-one, for instance, in the ten-based system is, of course, *three* times ten plus *one*, or thirty-one. In the eight-based system, however, it is *three* times eight plus *one*, or twenty-five.

"We can therefore write" – he used the menu again – "31 (eight-based) = 25 (ten-based)."

He went on, "The different number bases are sometimes given names derived from the Latin names of the numbers. The Latin for ten is 'decem,' so a ten-based number belongs to the decimal system. The Latin for eight is 'octo,' so eight-based numbers belong to the octal system. We can therefore write this – 31 (octal) = 25 (decimal).

"By coincidence, in 'octo' and 'decem' we have the months October and December –"

Rubin roared in sudden delight. "No coincidence at all. The Romans before Julius Caesar's time started this year in March. By that system, October was the eighth month and December the tenth month, and they were named accordingly."

Henry nodded his head and said, "Thank you, sir. If, then, we abbreviate the terms 'octal' and 'decimal' in a natural way and omit the parentheses we have – 31 Oct = 25 Dec. How can this be described better than by saying that Halloween, which falls on 31 October, is *precisely equal* to Christmas, which falls on 25 December."

Alexander's mouth had tended to slacken through this but now he tightened his jaw muscle and said, "Are you trying to tell me that the thief, blurting out his remark without thinking, gave away the fact that he was a computer expert?"

"Yes, sir," said Henry. "It was not out of embarrassment that a look of alarm crossed his face and that he left as soon as he could. It must have been out of fright at the thought of having slipped into his real character. – At that moment, if the significance of his remark had been seen by you, it would have been wise to arrange for his arrest."

Alexander looked chagrined. "Well, I didn't see it – I interpreted it the wrong way. – But wait, all this is clever and may even be right considering that the man in question proved to be the criminal, but how would you account for that look of love on his face? *That* was what threw me."

Henry said softly, "You are a family man, sir, and that is your point of view. You naturally interpret love in human terms alone. I, myself, am not a family man, and I know that love is broader than that. Even a misanthrope who hates the human race could love, and deeply too."

"Love what?" said Alexander impatiently.

"The beauty and surprises of mathematics, for one thing," said Henry.

Edward D. Hoch

Captain Leopold and the Impossible Murder

Captain Leopold has a penchant for "impossible crimes." Perhaps they come this way because he secretly likes them – they are baffling and frustrating, and they test his innermost resources. And this one was a beaut – it challenged his shrewdest jigsawing.

How can a man be murdered in his own car, strangled by a cord in the midst of a traffic jam, with no one else in the car and no one else seen entering or leaving the car? It couldn't have been suicide – but then how can a dead man drive a car? As Captain Leopold put it: "It was one hell of a case!"...

"Automobiles!" Leopold was to remark long after it was over. "I never had a case involving so many different automobiles! The crime, the clue, the capture, the confession – each involved a different car. There was an auto driven by a dead man, and another that hadn't been driven by anyone in thirty years. It was one hell of a case!"

It began at dusk on a November afternoon when Leopold's own car was in the garage for some minor repair work. Lieutenant Fletcher had offered him a ride home, and they'd chosen the Eastern Avenue route to avoid the rush-hour traffic on the expressway. But the usually deserted street was jammed with cars, and as they approached a familiar curve by an embankment Fletcher spotted some trouble ahead.

"Looks like we gotta go to work, Captain. One driver's out of his car. It could be a fight."

"All right," Leopold sighed. "I wasn't hungry anyway. Turn on your flasher."

They left the car and walked up to the scene of the trouble. A sandy-haired young man, standing at the open door of a late-model hatchback was gesturing wildly to a motorist in the next car. "What's the trouble here?" Fletcher asked. "We're police." Leopold followed behind him, feeling just a bit like a traffic cop.

The young man turned in obvious agitation. "I think this driver is dead!"

Fletcher reached in and felt for a pulse. "What happened?"

"We were caught in this traffic jam for like

twenty minutes, just inching along. Finally, when it began to clear up and move, he just sat there ahead of me. I got out of my car after honking a few times, to see what the trouble was. God, I think he's dead!"

Fletcher straightened up and glanced at Leopold. "I'll radio for an ambulance."

Leopold lowered his voice. "Is he –?"

"Dead as he'll ever be, Captain."

"Heart attack?"

Fletcher shook his head. "He's got a cord wrapped around his neck. Somebody strangled him."

Leopold's eyes widened. "In the middle of a traffic jam?"

"You figure it out, Captain."

The young man's name was Sam Prowdy, and he told a straightforward story. He was a plumber, employed by a building contractor, and he'd been on his way home from work along with everyone else when an accident on the expressway forced them into a traffic jam on Eastern Avenue. He'd noticed nothing unusual about the little green car ahead of him, and certainly hadn't seen anyone leave it in the middle of the traffic jam.

"Sure, I'd have noticed," he insisted back

in Leopold's office. "Somebody gets out of a car ahead of you, you notice it, don't you?"

"It was just getting dark," Leopold pointed out. "You could have missed it."

"I didn't miss a thing! The guy was alone in the car, and he was driving it. Then we were stuck for about five minutes and he stopped moving. I honked and got out to check on him and that's when you guys came up."

"Did you know the dead man?" Leopold asked.

"Hell, no! I still don't know him. Who was he?"

"His name was Vincent Conners. Thirty-two years old, with a wife and two children in the suburbs. Worked as a stockbroker with Bland and Burnett."

"Never heard of him!"

"All right," Leopold said with a sigh. "We'll probably be contacting you again, but you can go now."

When he was alone with Fletcher he said, "There was nothing to hold him on. A woman in the next car confirmed that he'd just opened the door of Conners' auto when we arrived. He couldn't have done it. Besides, Conners had already been dead anywhere up to a half hour according to the preliminary medical report."

Fletcher snorted. "Where does that leave us? With a dead man driving a car around town?"

"I don't know," Leopold admitted. "But I guess we have to talk to Mrs. Conners."

The home was in a suburb touching Long Island Sound, the sort of area in which local stockbrokers were expected to live. Lights burned in every window, and a neighbor opened the door as Leopold and Fletcher approached. "Mrs. Conners is in the kitchen," the woman said. "The children are over at my house."

Leopold nodded and went into the brightly lit kitchen. A few others, neighbors and relatives, stepped aside to let him pass. It was a gloomy setting for all its brightness, and the heavy atmosphere was one he'd encountered too many times before. Sudden violent death had a way of settling over lives like a somber fog.

Linda Conners was small and fragile-looking, with long dark hair and high cheekbones. Only one man chose to remain in the kitchen while Leopold spoke to her, and that was one of her husband's employers, Frank Bland. He looked like a stockbroker too. He might have been another Conners, ten years older and forty pounds heavier. "She's had a great shock," he explained to Leopold. "They were very close."

"I'm sure they were. Mrs. Conners, I hate to bother you, but I know you want to help in finding your husband's killer."

She took a sip of coffee and gazed up at him with pale eyes. "There's nothing I can tell you. No one had a reason for killing Vince. Everyone liked him."

"It must have been a car thief," Frank Bland suggested. "Someone Vince caught in the vehicle, who strangled him from behind."

"We have a bit of a problem because no one was seen leaving the vehicle," Leopold said. "Yet your husband couldn't have driven it after he was strangled." Even as he spoke the words, he was aware of how incongruous this suburban kitchen setting was with talk of an impossible crime.

"He once told me he'd probably die in his car, the way his father had."

"You needn't get into all that, Linda," Frank Bland cautioned. "The Captain is only investigating this case."

But Leopold was interested. "What happened to Vince's father?"

She tried to take another sip of coffee but the cup was empty. Bland refilled it from a nearby pot. "Well, he was shot in a hunting accident. Thirty years ago."

"What did that have to do with a car?"

"He bled to death on the back seat, while he was being rushed back to town. The car belonged to one of Vince's aunts, and they never used it again. It's still up on blocks in their garage."

"You say this happened thirty years ago?"

"Yes."

"Then your husband would have been around two years old."

"Yes."

"Is his mother still living?"

"She remarried, moved out West somewhere. He never sees – saw her."

"Is this aunt still alive?"

"Oh, yes. There are two of them. They live together in the family homestead."

"They're his closest kin in this area?"

"*I'm* his closest kin. And the children."

"Of course," Leopold corrected himself. "I meant besides you."

She nodded. "Yes, Aunt Gert and Aunt Flag."

"Aunt Flag?"

"That's what they've always called her."

"Perhaps you'd better give me their address."

"Certainly. Frank, could you hand me a piece of paper?"

She wrote out the address and handed it to Leopold. "I hope you find the killer," she said quietly.

When they were outside, Fletcher asked, "We going over to see the aunts now, Captain?"

Leopold looked at his watch. It was already after ten. "No, it's a bit late to be upsetting a couple of old ladies. We'll see them in the morning."

Connie Trent was in the office before Leopold, checking out a shooting at an all-night restaurant. "I heard about last evening," she said. "You and Fletcher drop right into them, don't you?"

Leopold nodded. "Can't even get home at night without finding a murder on the road. How about it? Any ideas how a man can be strangled to death in a car in the middle of a traffic jam? While he's alone?"

She thought for a moment. "If the window was open someone could have lassoed him."

"The window was only open a couple of inches, and none of the other drivers saw anything like a lasso. But thanks anyway."

"Any time," she said with a smile, and went back to typing her report.

Leopold and Fletcher reached the Conners homestead just after eleven and went up the crumbling sidewalk to the front door. The woman who answered was not as elderly as they'd expected, but she moved slowly, with a hint of some hidden disability.

"You'd be police," she said without looking at Leopold's identification. "My sister and I have been expecting you, ever since we heard about poor Vincent. Come in – I'm Gert Conners."

"We're sorry to bother you like this, Miss Conners. But outside of his wife and children you're the closest kin. We don't mind admitting we're baffled as to a possible motive."

Gert Conners pushed back a stray wisp of gray hair. "They said on the news he probably surprised a car thief."

"Well, that's one theory. But it doesn't cover all the facts."

She'd led them into a musty sitting room with lace curtains on the windows. A second gray-haired woman was seated in a rocking chair, busily knitting something long and blue. She smiled as they entered but didn't rise. "This is Aunt Flag," Gert Conners said.

Aunt Flag nodded as Leopold and

Fletcher introduced themselves. "I know you'll find out who killed our nephew," she said. "He was a good lad. Always came to see us."

Aunt Flag was perhaps ten years older than Aunt Gert, and obviously feeble. "You have an unusual name," Leopold commented.

"It's really Flagula, but that's a terrible name for a person. I've been called Flag all my life. We were always Aunt Flag and Aunt Gert to Vincent."

Leopold had taken a seat at one end of the claw-footed couch, and Fletcher gently lowered himself into position at the other end. "Do either of you ladies know any reason why Vincent might have been murdered? Any troubles, any enemies? Perhaps a feud from long ago?"

"There was never anything like that," Aunt Flag assured them. "He was always very honest and open, even as a child. We saw a great deal of him as a child, because of course his father died when he was only two."

"That would be your brother?"

Aunt Gert nodded. "Our brother George – our only brother."

"Just how did George die?"

There might have been a look that passed

between the sisters before Aunt Gert replied. "It was a hunting accident, one of those foolish things. They were out shooting pheasants and George dropped his shotgun somehow. It went off and hit him in the stomach. His wife helped him back to the car and put him on the rear seat. They hurried back to town as fast as they could, but poor George was dead by the time they reached the hospital. He'd bled to death on the back seat of the car."

"It was your car?" Leopold prompted her.

Aunt Gert frowned. "Who told you that? No, actually it was Aunt Flag's car. It was right after the war and cars were still scarce. George didn't have one of his own, so he borrowed it."

"We never used it again," Aunt Flag said. "It's back in the garage."

So both father and son had died violent deaths in automobiles, separated in time by 30 years. Leopold wondered about it, wondered what effect the father's death might have had on the son. "Thank you," he said. "You've been very helpful."

Aunt Gert walked outside with them, kicking a stone from the crumbling walk. "I really must get this fixed," she said.

"Is Aunt Flag confined to her chair?" Leopold asked.

"Oh, she gets around but she's very feeble since her stroke. I do all the shopping and I take care of her."

"That must be hard on you."

"She's my sister."

"Of course." Leopold looked up at the dappled sky, wondering if the sun would break through. "When did you last see your nephew alive, Miss Conners?"

"Oh, it must have been about a week ago."

"When he came to visit you, did he ever go out to the garage and look at that car his father died in?"

"Why would you ask a question like that? Of course not! He came to see us, not to stir up memories of the past."

"Did his wife come with him last week?"

Aunt Gert avoided Leopold's eyes. "Not last week, no."

"But she did come sometimes?"

"Not often. She has no use for old people."

"You're not old," Leopold reassured her, climbing into his car while Fletcher got behind the wheel.

"Thank you. You're very kind."

"Just one other question. Who was with your brother George the day of his hunting accident?"

"With him? No one was with him, only his wife. There were just the two of them out there when it happened."

It was Connie who tracked down the information and brought it to Leopold's office later in the day. "I ran up a small fortune in long-distance phone calls for this," she said. "I hope it's worth it."

"If it helps solve this damned case it's worth it. What have you got, Connie?"

"George Conners served in the European Theater of Operations during World War Two, and took part in the D-day invasion of Normandy. He met and married a British girl named Jean Hemmings. Apparently it was a rush marriage – their only child Vincent was born two months later, near the end of 1944. Conners and his wife returned to America in the spring of '45, when the European war ended. It was the fall of 1946 when he was killed in the hunting accident, just after Vincent's second birthday."

Leopold interrupted. "Was there any sort of police investigation at the time?"

"Just routine, apparently. Anyway, the widow Jean remarried soon after – within a year – to a car salesman here in town. I don't think Vincent was ever close to his mother and stepfather. When he was eighteen he went off to college and they moved out West. Except for occasional brief visits he never lived with them again."

Leopold grunted and stared out the window. "What are you thinking, Captain?" Fletcher asked. "That his wife shot him?"

"Like in that Ernest Hemingway story," Connie said. "The one about Macomber."

"She shot him and married another man," Leopold said quietly. "And thirty years later his son dies in another car. Did his wife kill him too, in order to marry another man?"

Fletcher snapped his fingers. "That guy Frank Bland! I thought he was being awfully chummy for an employer. Do you think –?"

"Check on him, Fletcher. Talk to Conners' coworkers. See if there was any gossip around the office."

"But the two crimes are entirely different," Connie pointed out. "Knowing about the first one doesn't help us in the least toward solving the second one. How could they possibly be connected?"

"If Vincent suspected his father was murdered all those years ago – suspected it through something he overheard or half remembered – he might have mentioned it to his wife. That might have planted the idea in her mind."

"It's all guesswork," Connie said.

Leopold agreed. "But in this case we've got nothing to go on but guesswork."

Both Connie and Fletcher had duties involving other cases, and after Fletcher's report on Frank Bland the following day the investigation was left pretty much in Leopold's hands. Fletcher hadn't come up with anything concrete about Bland. He was divorced, and he occasionally dined at the Conners' home – but this could have been nothing more suspicious than the time-honored custom of having the boss to dinner.

With the Conners funeral only a day away, the medical examiner still had not ruled on the cause of death. Speaking with Leopold, he was inclined to rule it a suicide, simply because "It couldn't be murder, could it, Captain?"

To which Leopold replied, "Doc, did you ever hear of anybody committing suicide by strangling himself with a cord while driving in a traffic jam?"

"I guess not," the medical examiner agreed.

Leopold picked up the murder weapon and examined it once more. It was a loop of knotted cord that they'd had to cut away from the dead man's neck. It fit the most likely newspaper theory of the case – that a car thief had been trapped in the back seat by Conners' unexpected return and had strangled Conners from the rear.

But that left a big question mark.

If the thief left the car immediately, how did a dead man drive the automobile for nearly a half hour? And if the killer was still in the car when it was caught in the traffic jam, how did he leave it without being seen?

It was as close to an absolute impossibility as anything Leopold had ever encountered.

So he went back to the medical examiner again. "Doc, can't you be more precise as to the time of death?"

"We're talking about minutes here, Captain. Remember it was nearly an hour after you found him before I saw the body. I'd be inclined to say he died twenty to thirty minutes before you found him, but if you say that's impossible I'll cut it to a shorter period."

Leopold accepted that and went in search of a new lead. In the police garage where the murder car was impounded he had a mechanic sit in the front seat while he sat in the back and went through the motions of strangling the mechanic. But that didn't satisfy him. It was all wrong. Finally he decided to follow up Fletcher's investigation by calling on the dead man's employer.

Frank Bland greeted him with a wan smile. "Still at it, Captain?"

"Still at it." He glanced through the glass wall of the office at the lighted display board of noon stock quotations. "I imagine this is a profitable business."

The stout man shifted uneasily. "We have our good years."

"I mean, Vincent made a comfortable living here."

"The salary and commissions are good, and we have a generous life-insurance program which will benefit his widow. He had no reason to complain."

Leopold chose his words carefully. "He gave no hint of anything wrong on the day he was killed?"

"Nothing. He left early, right after the market closed. I was surprised he wasn't home long before he was killed. But there was nothing else unusual."

"And you say his wife would benefit from the insurance?"

Frank Bland half rose from his chair. "Surely you're not implying that Linda had anything to do with this terrible thing!"

"No, no – don't misunderstand me. I was only thinking that Conners was well off financially. I visited his aunts and they would seem to be part of a monied family. And you've confirmed that Conners had a good income here. Of course if his wife divorced him she'd lose most of that."

"I can assure you Linda was happily married. I saw a great deal of them and they were very close."

"Were there any tensions among his fellow workers? Any clients he steered onto a bum stock?"

Frank Bland sighed. "I thought your Lieutenant Fletcher had been all over this matter. As I told him, I can contribute nothing to the investigation."

"All right," Leopold said. "One more question and I'll be on my way. Did Vincent Conners ever mention his aunts to you? Or the hunting accident that took his father's life?"

"Nothing was ever said about the accident. He may have mentioned his aunts in passing once or twice. I remember asking him one time if he couldn't bring them in as clients."

Leopold rose to leave. "Thank you, Mr. Bland. I hope I don't have to trouble you again."

He got his car out of the parking lot across the street and went back to visit the aunts. On the way he thought about Bland's denial that Vincent had mentioned the hunting accident. Bland had seemed to know about it earlier, and that indicated he'd heard it from Linda.

It was one of those sunny November days when it seemed as if summer was staging a comeback, and he found Aunt Gert trimming rosebushes in the side yard of the house. "So it's you again," she said by way of greeting.

"It's me again. I don't mean to interrupt your work."

She straightened from her task, brushing some loose soil from the knees of her slacks. "The garden takes a great deal of time. Aunt Flag used to help me with it when she was able to."

"I'll try not to take up too much of your time," Leopold said. "But we've come up against a dead end in trying to trace Vince's mother and notify her of his death. Do you have any idea at all where she might have moved out West?"

Aunt Gert shook her head. "We've lost all track of her. I know for a time they were in California, but then Vince told us once his mother had moved to New Mexico. He never said where, though. Doesn't Linda have an address?"

"She claims not. We've asked the police to check the last-known address in Los Angeles."

"It was too bad about Vince and his mother. But it was his step-father's fault they drifted apart. He never took to the lad."

"I was wondering, Miss Conners – as long as I'm out here again, do you think I could have a look at that old car in your garage? I'm something of an antique-car buff –"

"You'd hardly call it an antique," she said. "It's a 1941 Packard, made just before the war."

"Could I see it anyway?"

She hesitated just a moment. "I'll get the key to the garage."

When she opened the garage it gave off a musty odor even more overpowering than the one in the house. It was a cramped one-car garage, separated from the house, as all garages had been back in Leopold's youth. The car was a dull shade of green. Its tires had been removed at some time in the distant past and its axles rested on concrete blocks.

"It seems in good condition," Leopold observed. "You could probably still drive it."

"Never had a license. Never wanted one."

There was no overhead light, but the sunlight coming through the side window was strong enough for him to study the vehicle. He opened the rear door and looked at the back seat, where Vincent Conners' father had bled to death 30 years ago. There were two large bloodstains on the upholstery, about a foot apart. The one on the left was slightly larger.

"You should have sold the car," Leopold suggested. "It does no good remembering."

"He was our brother. Some things have to be remembered."

"Did he really shoot himself, Miss Conners?"

"She said so."

"What do *you* think?"

She was silent for a long time, staring out the driveway at a playful dog across the quiet street. Finally Gert Conners said, very softly, as if it was the first time her tongue had dared give voice to the words, "I think she killed him."

Leopold took a deep breath. The air in the garage seemed suddenly even closer. "And Vincent? Your nephew?"

She looked up at him, puzzled. "How could –?"

There was a noise from the house, a tapping on the rear window. They could see Aunt Flag motioning. "She wants me," Aunt Gert said. "I must go now."

He waited while she locked the garage door, then said goodbye and went back to his car.

Two deaths, with 30 years between. Different, and yet somehow the same.

That afternoon he told Fletcher to put a tail on Linda Conners. "The funeral is tomorrow morning. For the next few days I want to know where she goes and whom she sees."

Oddly enough, Linda Conners phoned Leopold less than an hour after he'd issued his order. Her voice was firm and she seemed in good control of herself. "Captain, I'm calling from the funeral parlor. I understand you've been trying to locate Vince's mother."

"That's right, Mrs. Conners."

"I've found an address that may be her current one. I'll read it to you."

Leopold copied down a street address in Santa Fe, New Mexico. "Do you want to try calling her, Mrs. Conners, or should we contact her about her son's death?"

"I wish you would, Captain. I've only met the woman twice in my life."

"We'll take care of it. Thank you for the address, Mrs. Conners."

Connie was assigned the task of informing Vincent Conners' mother of her son's death. It was not until the following morning, at about the time of the funeral, that Connie managed to reach the woman. "They certainly weren't close," she reported back to Leopold. "She expressed regrets, but that was all. I might have been reporting the death of a distant cousin instead of her only son."

"She has a new life for herself now," Leopold said. "She doesn't want to be reminded of Vincent Conners, or of his father." He was remembering the car in the garage, with its bloodstained back seat – the car that hadn't been driven for 30 years.

"Fletcher says you've put a tail on Linda Conners."

"That's right. I want to know if she sees Frank Bland."

"What will that prove, if we still don't know how Vincent was killed?"

"If we know who, we'll figure out how."

But the two cases – the old one and the new one – were still intertwined in Leopold's mind, and he couldn't help feeling that the answer somehow rested on that bloodstained back seat.

Nothing happened for two days.

Vincent Conners was buried, and Linda Conners cried. Frank Bland attended the funeral and put his arm around the shoulders of the grieving widow.

But you can't arrest a man for doing that.

Finally Leopold telephoned Vincent

Conners' mother in Santa Fe. It was late on Friday, and the autumn sun had already set.

Her name had changed from Jean Hemmings to Jean Conners to Jean Quinlan, but she still retained her British accent. After Leopold had identified himself, she asked. "Is this more about my son's death?"

"Not exactly, Mrs. Quinlan. It's about your husband's death."

"That was thirty years ago!"

"Yes."

"Well, what about it?"

"I realized that the shooting was an accident, and we're not attempting to reopen the case, but I have to ask you one question. It'll help us a great deal with the investigation of your son's killing."

"What is it?"

"Mrs. Quinlan, did you shoot your husband?"

"Shoot him? Of course I didn't shoot him! My God, I loved him – he died in my arms!"

"Yes," Leopold said, "that's exactly what I suspected." And then he asked her one more question, although he already knew the answer to that one too.

As he hung up the telephone, Fletcher hurried into the office. "She's moving, Captain. She left the house by a back door and went through the yards to the next street. Someone picked her up there in a car."

Leopold was on his feet. "Damn! Vincent's hardly cold in his grave. Let's go!"

The unmarked car that was following Linda Conners was put into contact with Leopold's vehicle. "They're heading south on Grand Street, Captain – toward the Sound," the radio crackled.

"Finding them together won't convict anybody of murder," Fletcher reminded Leopold.

"No, but if we show up unexpectedly Bland might panic. If she's sneaking around to meet him, she's got something to hide."

The car had parked for a time on a dark street near the water, but neither of them emerged. And by the time the radio had directed Leopold to the spot they'd started up again.

"We're close to them," Fletcher said.

"Don't let them spot the car. She might remember it."

The radio crackled into life again. "They seem to be just driving around, Captain. Should I keep with them?"

"Keep with them. Where are you now?"

"Just turning back onto Grand, at Maple."

"We're only four blocks away. Are they headed north again?"

"Right."

"We'll join a few blocks up."

Fletcher was driving Leopold's car, and he turned onto Grand Avenue a block and a half behind the red tail-lights of their quarry. "Looks like they're heading back toward her neighborhood," Fletcher remarked.

The car turned off Grand and before long Leopold could see that Fletcher was correct. He was taking her back home. If it had been a lovers' meeting it was a brief one.

"He's stopping a block from the house," Fletcher said. "Must be letting her out."

The door on the passenger side opened and Linda Conners appeared. She bent down for a final goodbye and then slammed the door shut. Something gnawed at Leopold's memory as he watched.

Then he had it.

"That car, Fletcher! That car!"

"What is it, Captain?"

"Head him off! Don't let him get away!"

Fletcher cut across the lawn of a corner house to beat the car around a corner, then slammed on the brakes to block the narrow street. The other car screeched to a halt as the driver hit his brakes. Then his door came open and he tumbled out, trying to run.

Leopold and Fletcher were on him then, with guns drawn.

It wasn't Frank Bland.

It was the man who had found the body – Sam Prowdy.

Leopold pulled the car up before the Conners homestead the following morning and tapped lightly on the horn. Aunt Gert looked up from her task of tying the bushes in burlap, recognized him, and walked over.

"My, you're getting to be a regular visitor here!"

Leopold smiled. "Could you get in the car for a minute, Miss Conners? Then we can stay warm while we talk."

"I saw in the papers that you caught the man who killed Vincent," she said, opening the door and sliding into the front seat next to him. "But I still don't understand it all."

"His name is Sam Prowdy," Leopold explained, "and he's been Linda Conners' lover for some time. They killed her husband for a large insurance policy on his life. It's the oldest sort of crime, but at first we didn't recognize it for what it was. A bizarre chain of circumstances made it look like an impossible crime.

"You see, Prowdy strangled Vincent with

a cord in the Conners garage, and then put him behind the wheel of his car. He sat next to the dead man and drove over to Eastern Avenue with Linda following in his auto. Then they stopped for a minute while he tied the steering wheel of Vincent's car and got back into his own vehicle. Linda walked over a few blocks and caught a bus. Then Prowdy simply started pushing the car with Vincent's body in it down the straight road – pushing Vincent's car with his own car."

"And nobody noticed it?"

"Well, it was getting dark. And that portion of Eastern Avenue is rarely traveled since the expressway opened parallel to it. Prowdy's plan was to pick up speed until he reached the point where Eastern Avenue curves to the left, then take the curve with his car while Vincent's went straight ahead and through the guard rail. They were hoping Vincent's car would burst into flames going down the hill, burning both the cord on the steering wheel and the one around your nephew's neck. Whether they could have covered up the signs of murder completely is doubtful, but they might have pulled it off. What they didn't expect, though, was the traffic jam."

"It was caused by an accident?"

Leopold nodded. "An expressway accident that shifted all the rush-hour traffic over to Eastern Avenue. Sam Prowdy hadn't figured on that, of course. The traffic was bumper to bumper, with no chance for him to pick up speed or push Vincent's car through the guard rail unobserved. It was easy for him to keep nudging the other car along on a straight road, but with the curve coming up he knew he had to do something else.

"So he simply stopped pushing it, honked his horn, and got out in all innocence to see what the trouble was. When he opened the car door he had time to unknot the rope from the steering wheel and hide it under his coat in the near-darkness, but we arrived before he could get the rope off the throat. He should have removed that after he killed Conners, of course, but murderers don't always think of everything."

"And you figured all this out?"

Leopold smiled. "I wish I could take credit for it. I never bought the newspaper theory of a back-seat strangler, because late-model cars have a head-rest making it extremely difficult to strangle someone from behind and knot the cord around his neck. After I discounted a car thief as the killer I naturally shifted focus to Linda. We followed her when she met a man, but it wasn't till I finally recognized Prowdy's car that the whole method tumbled into place in my mind."

"I appreciate your coming out here to tell me about it," Gert Conners said.

"To be honest, that wasn't the only reason I came. It's been stuck in my mind all along that there was some connection between the deaths of Vincent Conners and his father."

"That was a long time ago," she reminded him.

"Of course. And obviously the same person couldn't have been responsible for both deaths."

"Responsible? Nobody was responsible for my brother's death. He shot himself."

"It's difficult to shoot yourself in the stomach with a shotgun, even when dropping it – though of course it could have happened that way. But then I looked at the car and saw those bloodstains, and they told a different story."

"What do you mean?"

"There were *two* bloodstains, Miss Conners, on the back seat of that car. Next to each other, but separated by about a foot."

"There might have been a blanket under him."

Leopold shook his head. "On the long trip

back to town that much blood would have soaked through the blanket. He was lying on the back seat, so if the blood simply trickled down his sides from the wound the stains would have been at the front edge and the back of the seat, not side by side."

"Then how do you explain it?"

"My first thought was that he was held in someone's arms during the car trip, that he bled to death in someone's lap. That would explain the twin stains – on either side of the seated person. I finally located his widow yesterday and spoke to her on the phone. She confirmed that George died in her arms."

"As I remember," Aunt Gert said, "that's the way it happened."

"But if they were out there alone, and he died in her arms on the way back into town, *who was driving the car?*"

She was silent.

"They weren't alone, Miss Conners. They couldn't have been. And that means you lied about it when you said they were. If your brother really shot himself – or even if his wife shot him – there would be no reason to lie."

"All right," Gert Conners said very quietly. "I did it. I shot him. I was aiming at his wife, and I hit George instead."

In one of the trees overhead two squirrels were hard at work on a winter nest of leaves. Leopold watched them and wished he was in some other line of work. He turned to her and said, "The lies never cease, do they? Thirty years of it and the lies never cease."

"What do you mean?"

"The other person out hunting that day, the one who shot your brother, was obviously the one who drove the car back to town while Jean Conners held her dying husband in the back seat. And you told me you never had a driver's license."

"I –"

"It was Aunt Flag who shot him, wasn't it? It was Aunt Flag you've been protecting for thirty years. It was her car, after all, and she was driving it that day. That was why she put it up on blocks and never drove it again. No use denying it – Jean told me on the phone that Flag was there, though she never knew exactly how the shooting happened."

Gert Conners was sobbing now. "God, it's like a family curse! First George and now Vincent! I asked Flag what happened that day and she told me. It was Jean she was trying to kill, of course – Jean who even then was cheating on our brother by having a sordid little affair with that man she later married. Flag said she deserved to die. But somehow George stepped in front of the gun. Perhaps he knew what was in Flag's mind."

Leopold glanced toward the house. "She's tapping on the window again. You'd better go in."

"You won't take her away, will you? Lock her up?"

"She needs someone to watch her, to confine her and make certain she never harms another person."

"She's already got that," Gert Conners said. "I've been doing it for thirty years." She brushed away the tears.

Leopold watched her get out of the car.

"Yes," he said, "I suppose you have."

He sat there for a long time, thinking about life and death.